HEARTS OF NEW ORLEANS

HEARTS OF NEW ORLEANS

Inspired by her love for her hometown, Lynn Lorenz, best-selling author of Gay Erotic Fiction, has set the stories in this collection in and around the very heart of New Orleans, the French Quarter. In this book, she parades us past a homeless shelter, an all-night diner, a French Quarter luxury hotel, and even one of the city's famous cemeteries, as the men in these tales fight for happiness and love like beads tossed from a Mardi Gras float. Grab this collection, settle in, and find yourself transported to the city that care forgot.

Previously available only in electronic format, these three stories of Gay Erotic Fiction have now been combined for a paperback edition! Included are the tales...

Pinky Swear

Matt and Lane have been best friends since they were ten years old, keeping each other's secrets, but neither has shared their biggest secret—that they are in love with each other.

"4.25 Stars! Ms Lorenz is a pro at grabbing the emotions of her readers, and *Pinky Swear* is no exception to the rule. Not only do we feel the connection between the two young heroes as they grow up together and struggle with their feelings for each other, but we are also struck by the emotional impact of the storm."

—Bookwenches

"The visual images Lynn created in my mind of Hurricane Katrina broke my heart but were a perfect point in life to bring these two men back together and for Matt to redeem himself. But trust me, Lane doesn't make it easy on him. If you haven't read *Pinky Swear*, you really need to get to it. This one will definitely be going in my Lynn Lorenz favorites list."

—EbookAddict

Breakfast At Tiffany's

Two young homeless men not only discover the best waffles and wings in town, but find love, hope and a home in each other's arms.

"5 out of 5 Stars!...If you would like to read a story that is unforgettable, one that brings a smile to your face and makes you thankful for your life, read *Breakfast at Tiffany's*—you will want to cheer at the end for Scott and Tony. Highly recommended."

—Reviews by Jessewave

"5 Stars!...It took me a lot longer to read this story than its comparatively short length would warrant. The truth was I kept pausing to savor it, as I didn't want to get to the end and have to say goodbye to these two delightful, special, and precious young men. Hats off to Lynn Lorenz for creating a story that will live long in my memory. This one's a keeper, folks."

—Rainbow Reviews

My Heroes Have Always Been Cowboys

When Charles spots Simon, he thinks he's found the perfect man in his fantasy game of Cowboys and Indians.

"5 Nymphs!...Lorenz knows how to write a well-plotted story with fascinating characters. *My Heroes Have Always Been Cowboys* is entertaining and well worth a read. Pick up a copy; you won't be disappointed."

—Literary Nymphs

"4.5 Stars!...A lighthearted story of kismet...with a little bit of well-directed opportunity. The story is a fun romp with plenty of sizzle. I always look forward to anything Ms. Lorenz puts out, and I am never disappointed. She has a knack for writing and entertaining."

—Bookwenches

ALSO BY LYNN LORENZ

The Avalon Patrol: The Road To Avea
David's Dilemma
No Good Deed

HEARTS OF
NEW ORLEANS

BY

LYNN LORENZ

AMBER QUILL PRESS, LLC
http://www.amberquill.com

HEARTS OF NEW ORLEANS
AN AMBER QUILL PRESS BOOK

This book is a work of fiction. All names, characters,
locations, and incidents are products of the author's imagination,
or have been used fictitiously. Any resemblance to actual persons
living or dead, locales, or events is entirely coincidental.

Amber Quill Press, LLC
http://www.amberquill.com

Layout and Formatting provided by: ElementalAlchemy.com

PUBLISHED IN THE UNITED STATES OF AMERICA

*Thanks to everyone at Amber Quill Press.
And to my friends and family
who love New Orleans as much as I do.*

TABLE OF CONTENTS

PINKY SWEAR

HEARTS OF NEW ORLEANS

CHAPTER 1

New Orleans
Riverbend
April, 1985

Lane stared at the human leg bone lying on the floor of the clubhouse.

"Is that what I think it is?" He tore his eyes from the grisly thing illuminated by the flashlight quivering in his hand and looked up at Matt.

"If you think it's a *human* bone," Matt intoned in his scariest voice, "you'd be right." As of the start of this school year, Matt had become Lane's first best friend.

A shiver ran up Lane's spine and he swore his hair stood on end. The dark shadows in the corners of the clubhouse seemed to hold things he'd rather not think about. Or dream about.

"Where d-d-d-did you get it?" Lane whispered. He'd known Matt was brave, far braver than he'd ever be, but the idea that he'd touched it, much less found it, raised Matt up even farther in Lane's eyes.

"The cemetery." Matt's grin reeked of smugness, reminding Lane of the Cheshire Cat in *Alice in Wonderland.*

"No shit." Lane let out a low whistle.

Matt nodded, crossed his arms, and sat back against the wooden slats.

"When?"

"Last night. Snuck out my window, walked right over to the cemetery, and climbed the fence." His voice took on a singsong tone as he told the incredible story. Lane leaned forward, his eyes wide, his ears straining to hear the soft words.

"Did you see him?" Lane had to ask, had to know.

"Old Singin' Joe?" Matt chuckled. "Yeah, I saw him, but he didn't see me."

Lane had to blink several times to wash the dryness burning his eyes from holding them wide open for so long. Matt was so cool, but Lane would never tell him that.

"No one goes in the cemetery without old Joe knowin'. And if he c-c-c-catches you—" Lane made a slitting motion with his hand across his throat.

"But he didn't. I was dressed in all black."

"Like a spy." Lane didn't bother to hide the awe in his voice. "Smart thinking."

"Sure. I knew what I was doing."

They stared at the bone again. Lane found it hard to breathe in the small makeshift clubhouse. The old blanket covering the doorway hung down, blocking out sight and sound of his house, just across the backyard. They could have been on the moon, in the middle of a jungle, or on a deserted island.

He needed some fresh air. They were breathing in "bone" air and there was no telling what was in that. Disease. Spores. Death.

"How'd you get p-p-p-past your dad?" Lane knew he should go inside, knew it was late, but the bone had somehow paralyzed him. Or maybe it had been Matt.

"He was drunk, as usual." Matt snorted. "I climbed out my window, got the bone, then climbed back in. He never moved from in front of the TV. Passed out cold."

Matt's father had scared Lane the first and only time he'd ever been in Matt's house. They'd gone there after school to do some homework, but Matt's dad had come home an hour later, drunk, mad, and fit to be tied about something.

When the yelling started, Lane had grabbed his book bag and high-tailed it out of there. He'd run the whole way home, around two corners, and didn't stop until he'd gone up the steps of his house and stood, hands on knees, sucking in air, on his front porch.

The next day at school, Lane saw the bruises on Matt's arms peeking from under his sleeves and noticed the way Matt had walked, favoring his side.

No, Matt's daddy was not a man he wanted to cross, and that Matt did it on a regular basis made Lane wonder if Matt was the craziest kid he knew or the bravest.

"What are you going to do with it?"

Matt shrugged. "Not sure. But I need to keep it here until I find someplace better at home."

"You're going to k-k-k-keep it?" Lane's voice squeaked. "Here?" He shook his head. "No way, Jose. Uh-huh. If my mom sees this, she's gonna have a *cow*."

"Just for a day or two." Matt looked deep into Lane's eyes. "You know I can't keep it at home."

"Take it back to the cemetery. That's where it belongs." Somewhere there was a ghost without a leg bone. Lane's throat tightened and he barely got out the words, "Do you think it'll come lookin' for it?" He stared at Matt.

"Shit, no. It's just a bone that floated up from a rotten casket. I got it in the section of the cemetery for the poor people. Found it lying right on the ground."

Lane nodded. The cemetery sat one block away, and he'd grown up playing all around it. There were four sections, each the size of one block, three filled with raised crypts, mausoleums, and graves. The fourth section housed the graves of the poor, who couldn't afford burial above ground. Its black iron fence and gates kept all but the mourners out and the dead in.

In New Orleans, bones float.

Matt grabbed Lane's arm. "You can't tell anyone."

Lane nodded and swallowed.

"I mean it." Then he let Lane go and stuck out his pinky, crooked like an upside down hook. "Pinky swear." Matt's eyes narrowed, focused on him like laser beams.

Lane's eyes just about popped out of his head. A pinky swear, second only to a double dare in its power. This was *really* serious. Things happened to kids who broke a pinky swear.

Lane licked his lips and hooked his pinky with Matt's. Both boys stared into each other's eyes, and Matt started counting out the years they had to keep the secret. "One, two, three…"

They pulled hard, trying to break the link between them. Lane strained with the effort, but Matt was bigger, stronger, and after all, it was his secret.

Lane's finger gave way at nine. Nine long years he'd have to keep the secret.

Matt gave him a solemn nod.

"We have to hide it here."

Lane shivered and looked around the clubhouse for a place to put the bone, but the place was empty. No pirate treasure trunks, no locked cabinets, nothing.

"Where?"

Matt stood and turned in a slow circle, the stopped. "Here. We'll put it here, in this box." He pointed to the cardboard box they used to hold a mess of stuff, like jump ropes, a few decks of cards, and assorted things they figured they might need in a secret clubhouse.

He dumped everything out, then picked up the bone, and dropped it in.

"Shit! You touched it!" Lane yelled, jumping up and backing into a corner.

"Shut up!" Matt hushed him. "You're such a baby, Lanie."

"No, I'm not!" Lane took a step forward, his fists clenched. "Just because I don't want any "death" germs on me doesn't make me a baby."

Matt shoveled the stuff on top of the bone to hide it. Lane made a mental note to never—*ever*—touch that stuff again. In fact, he'd throw it all away. Once he found something to touch it with, and after the bone was gone, because he sure wasn't going to touch anything in that box with the bone still in there.

Then Matt stood in the doorway, lifting the blanket before he left. "Gotta go or my old man'll kill me."

Lane nodded. Those were just the words he wanted to hear. He nearly pushed Matt out the door in his hurry to leave the clubhouse and put the bone far behind.

He paused for a moment to appreciate how Matt jumped, with an ease he could never display, over the fence that separated their backyards, then he went inside.

All that night, the blanket pulled up to his chin, he listened for any noise of the ghost coming back to claim his missing bone. Somewhere, somehow, in the middle of the night, he fell asleep.

*   *   *

Two days later

His mother was screaming bloody murder.

Lane sat upright in his bed. Jesus, Joseph, and Mary, the ghost had found them! He pulled the covers up to his nose and then curled into a tight ball on his bed, hoping the ghost wouldn't figure out it was him under there.

His father's voice rumbled, then shouted in surprise.

Silence. Lane's heart beat like a hammer as he counted the seconds, like thunder after the flash of lightning, to tell how far away the storm was, only this time it was his father.

"Lane!" he bellowed.

Heavy footsteps came down the hall, creaking on the wooden floor of the camel back's second story. Those were definitely not the feet of a ghost; Lane knew that much.

The door to his room slammed open. Lane lowered the blanket and uncurled. His dad stood in the doorway, red-faced and glaring. Oh, no, he was gonna get it now.

"Lane, boy, where the *hell* did that bone come from and what the *hell* were you doing with it?"

"B-b-b-bone?" Lane's young life flashed before his eyes, all ten years of it. He was gonna die right now, without ever having... Well, he didn't know what, but he did know he was too young to die.

"A leg bone. A *human* leg bone," his father ground out the words from between clenched teeth. "Your mother found it in the backyard." His father wiped his hand over his face. "The dog had it."

Lane choked. *Shit, the dog found the bone?* Oh, no, the dog had licked him and he'd had the bone in his mouth. *Bone germs!* Lane's stomach rolled over. He opened his mouth to say something, but only this weird gurgling sound came out.

"Your mother is hysterical. You know how she is." His dad came in and sat on the corner of his bed. "She's downstairs right now, calling the priest."

"Father Phillip?"

His dad nodded.

And sighed.

And gave Lane a cocked eyebrow that said, Come clean. Tell the truth.

Lane knew if he told the truth, told it was Matt, bad things would happen. He couldn't break the pinky swear. He couldn't betray his best friend. His mother would never let him play with Matt again; she'd already declared him "common," and to her that was the lowest of the low.

And if Matt's dad found out?

Matt would get a beating even he couldn't live through.

"I f-f-f-found it," Lane whispered. "I didn't think it was bad." His shoulders hunched up around his ears. His father had never laid a hand on him, his mom either, but this just might be the first time.

"It's okay, son." His father chuckled. "But your momma's upset. She's talking cleansing and exorcisms and"—he leaned forward and whispered—"maybe even voodoo."

Lane's eyes got so big he thought they'd pop right out of their sockets. Then he dry swallowed, the gulp loud in the small room, and whispered, "V-v-v-voodoo?"

His father nodded, got up, and went downstairs.

*   *   *

That afternoon

Lane stared at Father Phillip as he walked around the backyard, sprinkling holy water and chanting in Latin. His mother stood to the side, her hands folded in prayer, a rosary dangling from between them, and her lips repeating an endless string of Hail Marys. His father kept shooting looks at Lane that Lane would rather not translate.

The bone wasn't present. Wrapped in newspaper, his father had taken it back to the cemetery that morning, while Lane waited in the car outside the large white clapboard house that held the cemetery's office. Lane just knew if he had to go in there to see the caretaker, Old Singin' Joe, and tell him he'd taken the bone, he'd have peed himself.

The old priest had gone three times around the yard, and Lane could tell he was about done in from the heat of his robes. In April, it was already in the low nineties.

Now, just when it looked like it was all over, his mom opened her eyes and gasped. "Oh, no, Father, you have to do the clubhouse. That's where it was kept." She pointed to it, sounding as if they'd kept the devil himself in there.

The priest sighed, wiped the sweat from his forehead with a white handkerchief, and nodded. He approached the clubhouse, nothing more than white painted plywood nailed to some two-by-fours with a hodgepodge of shingles covering the roof. Lane and his dad had built it two years ago during summer vacation.

God knew it was going to be a long time before Lane went back in there.

After a good dousing with holy water, inside and out, the priest declared the little house and the backyard clean.

"And the dog." His mom pointed to the little poodle, sitting in the shade of the house.

The priest shared looks with his dad, then tromped over and sprinkled the dog, too. The stupid thing tried to lick the holy water off its fur and just wound up chasing its rear end.

But it seemed enough to make Lane's mom happy.

Lane exhaled. Thank God, it was over.

Father Phillip came up to him and looked down with world-weary eyes. "Lane, I hope this will be a lesson to you. The bones of the dead are not to be disturbed."

Lane nodded.

"For your sins, you must come to confession this Sunday, where I will tell you the penance you must make."

Any amount of rosaries, prayers or novenas would be fine.

Lane nodded.

"And I understand you'll be punished by your mother and father."

Lane nodded.

The priest took Lane's chin in his hand and raised it up. They stared at each other, and the old man seemed to bore right into his brain.

He leaned over and whispered, "And tell Mathew I want to see him on Sunday, too. In church. In my confessional."

Lane nodded.

Father Phillip patted him on the head, made the sign of the cross at him, and left with only a wave of his hand toward his mother, who followed him out to the street.

His father and he stood alone in the yard. His dad walked over to him and placed his hand on Lane's shoulder.

"You're grounded, Lane. One month."

Lane nodded.

"And that boy Matt? He's off limits from now on." His father's gaze shot to the back fence and the run-down shotgun house Matt lived in.

"But Dad!" Lane gasped out. "He's my *best* friend." He could do the grounding, do the confession, but do without Matt?

"Son, with friends like that, who needs enemies?" his father drawled.

CHAPTER 2

New Orleans
Riverbend
1992

Lane hurried through his homework. The priests had really piled on the assignments this week. He didn't find it hard, just tedious, but if he didn't hurry, he'd never be able to get to the clubhouse and give the answers to Matt in time for him to copy them down.

It wasn't that Matt wasn't smart…he was. It's just that he didn't have the time. Once school let out, Matt had to get home, clean up, fix dinner for his dad and him, and get to work at six at the Riverbend Winn Dixie. He couldn't be late or his father would beat him bloody.

Lane could say it now, knew just what it was Matt's drunk of a daddy did when Matt earned his anger. After seven years of living behind each other, he'd seen and heard enough to know the truth.

Matt would be waiting at the clubhouse. Lane did the final worksheet, then gathered up the papers, stuffed them in a notebook, stuffed the notebook under his shirt and shrugged on his jacket. He headed downstairs. At the kitchen, he grabbed an apple, a bag of chips and a soda, and headed outside.

"Dinner's at six, Lanie," his mom called from the front room.

"Okay!"

Lane let the screen door slam as he trotted down the back porch steps, his signal to Matt that he was on his way. He got to the old clubhouse and ducked under the blanket.

Matt sat on the floor, leaning back against the wall, jerking off.

"Shit!" Lane stared at him, frozen in the dim light filtering through the small frosted glass window they'd installed two years ago.

"Fuck, man!" Matt groaned, his hand working his dick. "Almost there." Matt's jeans were splayed open and shoved down on his hips.

Lane slid down to the floor, watching, unable to take his eyes off Matt's hand wrapped around his dick. *Matt's dick.* Shit, he'd dreamed of it and now, here it was. Of course, he'd seen it in gym class, and, hell, yeah, he'd looked. Not that Matt had *ever* looked at Lane's, but then, who'd look at him? He was just a scrawny kid with a stutter.

Matt was...well, Matt was gorgeous.

And so was his cock.

Matt looked down at a magazine, open on the floor. Lane couldn't see what it was, but it had to be a *Playboy* or *Penthouse.* Matt had brought them to the clubhouse and shown them to Lane ever since Matt had turned thirteen. Lane had taken one look at those naked, sexy women and felt nothing. Nothing.

That's when he knew he was gay.

Now, at sixteen, that was Lane's big secret. One he'd never shared with anyone, not even his best friend Matt.

Lane's gaze shifted back to Matt. Fuck, his dick went rock hard.

That was his other big secret. He was in love with Matt.

"Shit, I'm coming," Matt cried out, spread his knees apart, and shot a load of cum up into the air. It splattered across the floor as if someone had flicked paint from a brush.

Lane panted, his fists clenched to keep himself from grabbing his own dick. That had been un-fucking-believable. Matt coming. Letting him watch. Lane knew he'd be jerking off to that scene every night of his life. Forever.

Matt gave a shake of his head and a laugh. "Damn. Sorry about that." He pulled out a handkerchief and wiped off, then wiped up the floor.

"Must be some hot babe," Lane muttered, still trying to get himself under control. "Let's see." He reached for the magazine, but Matt snatched it up.

"No." He rolled it up and shoved it in his jacket.

"Hey, maybe I want to borrow it." Lane knew he had to say stuff like that to keep up the pretense, even around Matt. Especially around Matt.

"Not this one." Matt shook his head, giving Lane the look that said, You're too young, too much of a baby. Lane hated that look.

He lunged for the magazine, snatching it from Matt. Matt leaped at him with a yell, but for once Lane was quicker. He unrolled it and gasped.

"What the hell?" A man, dressed in nothing but a pair of black leather pants and muscles from here to heaven and back graced the cover.

"Shit, man." Matt grimaced and backed into a corner. He stared at Lane, eyes expectant.

Lane flipped through the magazine. In the centerfold, the man from the cover stretched out over a motorcycle, no longer in the leather pants, just naked. And fully erect.

Lane's dick filled again as he swallowed.

"Matt?" He held up the centerfold.

Matt blinked and looked away, his bottom lip caught between his teeth.

"You jerked off to this?"

Matt didn't answer.

Lane closed the magazine and slid it across the floor to Matt, who reached out and dragged it back toward him, then tapped his fingers on the shiny cover.

"Yeah," he whispered. Then his gaze came up to meet Lane's in a clear challenge.

Lane's thoughts tumbled around in his head. Matt knew he would be here; they had a schedule. He knew it. He'd heard the back door slam. He knew the signal. He could have stopped. Sure, he'd have a bad case of blue balls, but that would be better than being found jerking off to a picture of a man.

Lane's eyebrows rose with the realization.

Matt wanted him to find out.

"Matt, are you g-g-g-gay?" Lane spoke quietly, but without any recrimination in his voice.

Matt blinked back tears, his dark eyes and hair looking to Lane as if they blended into the shadows he hid in.

"It's okay if you are. I don't c-c-c-care, man. We're best friends."

"You can't tell, Lanie. No one. Ever." Matt's voice trembled, cracked. "If my dad found out, Lane, he'd kill me."

Lane knew that was true. It would be the straw that broke the camel's back, the one brick that toppled the wall, the thing that would make his dad snap.

"I won't tell."

Matt's lip trembled and he stuck out his hand, little finger up. "Pinky swear, Lanie."

Lane extended his finger, hooked it through Matt's, and they pulled apart. Matt started to count, but his voice broke on three.

Lane took up the chant. "Four, five, six…"

Both teens strained, yet both determined to make this last forever. To bury the terrible secret so deep inside, it would never hurt either of them.

"…nine, ten, eleven, twelve."

They broke apart, each of them hurtling backward, hitting the opposite walls of the clubhouse.

Matt sobbed into his hands.

Lane's heart broke.

When it was quiet, Lane waited until Matt had wiped his face clean of tears and snot, then pushed the forgotten notebook, homework, and snacks toward his best friend.

"Here. You'd better hurry. Not much t-t-t-time left."

Matt nodded, gathered it all up, and shoved the apple, chips and soda into his backpack.

"Just leave the notebook when you're d-d-d-done. I'll get it later."

Grateful eyes locked with his. Lane gave Matt a nod and left before he did something really stupid, like cross the small room and kiss Matt.

Or worse, tell Matt he loved him.

This wasn't about what Lane wanted, but about what Matt needed.

He needed a best friend.

*   *   *

April, 1994
Before senior year of high school

Lane hung up the phone, rushed to his closet and got down his secret stash of cash. He'd hidden it in an old lunch box on the top shelf, under a thick blanket.

He opened it and dumped it out on the bed.

Seventy-one dollars and change.

He'd been saving for a car, and without a job, it hadn't been easy.

None of that mattered. Not now. Not when Matt needed him.

He shoved the money in his pocket, went to the window and stared down at the old clubhouse. A light blinked from behind the broken frosted glass.

Taking a deep breath, Lane snuck out of his room, crept down the stairs, through the hall to the kitchen, lit only by the light over the stove his parents always left on. In the living room, light flickered from the television they watched. The ten o'clock news blared.

At the back door, he unlocked it, turned the knob, and opened it, then slipped out the screen door, pulling it shut behind him without a sound.

Crouched over, he ran to the ramshackle building and into the black doorway. The blanket had long since fallen apart, rotted by the elements and mildew.

"Matt?" he whispered.

"I'm here." Matt huddled in the shadows at the back of the room.

"Shit, Mattie, what's going on? Why do you need money?"

"He found out."

Lane didn't have to ask who or what. "How?"

"He found my magazines. He tore my room apart looking for more. All my stuff is smashed."

"Even your CDs?"

"All of it." Matt clenched his jaw, the muscles ticking.

"Damn, I'm so sorry."

"I have to leave, Lane."

"What?" Matt was talking crazy.

"He's going to kill me if I stay. He threw me out." He held up his backpack. "This is all I have."

"I brought the money, like you asked."

"Thanks."

Lane didn't move, but held out the cash for Matt to take, luring him out of the dark corner he hid in like a frightened animal.

Matt stepped into the faint light, and Lane gasped, his hand flying to cover his mouth, as he stared at Matt's ruined, bloody face.

"Oh, shit, Mattie." He lurched forward and engulfed his best friend in his arms.

Matt didn't hug him back, just put his chin on Lane's shoulder. He shuddered, and his hand came up and rested on the center of Lane's back.

Lane held him tighter, then let him go. "What are you going to do?"

"Go."

"Where?"

Matt shrugged. "I got some money, and with this, I should be able to buy a ticket on the bus somewhere."

"Forget it. Running away won't solve anything. Besides, what about our plans? What about going to LSU? Rooming together?"

Matt shrugged. "I was fooling myself, Lanie. Dad wasn't going to pay for it before, and he sure as hell won't pay for it now. My job doesn't pay enough, and I don't have near enough money saved."

"I don't care. You c-c-c-can't give up. I won't let you. It's your future."

"If I stay here, I won't have a future."

"If you leave, you won't have a future either."

They stared at each other, but this time, Lane didn't back down. "Come with me," he ordered.

"Where are we going?"

"To talk to my folks."

Matt's eyes widened. "No way." He shook his head, long dark hair flying. "I can't tell them. You swore, Lane. You pinky swore."

Even now that they were nearly eighteen, the power of the vow held Lane in its grip. "I won't tell them that. But we can tell them the rest."

"What for?" Matt made a noise. "So they can laugh at me? Tell me I got what I deserved?"

"No, stupid, so they can help."

"Your parents would help me?" Matt looked up from under his bloody brows and wiped a line of dark red from his cheek.

"You're my best friend, aren't you?"

Matt nodded.

"Come on." Lane held out his hand.

Matt didn't take it, but he did follow, stumbling after Lane in the dark to the back porch, up the steps and into the kitchen.

"Mom! Dad!"

His mom rushed into the kitchen from the living room and skidded to a stop. "Oh, my God! Matt, what happened?"

"His dad." Lane huffed. "Drunk again, but this time…"

"He threw me out," Matt whispered.

"What?" Lane's mom clearly couldn't believe it. "What did you do?"

Lane jumped in. "Mom, he didn't do anything. His dad's been coming home drunk for as long as I've known Matt and beating the crap out of him, just because he's a mean old bastard."

"Lane!" His mother gasped at his language, but he didn't care. "Matt needs help."

His dad came in and paused in the doorway. "Honey, let's get Matt cleaned up. He might need stitches."

She nodded and went to work, wetting a washcloth, sitting Matt in a chair at the kitchen table and wiping the blood from his wounds as Matt winced and hissed.

His dad sat opposite Matt. "He put you out?"

"Yes, sir."

"What if you go back?"

"He'll kill me." Matt stared straight into his dad's eyes, completely convinced of that.

Lane's dad sat back and ran a hand over his face, then glanced at his mom. They shared some sort of secret parent code look, and his father cleared his throat. "Matt, would you like to move in here with us?"

Matt stared at his father, then at Lane, and then down at his feet. Lane followed his gaze, never realizing before that his best friend was barefoot.

"All I have is in my backpack." Matt's voice, once so cocky and sure, had turned quiet and fearful. Beaten down. Battered.

It just about killed Lane.

"Never mind." Lane's mom waved her hand. "Let us worry about that. Now, what do you think, darling? Stitches?"

His dad peered closer at Matt's cuts. "No. Just some strips to hold the edges together and they'll be fine." He rose, got a bag of frozen peas from the freezer and handed it to Matt. "Hold this against your cheek, Matt. Lane, take Matt upstairs. He can have the guest room."

Lane nodded and grabbed Matt's arm. "Come on, man."

Matt let Lane pull him from the kitchen, up the stairs and to the room.

He opened the door and pushed Matt inside. "Make yourself at home. Get some rest. We've got school in the morning."

Matt turned to face him, dropping the bag of peas to his side. "Thanks, Lanie. I...you're the best friend in the world. I don't deserve you." He shook his head, his eyes dark and troubled.

"Of course you do. See you in the morning." He almost closed the door, then opened it and stepped back in.

Lane stuck out his little finger, hook up. "Pinky swear, Matt."

"What?"

"Pinky swear to me that you'll be here in the morning. That you won't run away. That you won't leave."

Matt took a step closer. They joined fingers and pulled.

"One, two, three, four, five…"

Matt broke the link between them. "Five years, Lane."

"After college." Lane nodded. "You're sticking around until then."

Matt nodded, his gaze never leaving Lane's until the door shut.

Lane crossed the hall and slipped into his bedroom. After undressing, he crawled under the covers, put his hands behind his head and stared up at the ceiling.

It was more important than ever for him not to come out to his parents about being gay. If they thought anything was going on between Matt and him, they'd put Matt out for sure.

Lane snorted. *Like that would happen.* Matt was so out of Lane's league it wasn't funny. And Lane knew, once Matt turned eighteen and hit college, he'd have more men throwing themselves at him than Matt ever dreamed of.

For Lane, Matt had been all he'd ever dreamed of.

CHAPTER 3

Louisiana State University
Baton Rouge
Freshman year, 1995

Lane opened the door to the dorm room and went in.

Matt lay stretched out on his bed, as some guy crouched between his legs and blew him.

"Holy shit!" Lane yelped and froze, unable to look away.

If he'd thought Matt was gorgeous before, Matt getting head was even better. How could someone look so sexy? Matt pressed his hand down on the back of the guy's head as it bobbed up and down on his stiff shaft.

He opened his eyes, glanced at Lane, and laughed. "Sorry, dude. I'm sort of busy."

"I can s-s-s-see that." Lane gulped, then stared at the floor as if he'd never seen it before in his life.

"Give me a few, huh?" Matt husked out, then groaned.

Lane nodded like a bobble head doll and backed out of their room, pulling the door shut behind him. He leaned against the wall to catch his breath and wait for his heart to stop beating, and his boner to go down.

He ran his fingers through his hair and decided this was the last straw. He had to say something, because, goddamn, he just couldn't take walking in on Matt and one of his hook-ups one more fucking time.

It killed him.

Matt had never made a move on Lane, no matter how many opportunities Lane gave him. Granted, Lane didn't have too many slick moves, not unless you counted getting undressed, or sitting too close to Matt on his bed, or giving him long, goofy looks.

They'd been sharing the room since their last semester, and if he wanted to keep Matt for a roomie and his sanity, something had to change.

Like Matt letting Lane kiss him or suck him.

Fat chance that would happen.

All of Matt's guys were the complete opposite of Lane in looks and probably brains. Lane knew better than Matt did what Matt's "type" of man was, and Lane wasn't it.

No one had thought Lane was his type. He'd spent the last few months trying to flirt with various guys, but hadn't had a single hit. Talk about a loser.

Maybe he came off as too desperate.

Maybe the minute he opened his mouth, the stutter killed any opportunity he might have had.

Maybe he was a toad.

Really, his looks weren't so bad, but there just wasn't anything sexy about him. Longish, straight, plain brown hair, brown eyes, small in stature, and no muscles to speak of, Lane figured with all the hot guys he'd seen around campus, he was the least hot of them all.

The door opened, and Matt and the guy came out.

"Thanks, dude." Matt grinned.

"My pleasure, Matt." The other guy winked and turned away, only for Matt to swat his ass as he left.

"Matt." Lane's tone meant business. He followed Matt back inside the room, tossed his backpack on his bed and put his hands on his hips.

"What?" Matt stretched out on the bed, hands behind his head, grinning.

"You know what."

"Hey, you knew I was gay." He shrugged.

"But I didn't know you were a slut." Lane's tone was all snark. Jesus, Joseph and Mary, Matt drove him nuts and brought out his "inner bitch" faster than anyone.

"Hey, I'm just figuring this whole gay thing out as I go. You wouldn't understand, Lanie." There it was again, the tone that said,

You're such a baby.

It riled him up; made him so mad he could spit.

That was it.

"I *do* understand, you asshole. I'm gay, too," Lane blurted out.

Matt stared at him, eyes wide. Then he laughed. Slap your thigh, roll on the floor, laughing.

Tears sprang to Lane's eyes as he reeled from his best friend's callousness.

Matt stopped in mid-laugh and sat up. "Hey, Lanie, what's going on? Is this for real?"

Lane nodded, afraid to speak. His couldn't control his stutter when he got emotional.

"You're really gay?" Matt grimaced. "Since when?"

Lane slumped onto his bed. "Since high school."

Matt took it in, processing the data; Lane knew that look.

"When I moved in?"

"Before that."

"Holy fuck." Matt ran his hands through his rich ebony curls. "I never knew."

Lane shrugged. "You were kind of busy."

Matt got off his bed, came over and sat next to Lane. "Hey, man, I'm sorry I laughed. Why didn't you tell me?"

If Lane hadn't known better, he'd swear Matt was mad at him.

And wasn't that just fucked?

"Because you were living in my house. Because you didn't want anyone to know about you, so don't you think I didn't want anyone to know about me?" Lane looked up into those deep blue eyes he dreamed about and closed his mouth before he said, Because I've been in love with you since forever and didn't want to get hurt when you rejected me. *Oh, well, too late for that.*

"Oh, yeah, sure. I get it. Your mom and dad would've had a cow."

Lane laughed. "No, they're cool with it. I told them at Christmas."

"When we went home?"

Lane always felt a tug on his heart when Matt used the word home when he talked about Lane's house. It had become his home over the last couple of years, and his parents had become Matt's mom and dad, too.

One big, happy family.

One mom, one dad, one dog, two gay boys.

Oh, yeah, that's the American dream right there.

"Yeah. I told Dad first, then we told Mom. Surprisingly, she didn't call the priest and have me exorcised."

Matt hooted, slapping his leg at Lane's joke. "Too bad. Maybe it would've worked."

"Naw, this is the way we are, Matt. There's no changing, no going back, no do-over." Lane stood. "So let's talk about some ground rules for the dorm room, okay?"

"Rules?" Matt frowned, his brows gathering together into one thick dark eyebrow.

"Yeah. Look, I'm tired of walking in on you. We need to work out a signal, like when we used the clubhouse."

"Sure." Matt brightened. "How about I get one of the signs that says Do Not Disturb?"

"That'll work." Lane nodded.

"And you can use it, too, if you need to," Matt added.

Lane looked up. Matt stared at him, waiting, his head cocked to one side as if trying to figure something out.

"Me? What would I need that for?" Lane snorted as he kicked off his sneakers.

"In case you bring someone here, dude."

Lane kicked his shoes under his bed at little too hard. "Like that's going to happen."

Matt, still sitting on Lane's bed, stared at him. "Why wouldn't it?"

Lane growled. Was Matt really going to make him admit what a loser he was? Say it out loud? God, sometimes he could be such a jerk. "I'm not exactly prime beef."

"I think you're cute." Matt grinned and winked at him.

Lane's heart did a flutter at the teasing.

"You're my best friend. You're supposed to say that." Lane rolled his eyes. "Anyway, I've decided I'm not giving it up on a one-night stand. When I lose my virginity, it's going to be to someone I love and who loves me."

Matt stared at Lane for a long time, then nodded. "I hear you. You're right, Lanie. You deserve the best. Someone worthy of you." He rubbed his hand on his jeans and bit his bottom lip. "Look, I need to get going or I'll be late for work."

"Sure. Are you going to come back tonight?" Matt worked at an all-night grocery store and sometimes he'd take the graveyard shift for extra money, even though Lane's parents were helping both of them with their tuition. Matt had promised to pay them back and he'd always worked hard, even as a teenager.

"Should be." Matt grabbed his jacket and snatched up the keys to the car they shared. "You don't need the car, do you?"

"Nope. Nowhere to go."

"Great! See you later." And before Lane could blink, Matt had left.

Lane unbuttoned his shirt and glanced at the clock. Seven o'clock on a Thursday night. Not exactly date night, but Matt had managed to score a hook-up.

There was only one thing for Lane to do. This Friday night, he would get a date if it killed him. And bring him home.

Maybe Matt wouldn't like it so much if *he* walked in on Lane and some guy.

Lane stripped off his jeans and crawled into bed. He pulled open the drawer to his nightstand and got out the lube. His cock, ready and raring to go, ached, and the first sliding touch of his slicked hand eased some of it.

What Lane needed was someone else to do this, to touch him, not just his own hand. What he needed was a boyfriend.

Closing his eyes, he made his own personal pinky swear.

He would start dating, find someone to bring home, and use that stupid Do Not Disturb sign.

CHAPTER 4

Senior year, 2000
Two days after graduation

Lane snuggled on the couch with David, his arm wrapped around his boyfriend's shoulder. They'd been dating for nine months; the longest Lane had ever been with anyone since he'd started dating. Not that he'd been with many guys. He hadn't.

Boyfriends had been few and far between, but at least he wasn't a total loser.

David's body warmed his at they watched the latest foreign film David had picked out. Every Friday night, they ate dinner, rented a movie, snuggled, and got off.

It was comfortable, and easy for Lane to picture a future with David, taking walks to the Café du Monde, watching movies in the French Quarter apartment Lane had dreamed of, having dinners they would make together.

Lane's eyes burned from reading the subtitles in the darkened room, but David insisted on using them, not the dub over. A bowl of microwave popcorn sat on the coffee table in front of the couch in David's apartment.

Lane had lived on campus in the dorm apartment with Matt his entire time at school. David had never complained about it, which thrilled Lane, because the last thing he wanted was to choose between his best friend and his boyfriend.

Lane wasn't quite sure who would win.

He really liked David, despite David's streak of selfishness, and hoped to take their relationship to a new level before he moved back home and started his new job. He'd decided to ask David to come to New Orleans and move in with him, and tonight was the night.

But he loved Matt, as a best friend, so deeply he couldn't imagine his life without him.

Like he'd promised, Matt had stayed, but the end of their five years was almost up, and Lane knew Matt would leave. He'd been talking about nothing else but going to the West Coast and putting his journalism degree to work.

Junior year, Lane finally admitted to himself that he'd never have Matt, so why not just get on with his life. And he had. He'd met David at the library while doing research for an English paper. David was an English major who planned to teach junior high school. He could teach in New Orleans and they always needed teachers.

Lane planned to return to New Orleans, hire on with an oil and gas company as a geologist, find the next big oil discovery in the Gulf of Mexico, and if he could do it with his boyfriend in tow, all the better.

David was Lane's first real long-term boyfriend, not just a guy he dated; someone Lane could have a future with, someone who'd share Lane's life. They shared common interests, goals and dreams of the future.

But so far, David had not shared much of his body. They'd been moving slowly, taking time getting to know each other. Not that they didn't have sex, but it just consisted of jerking each other off, or rubbing against each other naked, but no oral sex and definitely no fucking. That would change when David agreed to move to New Orleans and live with Lane, he was sure of it.

The movie ended, and Lane rubbed his eyes.

"Tired?" David asked, moving so he could massage Lane's shoulders, if a bit too hard.

"No, it's the glare from the television in the dark." Lane winced at the fingers digging into his muscles. David seemed really nervous.

"Sorry."

Lane doubted that because he'd told David about it each time and it was really starting to annoy Lane. David was great in so many ways, but he never seemed to be all that in tune with Lane.

Not like Matt. Shit, they finished each other's sentences.

Not wanting to think anymore, especially about Matt, Lane twisted around, pulled David back onto the couch and rolled on top of him. David tensed and frowned as if he didn't want Lane to touch him.

That had been happening for a few weeks, and Lane hadn't a clue what it meant.

Now Lane didn't know what to expect. David didn't stop him, so Lane sighed, closed his eyes and focused on kissing David, getting hard as if by rote. David relaxed and rubbed against him, his hard dick at least some proof of desire.

Lane pressed down to meet him, lancing David's belly with his prick.

David moaned, and Lane swallowed it down as they kissed.

Now this was more like it; they slipped into their routine. He unzipped David's jeans, reached in and grabbed his cock. David returned the favor, grasping Lane's prick in his soft hand, and sliding up and down.

They lay on the couch, grunting, stroking, kissing, and working to bring each other to orgasm.

Lane's cock throbbed, aching for more than just David's hand. Why couldn't they suck each other? He'd had one or two blowjobs before from guys he'd dated. Shit, he wanted someone to suck him off. Didn't David want that, too?

He didn't have to fuck David, and David had never asked to fuck him. As far as Lane knew, they were both virgins. And that was cool.

Lane had been saving himself for the right man and he thought David was it, and for the first time, Lane thought he might be David's Mr. Right.

Lane's arousal grew as he went through the needed mental gymnastics to get off, but he needed more this time. He bent, pushed up David's shirt, and took David's nipple in his mouth.

David cried out, arching not into the touch, but away.

"Hey! What are you doing?" He sat up, jerking his shirt back down like a frightened girl getting groped in the back seat of a car.

Lane frowned at his boyfriend. "Making you feel good. Doesn't it feel good?"

"Not really." David grimaced, and rubbed his chest through his T-shirt as if Lane had bitten him.

"It doesn't?" Lane couldn't figure out what was going on. "Is something wrong?"

David's face flushed, and not with arousal. "Uh, we need to talk, Lane."

Oh, shit, that can't be good. Lane's stomach coiled in on itself and his heart beat faster.

"What about?" Whatever it was, Lane really didn't want to know about it.

"I can't see you anymore." David huffed out a breath and leaned back.

"Oh." Stunned, Lane couldn't think of anything else to say, so he stood and gathered his things. "Sure."

He should have expected it. It had been too good to be true. Sure, Lane didn't have Matt's good looks, but he wasn't an ogre. Still, he should have known this wouldn't last. He shouldn't have had all those stupid daydreams of a life with David.

"I *so* sorry." David sounded as if he really meant it. "But it just happened." He shrugged. "He swept me off my feet." What David really meant was he'd just been with Lane until something better came along.

Lane took a deep breath, held it and then let it out. "I understand." He moved toward the door, the urge to flee building in his body, along with the tears in his eyes.

He would *not* let David see him cry. Thank God, he hadn't asked him to move to New Orleans. At least he'd saved himself that embarrassment.

"We fell in love. It wasn't like I was looking for someone else." David followed him, still explaining. Lane wanted him to just shut up, afraid David would tell him how good-looking this guy was, how strong and manly, what a genius and how he didn't have a problem reading subtitles in the dark.

"What do you want me to s-s-s-say?" Damn, his stutter had returned. Not a good sign. He'd worked so hard at conquering it these last four years. He blinked back burning tears.

Matt would call him a baby right about now. He'd tell him to man up. He'd tell David to go fuck himself. Maybe even punch the guy out.

David stood with his arms at his sides, unable, unwilling to answer.

"How long?" Lane felt so damn tired.

"A month." David blushed.

How could Lane not have seen the signs that David had been cheating. *Shit.*

"Are you s-s-s-sleeping with him?" Lane didn't know why, but he had to ask, had to know, even knowing the answers would hurt.

David paused, his eyes screaming pity at Lane.

Oh, yeah. They'd fucked. "I see." Lane reached the door, opened it and stepped out into the hall.

"I'm so sorry." David hung in the doorway, looking like he'd kicked a puppy.

Lane just wanted him to go back inside and leave him alone. "You said that." Should he say something noble, like, I wish you and your new boyfriend happiness? It wasn't in Lane, so he just turned his back and headed for the elevator.

*   *   *

Lane reached the dorm room, his feet dragging. Matt's Do Not Disturb sign hung from the knob.

Just fucking great. Matt had someone in the room.

Lane did *not* need this. Not tonight. Not when he'd just been dumped by the only guy during the entire four years of college that he'd thought he might have a future with.

That had not been a problem for Matt. He could have any man he wanted, and he did. Repeatedly. No one stayed for long, but they all left smiling.

Lane closed his eyes, dropped his bag on the floor, leaned against the wall and waited.

Thirty minutes later, the door opened and a guy stepped out. He shut the door, took one look at Lane and grinned.

"You must be the roomie," he said.

Lane recognized him as a tennis player on the college varsity team. Tall, blond, muscles in all the right places. A typical Matt hook-up.

The complete opposite of Lane.

"And you must be tonight's entertainment." Lane couldn't help himself, but damn it, it killed him. No matter how many men came and went from their dorm room, though, Lane loved Matt. What was wrong with him?

"That's me! And let me tell you, I was *very* entertaining." He licked his lips, wiggled his fingers at Lane and then strode down the hall, his tight ass looking so perfect it hurt.

Everything about tonight sucked.

It wasn't going to get better when he went inside. Lane turned around. Maybe he'd go back to the car. Sleep there tonight.

The door opened. "Hey! Thought it was you."

"Hey." Lane sighed, picked up his backpack and came in.

28

"Man, you look like you just lost your best friend." Matt chuckled as he tucked his white button down shirt into his jeans.

Only every fucking time Matt had hung up that goddamned sign.

"I got dumped." Lane went to his room, tossed his bag on the floor and fell face down onto his bed.

Matt came to the door and leaned against the frame. "No shit. David?" He rolled his eyes. "Man, that dude is nuts to let you go."

"He fell *in love* with someone else."

"While he was with you?" Matt sounded as if he couldn't believe it, but Lane knew that was his best friend talking, not reality.

Lane nodded. He didn't want to talk about this; couldn't stand to see the pity in Matt's eyes. And he was never going to tell Matt he'd been on the verge of practically proposing to the guy.

"Well, *fuck* him. Hey, you want me to go over there and kick his ass?" Matt's curled fists and stiff shoulders said he meant it, too.

"No." Matt's bravura almost forced a chuckle out of Lane. Almost.

"Well, you can't lay there and mope about it."

"Watch me." Lane spoke into the mattress.

Matt crossed the room and sat on the edge of Lane's bed. "You know you didn't love him."

Lane sighed. "No, I didn't. And he didn't love me. I *know* that." He rolled over and pulled his pillow over his head.

Matt jerked it away. "So, what's all the pouting about, Lanie?"

Lane pushed up and glared at Matt. God, how could anyone be so fucking dense?

"Pouting? First, I'm not pouting. I just got my emotional ass kicked, so cut me some slack. He'd been seeing this guy while he was with me. All the time he wouldn't let me do anything but hand jobs, he was *fucking* this guy!" Lane's voice reached the territory only dogs could hear.

"He cheated on you? I'm going to kill him." Matt lurched off the bed and headed for the door, fists clenched, and Lane knew he meant business.

Lane raced after him and grabbed his arm.

"Look. It just hurt. That's all. That he didn't *ever* want me like that." Lane ran his hand through straight brown hair. Hell, no one had ever wanted him like that.

"Oh." Matt looked shocked. "I thought you two were doing it. I thought you said so."

"No, I just let you think that all this time so you wouldn't think I

29

was so lame."

Matt fell silent for a heartbeat, then his lips curled up, and his eyes crinkled. "I'm so disappointed in you."

"Well, you gave me so much shit about it, I just went along with it."

"So does this mean you're still a virgin?" Matt's gaze locked on Lane's.

Lane turned away to hid the truth coloring his cheeks.

"Aw, man. We need to get you laid." Matt slapped his hand on Lane's shoulder.

Lane nearly swallowed his tongue to keep from asking if Matt was volunteering, but he knew there was no way Matt wanted him. They were best friends, nothing more.

Lane shrugged Matt's hand off his shoulder. "No way. I'm not giving it up to a one-night stand or a pity fuck."

Matt laughed. "Okay, Lanie. Hey, I know this bar where I guarantee you can get blown."

Lane glared at him. "I do not need a blow job from a complete stranger."

Matt shrugged. "Suit yourself. Always makes me feel better to release a little sexual tension."

"I'm not sexually tense!" Lane shouted.

"Uh, right." Matt rolled his eyes. "How about we just go out and get a drink. Drown our sorrows."

"*Our* sorrows? From the look on that tennis player's face, it didn't look like you had any sorrows tonight," Lane snapped.

Matt rubbed his chin. "He's been chasing after me all semester, so I just let him catch me before I left."

"Just one for the road, right?" That's all Matt's guys were—one-nighters. Unlike Lane, Matt wasn't a "one guy" man. He'd be playing the field forever.

"Hey, he offered." He held out his hands.

"And you never refuse. What was it? Suck or fuck?" Lane really didn't want to know, but this is the game they played, talking about Matt's conquests. It hurt, but it reminded Lane of where he stood with Matt, and he needed that to keep it real.

"Suck." Matt shrugged. "Come on, let's go get that drink."

"Just one, right?" Lane wasn't a big drinker, and Matt never really drank more than one, afraid of becoming his father.

"Sure. Just one."

CHAPTER 5

Two a.m. the next morning

Lane half-dragged, half-walked Matt down the hall to their dorm apartment as he dug the keys out of his jeans pocket.

Matt giggled, hiccupped and staggered, as his knees gave out again.

"Damn, Matt, you weigh a ton." Lane shifted his grip on Matt's waist and lurched the rest of the way to their door. He leaned Matt against the wall, unlocked the door, and pushed it open.

Matt started to slide downward, a goofy grin on his face. "Oops!" He waved his arms at Lane.

Lane grabbed him and pulled him up, then dragged him into the apartment, and kicked the door shut behind him.

"Just one drink, huh?" Lane had never seen Matt drunk. Never. Not even graduation night at the senior party.

Matt stared into Lane's eyes, and Lane couldn't look away.

"Sorry, Lanie, but it's the end of an era, man. You and me together. No more. No more." Matt shook his head and, for one crazy moment, Lane thought Matt was going to burst into tears.

Instead, in an even crazier moment, Matt pushed Lane against the door, using his arms and body to pin Lane there.

"Lanie, I can't believe our time is up. Five years." Matt's breath puffed against Lane's face, and the smell of the whiskey he'd imbibed made Lane wonder what he'd taste like if they kissed. Matt, so serious, so sad, reached up and stroked Lane's face with his fingers as he pressed his forehead against Lane's.

Now Lane's eyes burned with tears. The thought of Matt finally leaving, walking away from him, going to the West Coast and living out his dreams without Lane by his side, destroyed Lane.

"I know. It's too soon." For Lane, a hundred years would have been too soon.

"Too soon." Matt nodded, then lowered his head. "You're the best, Lanie. Thank you. I wouldn't be here if it weren't for you."

Lane didn't know what to say. All he'd ever done had been purely selfish, to keep Matt with him. Matt had done the hard part—passed the courses, worked like a dog to pay Lane's parents back, excelled in his classes.

Matt's intent gaze fell to Lane's mouth. Lane's stomach whirled away as the surety of what might happen next hit him. He froze, terrified to do something that might change this, and terrified to let it happen.

Matt's lips brushed his, just the slightest, most tender touch imaginable.

Lane closed his eyes and raised his face to Matt, letting him know it was okay. It would be fine. It would be the best kiss of his entire life, just because it was Matt.

"Lanie," Matt whispered.

Lane thought he'd lost his mind; he heard such longing and desire in Matt's voice. *Man, Matt must be really drunk.* Maybe Lane was the one who was drunk and imagining things.

But, selfishly, Lane didn't care. He waited, pinned against the wall, his cock stirring in just the anticipation of a stupid kiss.

Matt came down on Lane's mouth, and Lane's cock stiffened in his jeans. When Matt ran his tongue over Lane's lips, he opened them, and Matt's tongue bullied its way inside. Lane went wild as it stroked and caressed and tasted.

Matt slid his hand up, twined their fingers together, holding him to the door, and buried his other hand in Lane's hair.

He broke their kiss. "Lanie."

"Matt, oh, God." Lane melted against Matt. And, oh, my God, Matt's dick pushed back into his belly, erect and demanding.

Now they kissed, open mouthed, as Matt ground against Lane's body, desperately pulling at his mouth, eating from it as if he were starving. Lane had never, not with David or any other guy, been so hot and bothered, so turned on, so ready to beg to be fucked.

If this is what happened when Matt got drunk, Lane wished it had happened more often. Wished he'd been with Matt every night since they'd started college.

What a waste of time, he wanted to cry out, frustrated and angry that they couldn't have had this, this passion, until now. At the end.

Matt grabbed his shoulders and pulled him away from the door. They stagger-stepped toward Lane's room. Matt reached around him and opened the door, then manhandled Lane to the bed.

The back of Lane's legs hit the bed and he fell back, Matt on top of him, their arms and legs tangled, their bodies still moving in the slinky dance of lovers.

"Fuck." Matt's breath exploded across Lane's face, as he tugged on the T-shirt Lane wore. "Sit up."

Lane obeyed. If Matt had told him to jump out off the Mississippi River Bridge, he'd have done it.

Matt ripped it off, then took off his own shirt, tossed it to the side and began unbuttoning Lane's jeans. Before Lane could blink, or think clearly, his pants and briefs hit the floor next to his shirt, and Matt was shimmying out of his own jeans.

Matt had gone commando.

Lane stared at the cock he'd seen for the first time so many years ago. But it had changed, become longer, thicker, even more beautiful than when Matt had been sixteen.

His own cock, just as long, but thinner, rode his belly, ready to do whatever Matt commanded of it. Lane would do whatever Matt ordered; he had only to speak the words.

Matt never said a word, he just fell back down on Lane, devouring, biting skin, sucking up marks on Lane's neck, his fingers twisting the hard points of Lane's nipples. Lane thought he'd come just from those hot, desperate touches.

But the best, sweet Jesus, Joseph and Mary, the best was the scrape and rub of their cocks together as they did the dance. Matt's big body overpowered Lane's just as he'd dreamed it would, and Lane gave into it, didn't fight it, let Matt take what he wanted.

Matt's hands glided over Lane's skin, traveling up and down, over and around, covering every patch he could with its width and hard calluses. It had to be the most glorious thing—having Matt's hands on him—Lane had ever known.

Lane shifted under Matt, spreading his legs, and Matt snuggled down between them. He clamped onto Lane's nipple and sucked it.

Lane cried out, arching into his mouth, wanting more.

"Harder," he begged.

Matt obeyed, and Lane's eyes rolled in his head at the sound of Matt slurping at his nipple, sucking and licking it, sending sparks of arousal shooting straight from it to his dick.

Matt pulled off, grabbed Lane's cock in his fist and pulled it upright. He knelt on the bed between Lane's legs, and Lane's eyes nearly bugged out of his head as he watched Matt open his mouth and swallow Lane's dick.

"Holy fuck!" Lane gasped and fell back on the bed, his head hitting the headboard. The only thing he felt was the pure pleasure of having Matt's warm, wet mouth on him, just like in his fantasies. Just like in his dreams.

That was it. This had to be a dream. It was the only explanation Lane could think of to explain Matt's behavior. Drunk and dreaming, oh, yeah, that had to be it because a man like Matt never looked twice at a dork like Lane.

Matt groaned, and the vibration shook Lane to the core. Matt's hand splayed open on Lane's thighs, worked like a cat's paws, kneading his skin as he milked Lane's cock. His dark-haired head bobbed up and down, cheeks hollowed on the pull up, mouth open on the stroke down as he took the entire length in. God, it was all Lane could do to keep from coming, but he didn't think Matt wanted him to do that, not in his mouth anyway.

Shocked, Lane could only experience Matt. He'd always thought he'd be the one on his knees in front of Matt, giving him head, not the other way around. Matt had taken Lane's dreams and exceeded them.

"Matt," Lane warned as his arousal built to ball blowing heights. Any more and he'd shoot like the virgin he was and that would be too fucking embarrassing.

Matt pulled off with a sloppy kiss, and Lane's spit-soaked prick slapped against his belly. Inside, Lane died a little knowing Matt didn't want to swallow his spunk. Why would he?

Instead of getting Lane off with his hand, Matt reached past him, jerking open Lane's nightstand drawer. Lane held his breath. Matt rummaged around in it, grabbed the slick Lane kept there, popped the top and squirted some out on his hand.

Without a word, no questions and no asking, Matt pushed Lane's legs wider. He covered his cock with the gel, spreading it out, using that same fisting motion Lane had watched all those years ago as Matt jerked off in the clubhouse. Matt's eyes closed as he stroked himself, then he opened them, stared into Lane's eyes and ran his slick covered fingers up and down Lane's crack, from balls to his hole.

Lane shuddered, closed his eyes against what he saw in Matt's heated gaze, and whimpered like a slut begging for it.

He didn't have to beg for long.

Matt's finger ran over his hole, teasing. He pushed into it as it danced over his opening, begging Matt without words to slip the finger in.

Matt pushed in, just a bit.

They both groaned.

Lane spread his legs even wider and tried to relax. He'd fucked himself with his own finger, and if Matt had searched a little harder in the drawer, he'd have found the rubber butt plug Lane used when the need to be fucked got so bad he couldn't stand it.

"More."

Matt slid it in farther, and Lane took it. His body seemed to suck it inside, and Matt gasped. He lowered his head against Lane's thigh and rested, shoulders shaking.

Lane reached out and petted Matt's shoulders. "It's okay if you don't want to." Matt had to be sober by now; maybe he'd realized what he was doing.

"Shut up, Lanie." Matt's voice, hard and hoarse, trembled.

Then he pushed another finger inside and hit Lane's gland.

"Oh, fucking God!" Lane arched off the bed, his fingers twisting the sheets in his ecstasy.

CHAPTER 6

"I can't wait." Matt gave his gland another hit, Lane groaned, and then Matt pulled his finger out.

Matt reached over the bed, grabbed his jeans and rummaged through them, pulled out his wallet, flipped it open and retrieved a condom.

Lane's eyes widened. This was really it. They were going to do it. Matt had a rubber in his hand and intent in his eyes. And lust.

Lust? For Lane? No, that had to be something else, something drunk and wild and filled with I'm going to regret this in the morning.

Lane closed his eyes, and took a deep breath. Should he call a halt to this?

Hell, no. Had he lost his fucking mind? This is what he'd waited his entire life for, his first time. And it was with Matt. Just as he'd always dreamed it would be.

Only Matt was drunk.

The sound of the foil ripping on the condom brought Lane's eyes open.

Matt knelt between his legs, rolling the latex onto his jutting cock, and Lane thought he'd never seen anything so sexy as Matt, hair falling into his eyes, his firm body posed over him.

Then Matt took his dick in his hand and guided it to Lane.

Matt inhaled and looked up into Lane's eyes. "Tell me to stop, Lanie."

Lane couldn't speak. Didn't trust himself to say the same thing he'd fought not to say since he was fifteen. *I love you.*

Lane shook his head and pulled his legs apart.

"Thank God," Matt muttered. With a toss of his head to kick the hair out of his eyes, he licked his lips and pressed in.

Incredible pressure. Lane tried to relax, just like when he took his butt plug, but this was Matt, and he couldn't. He could barely breathe. Could barely think.

Something inside him short-circuited and all he could do was feel Matt's cock pressing into him, spearing him, forcing that tight ring of muscles to open for him.

Lane pushed, and Matt slid in.

"Lanie, oh, God," Matt crooned, eyes shut tight.

It felt different than Lane's plug, warmer, so much warmer, fuller, more stretched, more exciting, just so much *more*.

Matt squeezed Lane's hips with his hands, holding back whatever it was that played over his face. Would he ever take his first stroke?

Lane needed to be fucked. Now.

He pulled back and thrust forward onto Matt's prick, and Matt's eyes shot open. Their gazes locked, and Lane tried to send a telepathic cry of, *Fuck me now*, to Matt.

Message received.

Matt snapped his hips, and Lane groaned. He did it again and again, and before Lane could think about it, Matt was fucking him. Slow and controlled, as if Matt had all the time in the world to spend with Lane, when they really only had until Matt sobered up.

Lane didn't give a shit if Matt never sobered up, if he could have Matt like this forever.

Lane wrapped his legs around Matt and held on. Matt lowered his head to rest on Lane's and shuddered as his hips, with a mind of their own, kept snapping, kept thrusting in and out, working Lane's tunnel until Lane was on the very edge of coming.

Not yet! His mind screamed at him to hold on, to give him more time. This couldn't be over so soon. Even if he was a virgin, Lane set his jaw, determined to ride it out as long as Matt did.

Matt looked like he might not last long after all. He shook and trembled. Must have been the alcohol. Even young guys felt the effects of drinking on their libidos.

Lane figured what the hell. He reached up and stroked Matt's cheek. "Matt, I—"

Matt crashed his mouth down on Lane, cutting off his next words.

Lane's brain couldn't function, not with Matt's dick in his ass and Matt's tongue down his throat, and he couldn't breathe either.

Jesus, Joseph and Mary, let me die right now.

Matt clung to Lane, his hips jerking faster, his desperation bleeding through every touch of Matt's tongue along Lane's mouth, then their kiss broke, and Matt buried his face in Lane's neck, sucking and biting and gasping.

Lane realized his hips were matching Matt's motion, all on their own. He hadn't thought about it once, no command to move his hips. Just his body's reaction to being taken wherever Matt wanted it to go.

He thrust up as Matt thrust down. They worked in such perfect rhythm, Lane thought he'd die from the sheer perfection of it. For once, Lane wanted Matt to know he could give back as good as he got, that he wasn't some baby, and that this wasn't his first time, even if it really was.

With a cant of his hips, Matt nailed Lane's gland. "Oh, fuck, yeah. That's it, Mattie, that's it." Lane's voice sounded odd to his ears. He sounded like a slut, with a strange purr-beg-whimper that he'd never heard before.

Matt drove into him, hitting it, slapping his balls against Lane's ass, the smack punctuating each mind-blowing thrust, and Lane knew it would only be a few moments before he blew his load all over Matt's chest and his own belly. And wasn't that fucking hot?

Matt pushed up on his arms and looked down into Lane's eyes. Tossing his head back, Matt groaned and his arms shook with strain.

"Lanie, gonna come," he ground out between clenched teeth.

Lane gasped and whispered, "Give it to me, Mattie."

Matt gave three quick thrusts, then froze, opened his mouth, closed his eyes and emptied into the condom as a wild, guttural, feral groan emanated from his throat.

Without a single touch to his cock, Lane came, shooting between their bodies, painting his own belly. Just from Matt's fucking and his cries. Lane had never heard anything more erotic, more arousing, than Matt at that one sacred moment, when his face became even more beautiful than Lane had ever seen it.

Matt hung there for a long moment, then pulled out.

"Shit." Matt grabbed at the condom. "It slipped off."

Lane froze. "How off?"

"It's okay. Don't worry. I'm okay."

Was Matt nuts? He fucked anything that moved. "Matt…"

"I said I'm clean. I'm very careful, Lane."

"B-b-b-but," Lane's stutter returned. "How can you be so sure?"

"I just am, all right." Matt rubbed his hand over his face and flopped back on the bed. "Just trust me, okay."

Trust him? Could Lane do that? He'd shared everything with Matt, his hopes and dreams, his successes and failures. But this? This was life and death.

It was done and nothing could change it.

"Okay, Matt, if you say so." Lane relaxed and exhaled. If he'd said no, if he'd made a bigger deal about it, it might have shredded their friendship.

When he returned to New Orleans, he'd just have to get tested. That's all.

Matt lay next to him, his breathing slowing. Maybe a few inches separated their bodies, but to Lane, it seemed as if it were the Grand Canyon. Huge. Too big to cross?

Lane reached out and touched Matt's hand.

Matt twined their fingers together. "Let's get some sleep, huh, Lanie?"

"Sure, Matt."

Matt closed his eyes.

Lane lay there, listening to Matt's breathing. Knowing just when he'd fallen asleep. Lane closed his eyes, but damn, his brain wouldn't shut down, wouldn't turn off as a thousand thoughts ran in circles in his mind.

Lane knew Matt had his ticket, had nailed the interview for the small Los Angeles press, knew in three days Matt would pack his things, and he knew the minute when Matt's plane would take off from the airport in New Orleans.

What he didn't know was if Matt would still leave after what had just happened between them. Lane didn't know about Matt, and he knew it had been his first time, and with the love of his life, but Jesus, Joseph and Mary, it had been incredible.

The kind of sex you read about.

Well, at least it was for Lane.

For Matt? Probably nothing special. Besides, he was drunk.

Would Matt remember this in the morning?

Would Lane see regret in Matt's eyes? He'd die if he did. Just curl up into a ball and die.

What would this mean to their friendship?

*   *   *

Lane woke up when the sun hit his face. He blinked, rolled over and reached for Matt.

No Matt.

He pushed up and looked around the room. "Matt?"

Lane's clothes lay on the floor, right where he'd left them, but Matt's jeans and T-shirt were gone. All signs the man had even been in his room were missing.

Maybe it had all been a dream? Maybe he'd been the one who'd had too much to drink? But he remembered last night, right down to the sounds Matt made when he came, the look in his eyes and on his face.

No way in hell that was a dream.

Lane got out of bed, tugged on his jeans and opened his bedroom door.

"Matt?"

The door to Matt's room was cracked open. Lane crossed the living room to it and paused. He took a deep breath, pushed it back and stepped inside.

Matt's bed had been made.

And his stuff was gone. Lane zombie-walked to the closet and pushed the sliding door to one side. Nothing but hangers and a crumpled candy bar wrapper.

He turned and stared at the dresser.

A piece of notepaper had been stuck in the side of the mirror, between the glass and the wooden frame.

Lane in bold block letters gave Lane's stomach a roll.

This couldn't be good.

He shuffled back to the dresser, staring at himself in the mirror. His hair stood out, spiked and bed-headed, his skin paler than usual, his eyes… Well, they just looked sad. Resigned.

He snatched the paper and fell onto Matt's bed, staring at the small folded sheet of college-ruled notebook paper.

Did he really need to open it to know Matt had left?

Yeah, he was a glutton for punishment.

Lane opened it and read.

Lane,

I'm so sorry about last night. I don't think I should ever drink.

Decided to cut out of here. No point in waiting.

Keep in touch.
Matt

Tears spilled over and Lane did nothing to stop them.

Bad enough Matt had left, but did he really have to say he was sorry about last night?

"I'm not sorry, Mattie," Lane said to nobody. "I'll never regret it." Hell, how would he ever forget it? How could he ever forget Matt? How could Matt have just left him? No goodbye. Nothing.

The sob that burst from his throat surprised him, then he gave in to it, his head hanging, his hands gripping the letter so tight he tore it in half, his shoulders shuddering with each deep breath he took in to fuel the next sob.

He fell back on Matt's bed and stared at the ceiling. Matt was gone. He just couldn't believe it.

"He's really gone." He had to hear it out loud, for himself, with his own words and voice, just to make sure that there wasn't a single piece of his heart that hadn't been broken.

He crumpled up two pieces of the note and threw it against the wall.

Fuck. Anger swelled in Lane's chest. Hard, cold, heart-closing anger.

Matt had left—no, Matt had run as if his ass were on fire—to get away from his past, New Orleans, and Lane. Especially Lane.

The son of a bitch couldn't even face him.

He'd fucked him and run, as if Lane were some piece of ass he'd picked up in a bar, had sex with, and was too embarrassed about it to hang around one second more than he had to.

Lane stood and left Matt's room, shutting the door behind him. He walked to the bathroom they'd shared, turned on the tap and splashed cold water on his face.

"Why would he stay? Not for you." Lane looked into his reflection in the mirror over the sink. He didn't even bother to finger his hair into place.

He leaned forward, searching deep into his own eyes.

Matt had treated him, his best friend, like a cheap pickup and made Lane feel worthless.

Another wave of anger buffeted Lane, drawing his mouth into a hard, straight line. "Pinky swear, the next time I see that son of a bitch,

I'm going to deck him."

By force of habit, Lane extended his pinky in a hook, but there was no one to wrap his finger with and pull.

He stared at his hand in the mirror, curled the fingers into a fist, and turned away.

CHAPTER 7

New Orleans
French Quarter
August 27, 2005

"Come on, Sebastian, we need to leave today. If we wait any longer, the roads will be so congested we'll be sitting on the interstate when the hurricane hits." Lane ran his hand through his hair as he tried for the last time to get his elderly landlord Sebastian LaGrange to leave their house on St. Phillip. The interstate had been packed with people fleeing the city for the last day or so.

"Dear boy, I told you before, I'm not leaving." Sebastian sniffed and dabbed at his forehead with his white cotton hanky. "I've lived in this house for almost fifty years and I've never once run from a hurricane." He glared at Lane down the long length of his nose. "And I'm not going to do it now."

Lane leaned back in his chair and shook his head. There was no way he could leave Sebastian alone. The man could barely walk, much less deal with the hurricane bearing down on them.

"Besides, dear boy, the French Quarter is the highest point in the city, bar the levees and Monkey Hill in Audubon Park." He chuckled. "I'm safer here than on the highway in your car."

Exhaling, Lane knew the old gentleman wasn't going to budge. He might have been eighty, but he could dig in his heels better than the most determined debutante could.

"Okay. Fine. We'll stay." Lane threw up his hands and stood.

"You don't have to stay, Lane." He smiled at Lane with watery ice blue eyes. Even at his age, Sebastian could still turn a man's head, always immaculately dressed, with his thick silver hair and blue eyes. In his youth, when his hair was jet black and his skin was tight, tanned, and smooth, he had been the most sought after lover in the French Quarter.

"I'm not leaving you alone." Lane shook his head.

"You're such a dear lamb." Sebastian patted Lane's hand. "If only I were twenty years younger."

Lane snorted. "Twenty? I'm not even thirty and you'd be—what? Sixty?"

"Hush, child. Don't disrespect your elders. It isn't a good look. Makes your mouth all wrinkled and pruney." Sebastian pursed his lips to show Lane.

"I'll go make preparations." Lane walked to the back door.

"You do that. I've already filled my tub with water and I still have twenty plastic jugs of water to fill." He waved at his mudroom at the back of the Creole bungalow he lived in. "I have flashlights, batteries, candles, matches, and canned tuna. I'm set." He nodded at the kitchen table where his supplies lay.

Lane rolled his eyes. "Right. I'm going to the store in a bit, so do you need anything?" He opened the French door and hung on the edge of the steps.

"Well, pick up a few bottles for me. Bring back the boys."

"Boys?" Lane cocked an eyebrow.

"Johnny Walker, Jim Beam, Jose Cuervo." He waved his hand. "And don't forget my favorite, Jack Daniels."

"You know, with the city emptying, there won't be any hurricane parties."

"Of course there will be! This is the French Quarter, Lane. There's always a party somewhere." He cocked an eyebrow at Lane, then waved him out.

Lane laughed, pulled the door closed and walked across the bricked courtyard, skirting around the long reflecting pool with its large bronze fountain and its three statues of naked cavorting young men, to his apartment in the slave quarters behind the house. Rumor had it that Sebastian had modeled for one of the statues and each time Lane passed it, he tried to decide which one.

The small two-story had been his home since college graduation and Lane had fallen in love with the place at first sight. Two rooms down, two up and a narrow balcony, with a tiny kitchen built into one of the downstairs room and an even smaller bathroom on the second floor.

An alley led down the side of the bungalow from St. Phillip, with a locked iron gate that offered a tiny sliver of a glimpse into the lovely courtyard Sebastian was so proud of. A truly decadent courtyard, filled with flowering vines that kept the air perfumed with jasmine and roses, and that glorious fountain that nearly every gay man in the city lusted after, topped by the terracotta-colored stucco slave quarters.

Lane opened the tall wooden doors and went inside. He flopped down on the couch and rubbed his eyes. Okay, he hadn't planned on riding out the storm, so he hadn't made any preparations.

Having lived in New Orleans his entire life, he knew them by heart.

But as what little energy he had left fled his tired body, Lane put his head down on the arm, stuffed a pillow under it, and closed his eyes.

Just as he dozed off, his cell phone rang.

"Hello." He rubbed his eyes again, trying to pull himself fully awake.

"Lane? Why haven't you left yet?" His mother's voice crackled in his ear. "We've been in Lafayette for two days, and everyone's expecting you." His parents had fled to his father's brother's home days before to beat the traffic out of the city.

"Mom, I'm not leaving. Sebastian won't go, and I can't leave him here."

"But, honey, this looks like the one. They're predicting it's going straight up the mouth of the river, and you know what that means."

Lane knew. *Everyone* in New Orleans knew.

"I know. It doesn't matter. You know Sebastian; he's stubborn. And if it hits and anything happened to him, I'd never forgive myself."

"I understand that, but what about you?" Her voice needled him right between his eyes, like an ice pick.

There was a scuffle, and a muttered, "Give me that phone" and then his father's voice.

"Lane, stay put. It's too late to get on the road now anyway. I'm watching the news and traffic's backed up. Hunker down there and make the best of it." Always sensible, Lane's dad had a firm grip on the situation, and Lane trusted him.

"I will. Going out to get the last of the stuff now."

"Got your candles, flashlights, and water?" he barked.

"Yeah. Well, I need to do the water, but I have almost everything else."

His father's voice softened. "Good boy. And Lane, we love you. Keep in touch, okay?"

"Sure, Dad. Tell Mom I love her."

Lane flipped his phone closed and sat up. Time was wasting. There were plastic jugs, a tub and some buckets to fill with water. He'd pulled out his little hibachi to grill on, but he needed to get charcoal for it.

And a run to the store for some liquor.

It's New Orleans, so you can't forget the booze.

*   *   *

French Quarter
St. Phillips St.
August 29, 2005

Lane and Sebastian sat in the kitchen of the bungalow. Lane had given up the slave quarters when the storm hit to keep the old man company. It wasn't that Lane was afraid or anything; just that Sebastian might need him.

"So did Matt contact you?" Sebastian poured another shot of whiskey into his glass.

Lane shook his head. He didn't want to talk about Matt. Matt wasn't concerned with Lane, not anymore. Not since that night he'd bugged out of their college apartment.

"Why would he do that?"

They'd lost power a few hours ago and now they sat in the dark. Sebastian observed him through the light of an antique brass hurricane lantern sitting on the table. The old man could tilt his head, peer at you, and your entire soul would be laid bare for him to see.

"Because he's your best friend."

"Was. Was my best friend." Lane tossed back the last of his whiskey. Ever since Sebastian had befriended him, Lane had visited him, and they'd have a drink and chat. Over the last few years, Sebastian had taught him the finer points of drinking whiskey.

"Well, if what you've told me is true, a friendship like that never dies."

Lane snorted. "No, it just runs away in the morning."

Sebastian smiled. "Couple of young fools, if you ask me."

"I don't know about Matt, but that certainly fits me." Lane reached for the whiskey bottle. Outside, Katrina raged. Inside, Lane's regret swirled in the bottom of his tumbler.

Sebastian leaned forward and took the bottle before Lane could get his hands on it. "Look at me, dear boy."

Lane looked across into icy blue mirrors.

"He broke your heart, Lane. He ruined you."

"Ruined me?" Lane's brows furrowed.

"Ruined you for any other man. You can't get past him and you can't move on. No man will ever measure up to him, despite what he did to you."

Lane frowned as the words sank home.

"And you still love him. Perhaps even more than ever." Sebastian chuckled.

Lane's head shot up and he glared at his landlord. "So I'm weak and pathetic? I'm worthless, is that what you're saying? Sorry, no newsflash there. Hell, I knew that." He half stood and pulled the bottle from Sebastian's hand. "I knew that the morning he left."

"You misunderstand me, dear boy. You're anything but weak and certainly not pathetic. Most of your charm is that you honestly have no idea how attractive you are." He waved his hand. "You're just missing half of your soul."

"What?" Lane ran his hand through his hair. Honestly, had the man had too much to drink? He wasn't making any sense at all. Attractive? Half his soul?

"Matt was your soul mate, Lane. The man you were destined to be with." He sighed. "Some people don't believe in soul mates, but I do. I know." His gaze focused into the distant dark corner of the kitchen.

"A soul mate? You're kidding me, right?"

"I certainly am not. I believe if we're very lucky, we find one person—our soul mate—who completes us. Without this person, we're only half inside. Half a heart. Half a soul. Something's always missing, right? Isn't that how you felt when he left? Isn't that how you feel, even now?"

Lane stared at his feet. Yeah, that's exactly how he'd felt. Did feel.

"So I'm going to feel like this forever? Fucking great!" Lane slapped the table, and the lantern jumped, its flame flickering dancing shadows on the walls and cabinets.

"Watch your language, Lane."

Lane nodded primly.

47

"Probably. I'm eighty, and Frank died twenty years ago and I'm still half a man."

"Frank?" This was the first he'd heard of Frank.

"My partner. Well, we didn't call each other that back then. It was the eighties, and we were just coming out really."

"How did he die?"

Sebastian smiled. "There was a time when I could mention the death of a lover and every gay man would know how he'd died." He glanced down at his hands, then back up to Lane's face. "AIDS. He fought it for two years and then cancer took him." A mask of sorrow covered Sebastian's face, and he looked very, very old.

"I'm sorry." He touched the man's hand, feeling the papery yet soft skin. "He was your soul mate?"

"Yes. In every sense of the word. When he died, a part of me died with him."

"And you're saying Matt is my soul mate?"

"I believe it to be true, yes."

"Doesn't the other person have to think you're his soul mate?"

"Yes."

"Well, then, that blows that theory." Lane laughed. "Matt couldn't wait to get away from me, Sebastian. Not even for the three lousy days until his plane flight. Nope, he had to leave right then. Without a word, without a handshake, without so much as a goodbye." Even after five years, Lane's heart hurt so much it brought tears to his eyes.

Sebastian fell silent.

Lane sniffed and wiped his eyes.

"Can I ask you something, Lane?"

"Sure."

"Why didn't you ever contact him? Surely you knew where he was going, how to reach him?"

Lane shrugged. "What would I have said? Begged him to come back? It wasn't like we were dating or anything. He was drunk. It was a mistake. He was my best friend, that's all."

"That wasn't all, and you know it. He was the man you loved. Your first and only love. And you let him go."

"I didn't have a choice, did I?" Lane's voice rose. "Look, he didn't want *me*. I was right there under his nose all that time at my parents' house and in college. Right there. And he never made a move." Lane shook his head. "He didn't want me."

Sebastian shrugged. "Maybe not, but maybe he did. You'll never know now, will you?"

Lane poured another shot into his glass. "Nope. I'll never know." He took a sip and enjoyed the burn as the amber liquid seared away the emotion clogging his throat.

Sebastian sighed. "So much sorrow could be avoided if people would just talk."

Lane mumbled, "Some people talk too much."

His landlord shrugged. "It's my nature." And he winked at Lane, giving Lane a glimpse of the charming rogue he used to be.

"Let's turn on the radio again and see if we can pick up any news."

Sebastian nodded and pressed the power button, but all they heard was static.

CHAPTER 8

Los Angeles
August 29, 2005

His cell phone rang and danced across the nightstand. Matt reached out and slapped it, but it still rang. Groaning, he pushed the covers off his head, picked up the phone and squinted at it.

His boss, Richard Mansfield, editor-in-chief of the small indie paper he worked for. *Crap. What now?*

He flipped it open. "Yeah, Matt here." Matt sat up on the side of the bed and scratched his chest. "What time is it?"

"It's five A.M. You're from New Orleans, right?"

"Uh-huh." What did that have to do with anything?

"Get up and get your ass in gear. You're booked on a flight to Houston in two hours. From there, you're connecting with a National Guard unit. It's the only way we could get you into the city."

"Into Houston?" What was Richard talking about? This time, the man had gone insane. Too much of that designer coffee he drank, for sure.

"No. Wake up, Matt! Haven't you been following the hurricane?"

"Katrina? Yeah, so what? Just another storm." He shrugged.

"Matt, the levees broke early this morning. The city's flooding. Most of it's under water."

"Shit!" Matt stood and looked around for his jeans. "Why didn't you say so?"

"I just did. Look, you're our man-on-the-ground. Get your ass to Houston, Matt. Then hook up with the convoy heading from there to the city. You've got connections there, right?"

Matt thought about the only connection he gave a damn about, and he'd severed that one five years ago in the most colossal fuck-up of his life.

"Yeah." It wasn't exactly a lie, he knew people...or he had a few years ago. Matt knew a story like this didn't come along but once in a lifetime. Still, it hadn't been the story that got his adrenaline going; it was the thought of Lane, the only man he'd ever loved, trapped in the floodwaters.

*   *   *

Louisiana
Somewhere on I-10
August 30, 2005

"Is Lane there, Mom?" Matt shouted into the cell phone as the National Guard truck he rode shotgun in rumbled down the I-10 Interstate. They'd made the outskirts of Baton Rouge, and he could see the huge bridge that crossed the Mississippi River up ahead. Next to him, his camera bag jostled his arm as he shifted in his seat.

"No, Matt. He stayed behind. He didn't want to leave Sebastian."

Sebastian? Matt's brain fogged over and his heart thudded, then stopped. Lane had someone. *Sebastian.* Definitely a gay name. Probably some guy who owned an antique shop in the Quarter, or an interior designer.

What a fool he'd look rushing in to save Lanie.

"They're in the Quarter. On St. Phillip and Burgundy."

Of course they are.

Matt didn't know what to say. His mind spun in a thousand directions and all of them led back to the same place—Lane.

Another voice came on the phone. "Matt? Good to hear from you, son. Where are you?" It was his dad, or the man he'd called Dad since he was a teenager.

"Hey, Dad, I'm in Baton Rouge, heading into the city with the National Guard. My paper sent me to cover the flood. Mom says Lane stayed behind."

"Hold on." There was a pause. "Sorry, had to wait for her to leave. I don't want to upset her."

"Why?" Matt's stomach tightened into a hard ball. He knew that serious tone in his dad's voice.

"We haven't heard from Lane in two days. Power's out in the city and there have been riots and looting. We think the Quarter is pretty dry, but the rest of the city is under water."

"I'm sure he's fine. He'll contact you when the phone lines clear."

"You're right, Matt."

"Sure." Matt stared at the bridge growing closer. Once they crossed it, New Orleans would be about an hour or so away.

"Matt, find our boy. He needs you." His dad's voice faded. "You shouldn't have left him, Mattie." A tinge of anger painted Dad's voice, and Matt winced.

"I know." Matt leaned his head against the side of the truck.

"You broke his heart, Matt."

"What?" Matt sat up and stared at the phone, then put it back to his ear.

"I always thought you two would be together. I know it's none of my business, but was I wrong to think you were in love?"

Matt choked. He'd known Lane had come out in college, but he'd no idea their dad knew he was gay also. "You knew I was gay?"

A soft chuckle, then a sigh. "Son, I've known it since you were a teen. And about Lane, too."

"And you still let me stay in your house?" Matt ran his hand through his hair, then touched the window. He couldn't quite believe how wonderful the people who'd taken him into their home, like a second son, had been to him, but it shouldn't have surprised him. Their dad had always been sharp and one step ahead of them.

"You needed help. And I think I'm a pretty good judge of character."

"Thank you." He took a deep breath. "I don't know what Lane told you, but it was all my fault. I screwed up, not Lane. He was"— *Fantastic. Wonderful.* Everything he'd ever dreamed of—"the best friend anyone could ever have. I didn't deserve him."

"Nonsense. You and Lane were perfect together."

Matt didn't know what to say. They had been perfect. As friends. "Lane didn't want me that way. As more than a friend." He shook his head.

"Did he tell you that?"

"He didn't have to. I knew what he thought about me."

"Really? When did he tell you he'd been in love with you since you guys were teens?"

Matt swallowed his spit and choked. Dad had to be out of his mind. Or the connection was bad and they'd crossed lines or something.

"Matt, do you love Lane?"

He sighed. Here it was—the big question. Could he finally say it? And if he did, shouldn't he say it to Lane? But that chance had passed years ago.

"I'll find him, Dad. Tell Mom not to worry. My press credentials will get me into the city, and I'll make a beeline to the Quarter. I'll contact you as soon as I find him, okay?"

"Okay. Take care of yourself. Be careful. It's a volatile situation there. The police are non-existent, and people are desperate."

Matt said goodbye and closed his phone. He leaned back in the seat, not seeing most of Baton Rouge sliding past his window. The exit for College Drive went by and, in a heartbeat, he was back at school, in the rooms they'd shared, making love to Lane on Lane's bed.

To everyone around him, Matt had played the part of the "hot" guy. He'd had guys throwing themselves at him, when the only man he'd ever wanted and could never have lived in the same apartment as he did and slept just ten feet away.

He'd loved Lane from the time he was fifteen and realized he was gay. He'd taken a huge chance that time in the clubhouse, jerking off and letting Lane catch him. He'd played it out in his imagination for weeks before he did it. In one fantasy, Lane would find him jerking off and he'd get so turned on, he'd join him and they'd jerk off together. In another, Lane would take over and jerk him off. In his favorite, Lane would kiss him, tell him he didn't care that Matt's father was a drunk, or that he was poor white trash, and say none of that mattered.

None of that had happened. Lane hadn't exactly turned away in disgust, but at least he'd understood. Matt knew how lucky he'd been not to lose his best friend over that stunt and admitting he was gay.

Matt couldn't believe it when Lane had told him he was gay, too. At first, all Matt could think of was the wasted time and it pissed him off. Then he realized Lane knew he was gay, and if he'd wanted Matt, he would have said or done something.

But he never did. Never.

And why would he? Lane thought Matt was a slut. At least that's what Matt let everyone believe. It was easier that way, to pretend Lane not wanting him didn't matter. Sure, he'd had sex with a lot of guys,

but he'd never gone all the way.
    He'd saved himself for Lane.

CHAPTER 9

New Orleans
French Quarter
St. Phillip Street
August 31, 2005

Lane knocked on the screen door to Sebastian's cottage. He'd brought another gallon jug of water for the elderly man. They'd survived the storm—it hadn't really been so bad—but the power had been off for days, and the water wasn't safe to drink due to the flooding.

Because the city sat below sea level, all the floodwater stayed inside the levees. The pumps had failed when they'd flooded, and the city couldn't push the water back over the levees into the river or the lake as more water poured through the breaches in the levees.

He'd gone out, checked on a few neighbors and they'd told him rumors that twenty thousand survivors had crowded the Superdome and the numbers were growing. Word in the Quarter among those diehards who'd stayed was the crowds were looting shops and stores, but most of them had been flooded and the food contaminated, including the water.

The people in the Quarter were frightened the looting would extend to them. Some talked about defending their property, no matter what it took. Lane had kept quiet and headed back to Sebastian's, determined to avoid any such trouble.

He and Sebastian stayed locked in their quiet bungalow. Sebastian's house, like nearly all the Quarter's homes, had thick wooden shutters that closed the windows and doors off from the street, and they'd made sure they'd been secured before the hurricane struck and now, after the storm had passed, they still didn't open them.

Lane had padlocked the alley gate and, for the most part, he and Sebastian lived in the rear of the house and in the courtyard. At the end of August, with the temps hitting the upper nineties and no power for the small air conditioning units, the inside of the little house and the slave quarters had become stifling.

Sebastian hadn't been looking so good. Those two pink spots that usually sat on his high cheekbones were gone. The heat seemed to be taking a toll on him, and without water to bathe, they were both the worse for wear.

For now, they had enough food, but water was in short supply. They'd been using the tub water to flush the toilets, and Lane had been rationing their supply of drinking water ever since he'd heard talk about how long it might take for New Orleans to dry out.

In the meantime, there was no in or out of the city. Another neighbor mentioned buses lining up at the Superdome to take people away, but the crowds were out of control down there and three feet of water surrounded the building.

They'd have to wade there.

Lane knew there was no way Sebastian could handle that. Besides, Lane had a car parked just outside the house on the street. He could drive them to Lafayette to stay with his parents, but there was no way to get out of the Quarter right now.

High water surrounded them. They were cut off on the island that the French Quarter and the Marigny had become with no signs of rescue.

Sebastian came to the screen door and opened it. "Come on in, dear boy." His voice sounded quite frail, but he could walk. "I see you've brought me some water. Tell me"—he motioned for Lane to sit down at the kitchen table—"how much water do you have left?" He sat down as Lane joined him.

Lane shrugged. "Enough."

"I fear we've greatly misjudged our predicament, dear boy."

"We'll be fine," Lane said. He didn't want to admit how bad it really was to the old man for fear it would steal whatever fight he had left in him.

Sebastian shook his head. "Promise me, if anything happens to me, you'll just put me on my bed, fold my arms across my chest, and close the door. And if you could see your way into dressing me in my burgundy smoking jacket, I'd appreciate it."

Lane almost laughed at the air of melodrama Sebastian gave off. He must have been something in his heyday.

"Nothing's going to happen to you. I won't let it." Lane patted his hand. The once-soft skin had become as dry as a dead leaf.

"My will is in the top drawer of my desk. Everything you'll need is there also—my lawyer's name, the accounts, and the keys to the house." He leaned back and sighed deeply.

"Stop that, Sebastian. You're going to live at least another twenty years. By then, I'll be old enough for you." Lane winked at him.

"Foolish lamb." Sebastian shook his head, but shot him an endearing look.

"Here." Lane stuck out his pinky. "Pinky swear, Sebastian. Swear you're going to get through this, that you won't let that bitch Katrina get you in the end."

Sebastian snorted. "These days, no one gets me in the end." He posed with his nose in the air, as if highly affronted by the suggestion.

Lane groaned. "Not even your boy toy?"

The old gentleman laughed and slapped his leg, then he hooked his pinky, the one with the huge opal ring on it, around Lane's and they pulled.

"One, two, three, four." Lane could feel the old man's strength giving out so he hurried. "Five, six, seven, eight, nine, ten." They broke apart. "See, at least another ten years."

"You rushed through that count, dear boy."

"Did not. Just got excited about being your boy toy." Lane winked.

"Good Lord, lamb, I haven't had the need for a boy toy in, oh, five years." Sebastian winked back.

Matt laughed. "Five years?"

"Stamina, dear boy. I'm known for my stamina." He leaned close. "It's the raw oysters," he whispered.

*   *   *

Matt surveyed the parking lot on the edge of the city where the National Guard had set up a staging area. Someplace called Kenner. With army tents, vehicles and uniformed men, it looked like he'd landed in the middle of a war.

These soldiers carried guns.

Wasn't this supposed to be a rescue operation?

He pulled out his camera and started taking pictures. Did a few interviews with the men, asking where they were from and what their jobs would be on this mission of mercy.

He spotted what looked like the headquarters and hurried over to it. He needed transport to the city and, for now, the only ones going in were the Guard, local police and the press, but only with permission.

"I need to speak to whoever's in charge." He held out his press badge.

The soldier checked him out and told him to wait. After a few minutes, he returned and invited Matt inside. They introduced themselves.

"Another member of the press, huh?" An older officer looked up from the desk he sat behind. He offered Matt a chair.

Matt sat, placing his camera on his lap. "Yes, sir. I'm shooting photos for my paper on the West Coast. Rescue efforts, survivors, that sort of stuff."

"And you need what from me?"

"I need to get into the city, sir. The French Quarter. I understand it's dry."

"That's right." The man sat back and appraised Matt. "I'm not sure we can spare anyone to take you. Right now, we're overwhelmed with rescues, both air and water."

"I understand. How close can you get me?"

He shrugged, his gaze still boring into Matt. "Perhaps to the Superdome. We have some supplies to deliver there." He ran his hand over his jaw, and Matt noticed several days' growth covering it.

"That's close enough. I'll walk the rest of the way."

"You'll swim is more like it. There's three feet of water all through the business district. Canal Street has water, not much, but some."

"I don't care. I have to get there."

"Friends?"

Matt swallowed. He wondered if the "Don't ask, don't tell" policy carried any weight for civilians dealing with the military.

"Yes, sir. My brother." Lane was like a brother to him in some ways, so it wasn't really a lie, but right then, he'd have said anything to get to Lane.

The officer thought that over. "You have your press badge?"

"Yes, sir." Matt prayed.

"Do you think you'll need supplies?"

"I might. How bad is it?"

"Well, on a normal day, the city only holds about three to four days of bottled water and food. We're on day three and most of the stores in this town are under water."

Matt nodded. "Then I guess I need supplies."

"I'll arrange it. You'll leave in the morning. Corporal!" he called. A young man entered and stood at attention. "Take this man to the press tent and get him signed in. He's going out in the morning. Make sure he has a case of supplies."

The soldier saluted. "Yessir!"

Matt stood and extended his hand. "Thank you, sir."

"All part of the job."

Matt followed the corporal out and across the parking lot, dodging Jeeps, Hummers and tents, until they'd reached a large tent with a press sign on it and a huge generator next to it.

Matt ducked inside and looked around. Rows of cots against one wall. A row of tables with chairs, and a neat nest of cables for their computers with a few reporters typing away.

"You have to sign in over here," a woman called to him from behind a table.

He went over to her and filled in the forms.

"There's a mess tent at the other end of the parking lot." She took his picture, ran it through some little machine that spit out a plastic badge. After attaching a clip to it, she handed it to him.

"Great." Matt took it and clipped it on.

"Wear that at all times."

"Will do." He moved off toward the tables.

"How's the internet access?" he asked one of the men typing on a laptop.

"Spotty at best. Forget uploading," he replied with a shake of his head. "Cell phone lines are still jammed, too."

"Right." Spotting an unoccupied cot, Matt went to it, dropped his duffle bag and camera and sat. The weight of his situation hit him. He'd rushed here to find Lane, not thinking Lane had gotten on with his life. He had someone he wouldn't leave behind, even in the face of a hurricane.

That shouldn't surprise him. Lane had always been the strong one. Steady, sure and competent. He'd been the screw-up. Seems like he'd screwed up again.

Well, tomorrow he'd find Lane and his Sebastian. Deliver the supplies. Do his report and then get the hell out of here.

CHAPTER 10

"Can you get me a little closer to the Quarter?" Matt shouted above the noise of the Hummer's engine as they plowed through standing water down Poydras Avenue.

The driver shrugged. "We can get just about anywhere in this baby. Don't worry. I'll take you where you want to go."

Matt sat back, brought the camera up and continued snapping photos. "Go to St. Charles Avenue and up to Canal, if you can. I want to catch some shots of more familiar streets."

The Hummer cruised on, then turned on St. Charles as Matt shot more pics. He'd stopped crying by the time they'd reached the Superdome, almost immune to the crushing emotions that gripped his heart to see his hometown so devastated.

He'd just let the tears fall without bothering to wipe them away. The driver had given him a few glances, but just nodded when Matt had said, "I was born and raised here."

They reached Canal Street and the Hummer rolled to a stop in the dry portion of the neutral ground where the buses and streetcars usually ran. Matt hopped down and went to the back to grab his duffle bag and the carton of supplies, mostly MREs and liter bottles of water.

He put the duffle bag over his shoulder, then popped open a silver luggage trolley and placed the carton on it, tying it down with bungee cords. When he finished, he signaled to the driver and watched as the huge truck pulled away.

He turned to face the Quarter and took a deep breath.

St. Phillip and Burgundy.

Lane and Sebastian.

Would Lanie be surprised to see him? Hell, yeah, but not in a good way, that was for sure. Maybe he should offer the supplies first, sort of a peace offering?

He tried his cell phone again, hitting their dad's number, but that same damn busy signal he'd heard for nearly two days buzzed in his ear. He shut his phone, got his camera out, and started across the street.

He walked down Canal to Burgundy and traveled down it.

The streets were empty, except for parked cars. No one walked around; no one sat on the stoops. All the shutters were closed tight to the street. He knew if Lane and Sebastian had stayed, they'd most likely be living in the back of their house, just like the homes had been designed for. Built on a swamp, New Orleans had been rife with disease in the early years of the city. Designed to do all the living off the street, most of the houses had courtyards at the back in which to escape the heat and sickness.

Matt passed a bar. The door stood open. He stopped and stepped into a darkened, hot room. A few people, sitting at one or two tables, had gathered there and they looked him over. He could read the distrust in their gazes.

"I'm with the press. Can I get an interview?" he asked.

They motioned him over, and he introduced himself, then sat. They were a ragged lot in sweat-stained shorts, camp shirts, wife-beaters and flip-flops. None of them had had a bath in days, but then neither had he.

He snapped a few pics as he asked questions, enjoying the familiar N'awlins accent that took him right back to his former life here. When he'd gotten enough shots, he put down the camera.

"I'm looking for a friend who lives around here."

"Who's dat?" one of the women asked.

"His name's Lane."

They shook their heads.

"Sorry, dawlin' but don't know him." She looked over to the bartender. "Hey, Freddie, you got dat old phone book?"

The bartender nodded, went to the end of the bar and bend over. He came back up and dropped a thick phone book on the counter. "Here ya go."

"Thanks!" Matt rushed over to it, flipped it open, and searched for Lane's name, as he ran his finger down the listings. "Got it."

He memorized the address, closed the book, and slid it back toward the bartender.

"Want something to drink?" he asked Matt.

"What do you have?"

"There's not much left." He shrugged. "What I don't have is water and ice." He motioned to the rows of liquor. "But if you want a high ball, I can mix it with some soda. Still got a bit left in the canisters."

"Thanks. I'd take just a soda."

"It's hot," he warned.

"That's okay. I'll take it."

The bartender poured him a glass. "Four bucks."

Four bucks for a soda? Seemed high to Matt, but he didn't care—it was a soda.

Matt gave him the money and a dollar tip, then returned to the table. After finishing his drink, he gathered up his things, said goodbye, and left.

Out on Burgundy, he trooped along, pulling his carton of supplies behind him, counting off the streets he passed. He hit St. Ann and knew there'd just be a few more streets until St. Phillip.

Time to man up and face the music, or at least, Lane's wrath. As he walked, he relieved his favorite fantasy, the one where Lane welcomed him back as if they'd never been apart. Fat chance that would happen.

He'd settle for being friends, forget best friends, and with Sebastian in the picture, it's the best he knew he'd ever do. Lane had moved on, leaving Matt stuck in the morass of, in the words of one of N'awlin's favorite Saints' coaches, Jim Mora, "Woulda, shoulda, coulda."

*   *   *

Lane poured the last of his water bottle on the cotton washcloth, rubbed the bar of soap on it, then handed it to Sebastian. "Here, use this."

"Is this your subtle way of telling me I smell?" Sebastian took it from him and frowned. "Are you sure we can spare the water?"

"Yes, I'm sure. I have more water in my apartment, you know. Go ahead."

Sebastian rose, took it into the bathroom and closed the door. A few minutes later, he returned, holding the cloth out between his pinched fingers. The scent of his favorite cologne wafted around him.

"Take it if you dare." He had changed into a T-shirt that proclaimed "Suck my head, eat my tail" and had a huge red boiled crawfish on it.

Lane hid his snicker.

"Don't laugh. I'm down to the dregs of my wardrobe." He looked down at the shirt and made a face. "Normally, I wouldn't be caught dead in this, but…"

"You've got other clothes you haven't worn, Sebastian. If you hate the T-shirt, why not wear them?"

Sebastian's mouth dropped open. "And sweat in them? Heavens." He clutched at his heart as if in pain. "Those clothes weren't meant to be sweated in, dear boy." He shuddered. "In my current state of dishabille, these will do."

Lane chuckled. "Really, there's no way you smell worse than I do." He dropped the cloth in a small plastic pail of water and swirled it around to clean it. The water, already a light grey, darkened another shade.

"I'll have you know I can stink with the best of them." Sebastian grinned, then motioned to the back door. "I'm going to sit outside on the porch. It's cooler there."

"Sure. I'll be out in a bit, after I clean up." Lane took out the washrag and squeezed it out, then added some clean water and soap to it. After working up the lather, he pulled off his T-shirt, his modestly claiming "Acme Oysters," and ran the cloth over his arms, chest, belly, and his back. Then he scrubbed under his arms and dropped the rag into the pail again.

They'd been taking sponge baths for two days. It helped, but Lane could still smell himself. He got his deodorant and rubbed some in his armpits, hoping it'd help. Sure, there wasn't anyone around but Sebastian, but Lane took the old man's lead to cover up whatever smells still floated in the air around him.

He decided not to put his shirt back on and joined Sebastian on the porch where the man had stretched out on a wicker couch covered in thick, bright floral cushions. The sun beat down on the bricks of the courtyard and the fountain stood silent and waterless.

"So which one of those boys is you?" Lane grinned and pointed at the bronzes.

"All of them. I'd just turned nineteen and caught the eye of an older sculptor. I spent the entire summer being posed, sketched, and painted, among other things." He winked at Lane.

Lane snorted. "I'll just bet."

Sebastian gave a wave of his hand. "He grew bored with me and tossed me over for a man his own age." He rolled his eyes. "Can you imagine? Being dumped at nineteen for a man of forty-five?"

"Being dumped, yeah, I got that down. But older? That must've been a real blow to your ego."

"Of course not. I put it down to insecurity about his inability to satisfy me." He gave Lane a devilish smile.

"Stamina, right. I remember." Lane laughed.

They sat in the quiet shade for a while until someone pounded on the front door.

Sebastian looked at Lane and Lane looked at him. "Who could it be? The police? Rioters? Looters?"

"Knocking at the door? Not likely. I'll see who it is. Stay put," Lane ordered as he rose from his chair. He made his way through the house, and, despite his order, Sebastian followed.

Lane frowned at Sebastian, and he shrugged. "It's my house. It might be someone I know."

"Okay. Just stay out of sight, okay?"

"You're so protective. I like that in a boy toy."

Lane leaned against the door trying to hear anything at all. The banging started again, and Lane jumped, stumbling back into Sebastian, who pushed him forward.

"Stop that!" Lane whispered.

The knocking stopped and a voice called out, "Lane! Lane! Are you in there?"

Lane's heart stopped. Fucking stopped. He froze, eyes wide, mouth open, as all the color drained from his face down his neck, sliding out of his body to pool in his feet.

"It's for you," Sebastian whispered. Then he touched Lane's arm. "Are you all right, dear boy? You look as if you've just seen a ghost."

"I think I just did. I mean, heard, I mean…" He fumbled over his thoughts as they formed into words. *Matt.* Matt stood on the other side of the door.

Lane blinked and touched the cut crystal doorknob.

"Aren't you going to open it? Who is it?"

"It's Matt." Lane forced the words out.

"Matt? Your Matt? One glorious night of heaven and gone in the morning Matt?"

Lane shot Sebastian a look. "That would be the one."

"What's he doing here?"

"How do I know?"

The banging started again. "Lane! Please open the door. It's Matt."

It's Matt. As if, even after a hundred years, Lane would forget the sound of Matt's voice.

He turned the deadbolt. *Click.* Then twisted the knob and pulled the door open. He unlatched the shutter and it swung open also.

"Hello, Matt. What are you doing here?" Lane gripped the doorframe as if his life depended on it. His standing up sure did because, right at the moment, his knees had turned to Jell-O.

Matt stared at him, opened his mouth to speak, ran his gaze over Lane, and swallowed hard.

Lane's brain kicked into gear. He stepped forward and pulled back his arm, curling his hand into a fist.

"I'm here to find you, Lanie. I brought you some—"

His fist cut off Matt's words as it smashed into Matt's mouth. Lane felt Matt's lip split under his knuckles, the hard enamel of his perfect teeth, and watched as Matt's head rocked back with the blow.

"You bastard!" Lane growled and took another step forward.

"Fuck! Lanie!" Matt held his hand to his mouth as blood dripped through his fingers.

"Don't you dare say 'What was that for?' because you know damn well what it was for." Lane's chest heaved with anger and passion. The anger he understood, but the passion?

He didn't want to understand that at all.

How could Matt still look so damn good after all this time? How could his body still want to rub up against Matt? How could his heart sing and leap at the sight of the man who'd broken it?

Matt nodded. "I brought supplies." He pointed to the carton next to him as he still held his mouth. "Thought you might need them."

Sebastian called from behind Lane. "Did he just say he had supplies?"

"Yes," Lane said over his shoulder.

"Invite him in, Lane."

Lane sighed and stepped aside. "Come in. You can leave your bag here."

CHAPTER 11

Okay, it wasn't the fantasy reunion he'd dreamed of, but at least Lane had let him in the door.

Matt dropped his duffle bag and dragged the carton behind him as he followed Lane through the dark house. He'd heard Sebastian's voice behind Lane, but hadn't caught a glimpse of the man who made Lane happy.

Man, he deserved that punch. In spades. And he was ready to take whatever Lane dished out. He owed Lane that much. Actually, he owed him everything.

"We're in the kitchen...there's light in here from the back windows." Lane spoke without even turning to look at him.

"What did you bring us, dear boy?" That voice again. Culture, suave, sexy.

Matt grimaced. Everything he'd never be. Well, Lane had deserved the best, and now he had it, it seemed.

Matt wiped the blood from his lip. It had stopped bleeding. He stepped through the doorway and into the much brighter room. He blinked as his eyes adjusted to the light, then he looked around. Gleaming stainless appliances, granite countertops and a large antique farmer's table, surrounded by equally antique mismatched, yet perfect together, wooden chairs.

Of course, the guy had great taste, too. He'd picked Lane, after all.

Matt's gaze fell on an old man sitting at the end of the table.

"Matt, this is Sebastian." Lane moved to stand protectively behind the man.

Matt's mouth fell open. The guy had to be, what—eighty if he was a day? Yeah, he looked good, as good as someone in these conditions and his age could, but fuck, this is not what they meant by "older man."

"Hello, Matt. I've heard so much about you," he murmured. "And I can see Lane's description wasn't the fevered ramblings of a man who lost his best friend."

Oh, shit. He knew. Matt looked into that steely blue gaze and knew the old man knew it all. Everything.

Fire crept up his face, burning and telling Sebastian and Lane exactly what he felt.

Shame. Embarrassment.

Matt swallowed. "Very nice to meet you, Sebastian." Matt extended his hand and took the older gentleman's in his. Soft, but dry and almost lifeless. No wonder Lane wouldn't leave.

Lane would never leave anyone he cared about behind.

Matt had been the coward.

*   *   *

Lane stared at Matt, and Matt returned the gaze. The longer they stayed locked in on each other, the hotter Lane got. Aroused and turned on. Just as he did all those years ago when he'd see Matt.

Rock hard.

Fuck, this wasn't good. Whatever this was, it wasn't Matt coming back to him. It wasn't Matt taking his place at Lane's side, as his best friend and partner for life.

He didn't know what this was, but damn it, he wanted to know. With every fiber of his being, he wanted his Matt back.

Just goes to show what a wimp he was.

"So, are you going to stare at each other until your clothes spontaneously combust or you going to sit down and talk?" Sebastian chuckled.

Lane shot a glare in Sebastian's direction and pulled out a chair. Matt dragged his out also and they both sat.

"Now, dear boy, what brings you to New Orleans?"

Matt cleared his throat. "I work for a small newspaper on the West Coast. They knew I'm from the city and when the hurricane hit and the levees broke, they wanted someone here to cover it."

"Figures." Lane snorted and crossed his arms over his chest.

"My first thought was about Lane and his family." Matt concentrated on Sebastian because it hurt too much to see the anger on Lane's beautiful face.

"Of course it was." Sebastian nodded. "Not the chance to make your name at the paper."

"No…well, it's my job. I have to go where they send me. I'm just lucky they did because without my press credentials I'd never have gotten into the city. They're not letting anyone in, even the residents. No one back in until the National Guard restores order and the conditions improve."

"That'll take weeks," Lane griped.

"Yeah, probably months. It's a mess out there."

Sebastian leaned forward, interest and curiosity burning in his eyes. "Is it as bad as they say? Water everywhere? Looting and riots?"

"Yeah. It's bad." Matt glanced over to Lane and the message in his eyes said Don't go into details. Matt shut up. Whatever Lane wanted, he'd do.

"What did you bring?" The old man pointed to the carton he'd dragged through the Quarter. "Chocolate bars and nylons?"

Matt laughed. "Wrong war, Gramps." *Shit.* He didn't mean to say that. He checked out Lane's reaction, but Lane seemed fine.

"So many soldiers, so little time." Sebastian waved a hand as if he were the queen of…well, Bourbon Street?

"Mostly it's bottled water. There're some MREs. They're not so bad if you're starving."

"Water? Great!" Lane's eyes lit up, then he sobered. "Not that we're running out…"

"But we're running out," Sebastian finished. Lane sighed. "Did you think I didn't know?"

"I hoped." Lane shook his head.

"Lane, I spoke to your mom and dad. I called them when I couldn't reach you. They're very worried about you."

"I know, but the phone's out."

They looked at each other. Time crawled by.

Sebastian laughed. "You two!" He pushed to his feet. "Lane, take Matt and show him your apartment." He made shooing motions.

"This isn't your place?" Matt glanced at Lane as he stood.

"No, this is Sebastian's house. I live in the slave quarters behind the courtyard."

"Oh." Matt's brows furrowed. It was odd, but maybe it worked for them. Still, he couldn't get over the age difference and that Lane would want this old dude.

*   *   *

Lane opened the door and motioned Matt through to the porch.

Sebastian muttered, "Soul mates, Lane." And cocked an eyebrow at him.

Lane huffed and rolled his eyes.

"He came for you."

"He came for a story."

"Listen to him. Give him a chance."

Lane turned away, not wanting to hear any more, and joined Matt on the porch.

"Well"—he pointed to the small building—"that's my place. Its small, but I love it."

Matt and he walked around the lifeless fountain. "Neat fountain."

"Yeah. You should see it when it's on." He paused. "But you won't be staying, will you?"

"That depends." Matt shrugged.

Lane didn't want to know on what, so he let it drop. He opened the door to his home and the heat hit them.

"Sorry it's so hot. No power. Let me open all the windows. Since the storm, I've been living at Sebastian's. It's easier that way for me to take care of him." He moved through the house, opening the shutters and windows, filling the rooms with sunlight.

"It's really nice, Lane. So you." Matt smiled as he walked through the place, touching and taking everything in as if he were starving.

Then he turned that ravenous, hungry gaze on Lane, and Lane nearly fainted.

Probably just the heat.

Yeah, right. Fainted with a hard-on.

Lane sat on one end of his couch, and Matt sat on the other.

"Lane." Matt cleared his throat. "Are you in love with him?"

"In love with whom?" Lane tilted his head at Matt.

"Sebastian."

"Sebastian?" Lane's voice rose and cracked. Then he laughed and shook his head. "You think I'm in love with Sebastian?"

"Well, uh, yeah. Your mom said you wouldn't leave him. She said you stayed because of him."

70

"Of course I did. He's my elderly landlord and he's a good friend."

"Oh." Matt's face colored again.

Lane liked the way it looked on him.

Then Matt groaned and closed his eyes. "Sorry."

"Matt, what did you really come here for?"

Matt swallowed, and Lane watched, fascinated by the movement of Matt's Adam's apple as it bobbed. Of the day's growth of beard on his handsome face. On the way his dark hair still set off the blue of his eyes.

"I came for you, Lanie. All I could think about has been to get to you."

"Too bad you didn't think about that five years ago." There was no anger in Lane's voice, only sorrow.

"About that." Matt ran his hand over the back of his neck. It came away sweaty and he wiped it on his jeans. "I made a mistake that night."

"I know. Sleeping with me," Lane bit off the words. Maybe he'd just punch Matt again.

"No, Lane. For leaving. I never should've done that. I never should've left you." Matt shook his head as he took Lane's hand in his. "I was so scared. I knew you didn't want me like that, but I was drunk and I just took…" He looked at his feet and inhaled. "It was wrong, what I did, and want to apologize. I ruined our friendship. I ruined us." Matt's teary gaze came up and fastened on Lane.

Lane blinked. *Did he just say I never should've left you?* And that Lane didn't want him like that? Where did he get that idea? Matt was the one who didn't want Lane.

Despite his brain screaming it was crazy and wrong, Lane's heart did jumping jacks. Soul mates? Stupid, foolish soul mates.

"No, you shouldn't have left me," Lane whispered. "And I thought you didn't want me. You never came on to me. Ever."

"How could I? At your parents'? They'd have thrown me out and then I'd have lost you, two people I loved, and the best home I'd ever had."

Okay, that made sense. Matt's insecurity played a part in that.

"But when we went to college? We shared a room."

"Lane, as far as I knew for the longest time you were straight. Hitting on your straight best friend is a sure fire way to kill a friendship." He shook his head.

"But I came out to you."

71

"Sure, after I'd established myself as a total slut." Matt sighed and ran his hand through his hair. "A great guy like you…why would he want a slut like me?"

Lane stared at Matt. "Because I loved you, you idiot. I've always loved you, Matt."

Matt opened his mouth to protest, but Lane closed the gap between them so fast he didn't have time to speak. Lane's lips crashed onto Matt's. He pushed Matt back, and Matt toppled over.

CHAPTER 12

Lane took complete control of Matt like no one had ever done before. Lane's hands gripped his head in a lock and his mouth sealed over Matt's, taking his breath away.

The slide of Lane's tongue across Matt's lips drove his cock into pile driver territory. *Where the hell had Lane learned to kiss like this?*

Thank God, he had.

Lane's tongue bullied its way inside Matt's mouth and in a hard, bittersweet rush, the once tasted and never forgotten flavor of Lane filled him and nearly swamped his emotions.

Could this be happening? Lane loved him? Him? Not even his father had loved him.

Lane broke the kiss and held Matt's head in his hands. He stared down at Matt with fire and hunger and such incredible intensity Matt knew he'd give it all up to have Lane again.

"Are you going to leave me again? Answer me now. Right now, Matt."

Matt stared up into soft brown eyes that held a sharpness he'd never seen in them before. Lane had changed. He'd become stronger, bolder, more sure of himself than ever before, and that just blew Matt away.

It was like Lane times two. Lane to the power of three.

And fuck if he didn't want that Lane, even more than he'd wanted Lane before.

Matt wanted Lane to take him. This time, be the one to give it up to Lane.

And he knew what he said now, in this moment of passion between them, would alter his life forever.

"Never, Lanie. I'm never going to leave you."

Lane's breathing hitched and he released Matt's head. He stuck out his little finger.

"Pinky swear, Matt. Swear you're mine forever. That you're going to stay with me, here in New Orleans."

Lane asked for the world. Give up his job, the few people he hung with, his apartment. Matt thought for a second—no contest.

"I swear it." Matt hooked his finger with Lane's and they pulled.

"One, two, three, four, five…" By five, Matt stopped pulling, and so had Lane. They kept counting, fingers locked, staring into each other's eyes, counting.

"Twenty, twenty-one, twenty-two, twenty-three…"

Matt leaned forward and kissed Lane, as their lips still keep counting off the years they'd swear to be together.

"Thirty-one, thirty-two," Matt counted.

"Can we quit when we get to fifty?" Lane said against Matt's mouth.

"One hundred." Matt placed his bid as his tongue tangled with Lane's.

"How about seventy-five?" Lane countered.

"Sold," Matt whispered.

*   *   *

Lane had no idea how they got there, but they stumbled into his darkened bedroom upstairs and toppled onto the bed. Lane straddled Matt, pulling clothes off his best friend and soon-to-be lover.

Matt ran his hands over Lane's body, fingers touching his skin, sending shivers through Lane.

"It's too hot for clothes, Lanie."

"It's too hot to breathe." Lane bolted to the window, threw open the sash, and unlocked the shutters. After pushing them open, light and a soft breeze filled the room, and the heat seemed to lessen.

Matt pushed up on his arms and watched Lane as he crossed the small room. Hunger burned in Matt's hot gaze, and Lane's body responded. He wasted no more time and stripped off his clothes as he advanced on the bed.

"Take off your clothes, Matt."

Matt inhaled and finished the job Lane had started. Within a minute, he was naked and stretched out on the bed, his cock standing straight up as he ran his fingers through his pubes.

Lane stood at the end of the bed, just as aroused, if his own throbbing erection could be trusted. God, it throbbed, as if each beat of his heart were magnified in the pulse of blood filling his dick.

"You're staying?"

"Yes. I pinky swore." Matt grinned and stroked his cock.

Lane lowered himself to the bed and crawled on hands and knees to Matt. Since that one time with Matt, his first time, he'd been with a few guys, rubbing off, blow jobs, that sort of thing, but he'd never let anyone take him again.

"Do you remember that night?"

"I'll never forget it, Lanie." Matt shook his head.

"You were my first, Matt." Lane moved forward as Matt spread his legs to accommodate him. "My only."

Their gazes locked. If Lane told any more of his secrets, he should just rip his chest open and bleed them out. But they'd really fucked up before by not talking; he wasn't going to let that happen now.

"Me, too." Matt's face reddened.

"What?" Lane stopped and sat back. "Matt, don't lie to me. You'd been with tons of guys all through college and probably in high school."

Matt reached out and stroked his finger down the top of Lane's thigh.

"I lied to you, Lanie. There were guys, but it was just jerking off and oral sex. I never went all the way, not until that night with you." Matt bit his bottom lip and looked up into Lane's eyes. "I wanted you to be the first one. I wanted to be with you before I left." His finger trailed up Lane's chest, over a pink nipple, and then up to his throat.

"Are you serious?" Lane's mouth hung open, even as his body shivered with Matt's touch. "I can't believe that." He shook his head. "I wanted you to be my first. Always had, since I was fifteen and understood what that meant."

"You waited for me?" Matt shook his head. "No one's ever…" Tears filled his eyes, and Lane reached out to cup his cheek.

"Mattie, I'd wait for you forever. You're so worth it. Worth the wait, worth my love, worth the world to me."

Matt's eyes overflowed, and Lane brushed the first few tears away with his thumb.

"I just can't believe you wanted me. God, you're so gorgeous, and every gay guy on campus wanted you. I was so far out of your league." He shook his head.

Matt chuckled through his tears. "Out of my league? You mean the poor, white trash league? Not quite." He snorted.

"Don't say that, Matt. You're not your father."

Matt froze.

And it all snapped into place for Lane. Matt's father, that drunken bastard, had done more to Matt than just beat on him. He'd destroyed Matt's self-esteem and self-image. Matt had never thought he was good enough, or handsome or smart.

Lane cupped Matt's face in his hands and leaned down so close their noses touched, as if the words he would say would jump from his hands into Matt's head and heart.

"You. Are. Not. Your. Father." He'd say it as many times as Matt needed to hear it to believe it. "To me, you've always been my hero, Matt. My best friend. The bravest, smartest, kindest man I've ever known. The man I've loved since I was…hell, probably ten years old. I worshiped you then and I've never stopped."

Matt sobbed, and Lane swallowed it with his kiss. Matt's hands clung to his shoulders, fingers digging in desperation as he pulled Lane down on top of him. Their chests met, bellies, then the blessed heat of their cocks pressed together. After that, Lane's brain blew a fuse and all he knew was his body thrusting against Matt's and Matt's against his as they tried to climb into each other.

"Need you," Matt whispered. "So bad, Lanie."

"Matt, my Matt." Lane kissed his best friend and lover. "Now and always."

"Now and always," Matt repeated. He arched against Lane. "Please."

Lane shifted, Matt widened his legs, and the head of Lane's cock found its home. With a hiss and a moan, Matt grabbed Lane's ass and dragged him forward, his naked need to be taken so exposed and so beautiful, more than he'd ever been before, that it nearly sent Lane over the edge.

"Now, baby." Matt pushed forward and the head of Lane's cock slipped past the first tight ring.

Matt trembled, his mouth searching for Lane's, and Lane opened for him. Matt's tongue thrust inside, and Lane swallowed the soft moan just as Matt's tunnel swallowed him.

Lane gasped and broke their kiss. "Oh, God, Matt, you're so tight."

"It's for you, Lanie. It's always been only for you."

Matt surged forward, and his eagerness rocked Lane. No one had ever wanted him like Matt did. Had he always wanted Lane so badly?

Fuck, they'd wasted so much time, he wanted to pound something in frustration.

Instead, Lane pounded Matt's ass in a volley of hard thrusts and sharp withdrawals punctuated by Matt's sweet little noises of pleasure.

Lane couldn't believe he'd be the one on top driving his cock deep inside any man, much less Matt. But he was and, sweet Jesus, Joseph and Mary, he loved it. Better than any blow job, any hand job, the only thing that topped it was Matt's taking of him their first time.

The second time, Lane decided, was so much better. And, if he had his way, the next time and the time after that would be just as good. This—what he had with Matt—could only get better, deepen their friendship and grow their love.

"I love you, Matt." That single spark ignited in Lane's body and every sexual nerve ending coiled in preparation to fire. He looked down into Matt's eyes, blue surrounded by a ring of black, thick sooty lashes, and his heart nearly stopped at the love he found there.

"I love you, too, Lanie." Matt let go of Lane's hips and buried his hands in Lane's hair to pull him down in a soul-searing kiss.

Matt groaned, and Lane felt the tight squeeze of Matt's orgasm. It milked Lane's cock, setting off his explosion. He filled Matt's channel with his cum as Matt shuddered and spurted between them.

Lane trembled, sweat dripping from his body onto Matt's. "Oh, my God."

Matt sighed as Lane rolled off him. "If I thought being inside you was fantastic, it was nothing compared to you inside me." Matt rolled onto his side as he used the sheet to wipe the drying cum off his belly and chest, then did the same for Lane.

It was so touching and sweet the way Matt's face concentrated on cleaning Lane up, Lane's heart filled up to near bursting again. So much love.

They twined fingers between them, smiling at each other, and for that one perfect moment, they had it all.

Best friends.

Lovers.

Forever.

*   *   *

New Orleans
French Quarter
Christmas, 2005

"My dear boys, I never thought I'd see this day," Sebastian said as he raised his wine glass in a toast. "To New Orleans, the grand dame of the south. May she forever rise from the muddy waters."

They'd drained the city, the population had been allowed to return, and life had been slowly regaining a small taste of normalcy.

Lane and Matt raised their goblets, and they all toasted across the mahogany table in Sebastian's dining room. Above them, the crystal chandelier caught the glitter of the glasses, silver chargers and the eyes of the three men gathered beneath it.

"She might be waterlogged, but once she dries out, she'll be as beautiful as ever," Lane promised. "I couldn't have asked for a better Christmas present."

Matt grinned. "Me, too. And don't forget my front page story."

"That's right. Picked up by the national wire, mind you." Sebastian nodded. "It brought tears to my eyes, Matt. You did the city and her inhabitants proud."

"Thank you, Sebastian. It came straight from my heart." Matt gazed at Lane.

"So when do you return to L.A.?" The old gentleman rolled his glass between his hands, and Lane grew a touch happier to see him looking so well.

Matt reached across the table and took Lane's hand. "I don't."

"Not even to get your things?" Lane asked. Matt had been living with Lane in the slave quarters since Matt found him and Sebastian.

"There's nothing there I need to go back for. I gave my notice and told my landlord to sell my things or give them away." He shrugged. "Didn't have anything, really."

"Are you sure?" Lane frowned. "I didn't mean you couldn't go back to close up shop."

"There is nothing there I want. Everything I love and care about is right here, if not in this room, then in this city." Matt leaned over and gave Lane a kiss.

"See. I hate to say it, but I told you so, Lane. Soul mates." Sebastian looked decidedly smug.

Lane laughed. "When you're right, Sebastian, you're right."

Matt shrugged. "Hey, when Lane makes you pinky swear, it's the real deal."

"Hey, the pinky swear is nothing to play around with. Bad things happen to anyone who breaks his oath." Lane meant it. He'd always believed in the power of the pinky swear.

Matt twined his fingers with Lane's. "Don't worry. I've never broken any of the pinky swears we've made, Lane, and I'm not going to start now."

Lane pulled his hand away from Matt, and Matt growled at the loss.

"Pinky swear, Matt." Lane stuck out his finger with a sly smile.

Sebastian roared with laughter. "About what, dear boy?"

Lane looked into Matt's eyes. "That you'll be my best friend forever."

Matt hooked it with his, eyes shining. "Forever, Lanie, I swear."

Both Lane and Matt counted, "One, two, three, four, five, six…"

BREAKFAST AT TIFFANY'S

CHAPTER 1

Scott trotted down the steps of the homeless shelter, pulled up the collar of his threadbare windbreaker, and headed down St. Joseph Street to Magazine Street. At four in the morning, the street was deserted; all the action would be over on Canal Street, just bordering the French Quarter. His head swiveled back and forth, checking in the shadows of the buildings for signs of life.

Even though he didn't have more than five dollars on him, he knew there were addicts who would try to take it from you, beat you for it, leave you bleeding and hurt, just to get their next fix.

As he turned the corner onto Magazine Street and made his way toward the Quarter, he relaxed. The closer he got to it, the better he felt. In the Quarter, with its around the clock nightlife, bars, restaurants and tourists, he'd be safe, or at least safer than here in the deserted business district where the shelter he lived at was located. He hated being there, but the only other place to live would be on the streets. He'd tried that, and other men had pushed him against a concrete pillar, robbed, and raped him.

The shelter might smell, and the food sucked, but none of the other men bothered him there. None of them assumed they could take his ass whenever they felt like it. Like him, these men wanted only to keep to themselves, to lie on a warm cot with a blanket, and to sleep in safety.

Up ahead, the traffic light on the corner of Canal and Magazine shone like a beacon in the darkness. His shoulders eased from riding his ears.

Only three blocks to go.

*   *   *

Tony stood in the shadows of the alley between the two buildings and watched the skinny white kid walk down the street. Head down, jacket zipped up to his chin and collar up against the dampness of the early morning, the guy bustled down the street, in and out of the halos cast from streetlights placed just too far apart to make the illumination continuous.

In and out of pockets of darkness. Coming closer. Fading to dark. Closer. Fading.

Inhaling, Tony pulled back farther into his hiding spot. His stomach rumbled. Fuck, he hadn't had a thing to eat in two days and if he didn't get some cash soon, he'd have to go back to selling his ass on the street. Jobs for people like him were few and far between.

He'd already promised the memory of his grandmother, embodied in her silver cross around his neck, that he'd never sell his body again. And no selling drugs. *Uh-huh.* He was clean and he was gonna stay that way.

Running out of choices, he'd turned to thieving. Grandmama would forgive him that, Tony was sure of it. Which is why he now found himself on the outskirts of the Quarter, looking for someone stupid enough to be walking around down here.

Like this fool kid.

He had to be about eighteen, maybe twenty, but damn, the boy was skinny. Hair so black it looked blue in the lamplights, skin so white it nearly glowed. Skin so white that, next to Tony's ebony skin, the contrast between them would burn his eyes.

Somewhere a car horn blared, and the kid's head snapped up.

Shit, his eyes were pale, too. Almost without color. For a moment, he stared into the spot where Tony hid, but his steps never faltered. Then he dropped his head, dug his hands deeper into the jacket's pockets, and kept going.

Booking for the Quarter.

Maybe one of those rent boys on his way to earn a little cash in the clubs.

Maybe he had a little cash on him right now.

Maybe if Tony moved fast when the kid passed him, he could just reach out, grab him, and drag him into the alley. Tony easily had size and muscles over him. It'd be no problem.

Tony held his breath.

The kid passed him.

The scent of soap and something else filled Tony's nose, stirring a memory deep inside him from long ago. When he had a home, a momma who gave a shit, and two little brothers and a baby sister to care about.

Everything he'd lost in Katrina.

Tony struggled with the wave of grief washing over him, making his knees buckle and his gut ache even harder.

The guy continued on down the block.

*   *   *

A soft sniff broke the silence.

Scott swallowed and his ears pricked up. It had come from behind him, he was sure of it. He pulled his hands out of his jacket, fisted them, ready, just in case. As he strained to hear any sound other than his own footfalls, he never saw the hand reaching out from the alley he'd passed, grabbing him by the neck, and yanking him to the side.

He cried out, his own fists flying blindly, but another harder, bigger fist smashed into the side of his head, shooting pain and a warning to shut the fuck up or he'd get worse.

Strong hands cupped under his armpits, dragged him into the darkness of a narrow space between buildings, and dumped him like a bag of garbage on the cold, damp concrete.

Fuck. He'd almost made it to Canal.

Dark, feral eyes surrounded by yellowed whites stared into his face.

"Gimme yo money, muthafucka."

Scott nodded his head and reached into the pocket of his jeans. His ear stung from the blow, and a warm trickle ran down his neck. The back of his earring must have cut him. Lucky his attacker hadn't seen it and tried to rip it out of his ear. He leaned closer to the brick wall to hide it. No sense losing everything.

The black man, so much bigger than Scott, pushed his hands out of the way and dug around for the cash, bruising Scott's hip, crushing against Scott's cock, ignoring the gasp of pain from his victim.

He pulled out the money and looked at the few carefully folded ones Scott had, then straightened as he went through it. "Shit, man, you ain't got *shit*." He sounded so disappointed. Disappointment was bad.

Disappointment could get you killed.

Scott looked up from the ground and prayed the guy would just go away, not get any ideas, or get pissed and kick the living shit out of him. Or worse.

"Fuck you, you little faggoty cocksucker."

The man put his hand on the wall, leaned against it, and drew back his foot, aiming for a hard kick in Scott's ribs.

Scott curled into a ball, waiting for the first of many blows that would rain on him until he mercifully lost consciousness. Over the last few years, this wouldn't be the first time or the last. Nothing to do but duck and cover.

"What the—" The man's voice abruptly ended, cut off.

Scott peeked from behind his arms as they covered his face, protecting it.

A huge man, bigger than his attacker, had his hand around the throat of the guy, and his other hand, a tight black mallet of a fist, landed a punch in the guy's gut.

"Arggh!" The man's legs pulled up toward his belly, his hands spasmed open, and Scott's money fluttered to the ground.

The other man opened his hand and Scott's attacker fell into a heap, curling around his belly and retching.

A rush of relief followed by disbelief swept over Scott. He'd been saved by a total stranger.

Scott stared through the darkness at his rescuer. Barely discernable, the man had to be the blackest guy Scott had ever seen. His skin, what Scott could see of it, seemed to gleam in the dim light, as if covered in a fine coating of oil, like a bodybuilder.

"Thanks." Scott pushed against the wall, trying to get to his feet.

Without a word, the man leaned over, picked up the money the guy had dropped, and shoved it into his own pocket. Scott frowned. So much for his rescue.

He swallowed down the urge to declare that was his money, when a warm chocolate brown gaze, interested, but cautious, cast up and down his body.

Then the guy backed out of the alley and left.

What the fuck?

He'd been robbed. Then his robber had been robbed.

Shit.

He scrambled to the street and looked up and down it, but it was deserted.

Hoarse coughing brought his attention back to the alley.

Scott turned, fighting the urge to add his own kick to the bastard on the ground. But what good would that do? He'd only be waiting tomorrow night for Scott, and Scott might get the worse part. He shivered at that thought.

Maybe if he just left, the guy would think he had a protector and leave him alone. Scott didn't want to rely on anyone but himself; he'd learned that lesson the hard way. Still, even a pretend protector would be worth losing the five bucks.

He straightened his clothes, brushed off his jeans, and wiped the blood from his neck with his hand. Giving the alley a last look, he spotted a single dollar bill caught in the trash on the ground. He jumped over the man, grabbed the one, and then ran.

He didn't stop until he'd crossed Canal Street and entered the French Quarter.

CHAPTER 2

Tony broke from out of the shadows and dashed after the kid, staying far enough behind him to keep him in sight, and so he couldn't hear Tony's footfalls.

He crossed the wide neutral ground at Canal, where the buses and streetcars ran, then to the far side. Even at four in the morning, streetlamps illuminated the boulevard. The warning clang of a streetcar echoed in the night from down near the river, but he kept his gaze locked on the kid ahead of him on Decatur Street.

Tony's head buzzed with questions. Why the hell had he saved that skinny kid? And why was he still following him? Maybe guilt? Maybe some sort of feeling of responsibility? He hadn't been responsible for anyone but himself in the two years since Katrina. His good-for-nothing junkie momma had left his brothers and sister with him in their rundown shack of a house and saved her own skin, leaving town with her latest pimp, never to be heard from again.

Then the waters had risen, trapping the kids and him in the house.

Tears filled his eyes, but he dashed them away with the back of his arm. He wasn't gonna think about that. No way. That was done—over and done—buried in his past, buried wherever they had put the unidentified victims of the flood.

The kid had stopped running, and now he quick footed it. Tony managed to get within a block of him. They were coming up on the Café du Monde, and when the smell of the frying beignets hit his nostrils, his tummy growled. Yeah, they sure would taste some good right about now.

And he had the money to buy them. And a cup of good *café au lait,* too.

He licked his lips as he paused on the sidewalk across from the place. All he had to do was cross the street, sit in a chair, and order up some.

Tony glanced back at the kid. He'd crossed to the next block and soon he'd be out of sight.

With a deep inhale, Tony sucked in the aroma of the beignets, then took off, down the block to catch up with the white guy. He'd get the food on the way back, for sure.

He closed the gap between them. Where the hell was this dude heading? Esplanade Avenue was just ahead and once he crossed that he'd be in the Fouberg Marigny.

After stopping for a lone car, the kid crossed Esplanade, the shadows of the huge oaks plunging him into darkness. For a moment, Tony thought he'd lost the guy, but he stepped up on the far sidewalk and back into the light.

Tony smiled and hurried on.

Two blocks in, his target turned into an alley and disappeared.

Halting, Tony stared at the sign over the two-story building, his mouth hanging open, watering at the sight and the smells.

Tiffany's Waffles and Wings

Breakfast served all day

What the hell? That was a damned long way to walk for some breakfast. What was the kid up to?

Tony moved forward, scanning both sides of the street. Light poured out from the two large windows that fronted the sidewalk, the door to the place between them. Parked cars lined both sides of the street, belonging to either residents or customers; he didn't know which. Didn't care.

He crept to the window and peeked in.

The place was crowded, not full, but at four in the morning not bad at all. He glanced at the table nearest the window and moaned.

The biggest, most bodacious waffle he'd ever seen sat on a huge platter, three pats of butter melting on it, surrounded by three of the most golden, succulent-looking, mouth-watering, crispy fried chicken wings.

Sweet Jesus. He'd died and gone to heaven.

*   *   *

Scott pulled his apron over his head and tied it around his waist.

"Where y'at, sugar?" Miss Tiffany greeted him as she looked up from the counter where she tended a row of six waffle makers. "You late."

"Yes, ma'am." Scott nodded as he checked out her latest hair-do. This morning, she wore dozens of braids decorated with black and gold beads. They matched the black and gold Saints jersey she wore over black leggings. He'd never seen a woman with so many different ways to wear her hair, and he suspected most of them weren't really hers.

She frowned at him. A beep sounded, and she rotated a waffle machine to cook the other side of the waffle. Then she brushed off her hands and came over to him, snatching his chin and head in her large red-brown hands as she stared at the marks on his face.

"Who did this, dawlin'?" Storms swirled in her deep amber eyes.

"Someone jumped me and took my money. I'm fine." He knew better than to try to jerk away from her. She was strong as hell from lifting forty-pound bags of waffle mix and gallon jugs of milk. But the rest of her was round as a peach and soft as a goose down pillow.

"He got yo money?" She tsked, shook her head, and let him go.

"Just five dollars." He shrugged. He had more in a savings account in the bank, where he kept most of his money. But it was the weekend, and no banks were open. Any cash he'd need would have to come from his tips today.

"You call the po-po?"

"No. No police." He shook his head, and she nodded in unspoken agreement. What was the point in calling the police? The cops were over-worked and stretched thin. Scott and Miss Tiffany both knew nothing would be done and then you'd just have the cops noticing you.

Not good.

"Damn. Can't a boy walk down the street without gettin' mugged?" She gave him a quick kiss on his cheek and a slap on his ass as she turned him around. "Go on. Get in there. I got tables need busin'. Then you can wait tables."

"Yes, ma'am." He grabbed the bus boy cart and backed through the swinging doors from the kitchen to the dining room.

He scanned the room. Most of the usual customers were there. He nodded to some of them as he pushed the cart around to the first vacant, dirty dish-covered table. The dishes were always empty. No one left Tiffany's hungry, or without licking their fingers, or without a satisfied smile on their faces. He stacked dishes in one pan, silverware, glasses, and coffee cups in another and trash into the plastic garbage bag that hung on the back of the cart.

"Hey, blue eyes."

Scott looked up and smiled. His favorite regulars sat at a table in the far corner. He moved toward them, cleaning as he went. "Show's over?"

"Yeah, we're done for the night. Crowd's still too light for us to do a third show." Jimmy headlined at the Cage au Follies club over on Bourbon Street, impersonating Celine Dion and Barbara Streisand. Faint traces of make-up still marked his face. Scott thought the eyeliner looked hot.

"Money good?" Scott had thought about asking them if there was anything he could do there, because these guys always had lots of money. Dressing in drag and impersonating stars must pay well, but Scott couldn't think of anyone famous he looked like, and he sure as hell couldn't sing or dance.

"It's been better," Bob, a heavy-set man with mocha-colored skin, answered. He did an act that segued from Ethyl Merman into Bea Arthur, and ended with Bette Midler. Scott had been to the club as their guest once and seen all their acts. They'd sneaked him in the back because at nineteen he was under age.

All of the men lived here in the Marginy. Scott knew Bob and the Diana Ross/Whitney Houston impersonator Peter were a couple, but he'd never seen Jimmy with anyone. And the fourth of their group, Derek, had a lover who usually joined them.

"Where's Max?" Scott asked about the missing boyfriend.

"Out of town. He went to see his parents. They're still in Atlanta. Been there ever since Katrina." Derek shrugged and took a bite of his waffle.

"Aren't they ever coming home?" Jimmy asked.

"No. With the house gone and no insurance money…" He shrugged and didn't bother saying what they all knew. Other than the neighborhoods along the river, the French Quarter, and a very few others, there wasn't much to come back to. Rebuilding seemed to take forever, and no one had seen much of the promised money from the government.

"Atlanta's nice." Scott had never been there, but had heard several people say so.

"Yeah, but it's no N'awlins, dawlin'," Bob drawled.

Jimmy stood and sang in a sultry voice.

"Do you know what it means to miss New Orleans
I miss it both night and day
I know that it's wrong
This feeling's getting stronger the longer I stay away."

At the second verse, the others got to their feet and sang backup, giving an impromptu concert for the patrons. Their voices blended and filled the small dining room with the sounds of the melancholy song, capturing the nostalgia everyone in the place felt about their once-glorious city.

Most of the patrons gazed off into space or out the large front windows; a few wiped tears from their eyes. Even Miss Tiffany came out to listen, her hands clasped, her eyes closed, as the men sang.

Scott hummed along with the familiar tune as he bused tables, wiping each of them down until he'd gotten them all done. No, the city wasn't as it once was, but he had hopes that it would survive. If he could, then so could the city he'd made his home.

The performers finished the song to the applause of the diners, then sat back down.

"You go, girl!" Miss Tiffany clapped as she stood in the doorway of the kitchen. "You sure know how to sing it, Jimmy, you surely do." She chuckled.

"Thank you, Miss Tiffany!" Jimmy waved, stood and then after an elaborate bow, he flopped back into his seat. "Give it up for my girls!" He motioned to the other singers, and they all stood, did a perfectly timed curtsy, and then sat as the room roared with laughter and gave them another round of applause.

Smiling, Scott pushed the cart past his boss, into the kitchen, and over to the dishwasher. This had to be the best place he'd ever worked at and, despite being beaten and robbed earlier, just being around these people put a smile on his face. Miss Tiffany warmed his heart with her caring ways and the customers treated him special, like part of a family. At least, it's how he remembered a family should be and how it would feel like to have people who cared about you, since he'd never lived anywhere but group homes from eight years old on.

He loaded the dishes and set the dishwasher. That done, it was time to get out on the floor and wait tables. He might not be making the kind of money those guys did and he knew he could make more if he wanted to as a rent boy at the gay clubs, but this was good, honest work. His soul and his pride could remain intact, and that was all that counted to him.

CHAPTER 3

Tony leaned back and exhaled. He snaked his hand into the pocket of his jeans and grasped the folded money tight.

The kid's money.

He peeked again and watched the guy he'd saved push the dish cart around the room as muffled singing came through the glass. Inside, where it was warm, where delicious aromas teased, where the people looked happy to be alive, that's where Tony longed to be.

That life wasn't meant for him and he knew it. Most of his life he'd been standing on the outside watching the world go by. When he was a kid, he watched good people struggle…some made it, some faltered, but most fell. Then from the roof of a house, he'd watched bodies float past. Now, he longed to join the others on the inside of this little neighborhood restaurant.

Once upon a time, he had his brothers and sister there with him. Together, he thought they'd make it through anything. Even their mother's druggin' and hookin'.

That was until the perfect storm—the one every man, woman, and child knew would hit one day—slammed down on the city. The levees broke and a wet hell flooded the streets of his neighborhood, black water rising in a dark night, to wash away everything that had been good and clean in his life.

His chin quivered as he fought off the thought that this is all he'd ever be or have. No home. No family. No future. He closed his eyes to cut off the dampness gathering in them. The money felt hot in his hand, as if it burned to touch it.

That boy's money, his grandmama's voice whispered.

Tony took a chance at another look, not at the food, but for a glimpse of the skinny white guy with the ebony hair. He was nowhere to be seen, probably in the back, working in the kitchen.

He'd kill to work in a kitchen. To work anywhere. Things had to get better, didn't they? But it was two years later and things were as bad as ever in his old neighborhood. Wrecked cars. Wrecked houses. Wrecked lives. No one lived there anymore. No one but cats, rats and snakes. No businesses had reopened. Not even the po-po drove down those streets.

Maybe here they might have a job for him?

His stomach rumbled, reminding him of its need.

"Shut up," Tony mumbled at his belly. He rubbed his hand over it, but something scratched him. He looked down and groaned.

He had the cash still in his hand. Holding it up, he stared at it as if he'd never seen a few dollar bills before in his life. The wad of bills looked foreign in his hand, as if it didn't belong there. He curled his hand into a fist and shoved it into his pocket again, pushing the cash to the bottom.

He had the money to buy breakfast right here. He could just walk right into Tiffany's and order him up some waffles. And some wings. Maybe a cup of coffee.

Tony nodded, his decision made. He'd just go in there, sit down at a table, and order him some food. He pushed off the wall and headed to the door. Hand out-stretched for the handle, he froze. The guy had come back out of the kitchen and now stood next to a table, taking an order.

Tony's gaze locked on that kid again, like a homing pigeon flying straight to where it belonged. *Home.*

Shaking his head in denial, Tony backed up, spun around and hotfooted it down the block. Once he'd crossed Esplanade, he veered toward the river and slowed his stride, his heart still hammering in his chest. Dawn broke as he entered the old Farmer's Market, the sun coming up over the West Bank across the river. Tony stopped to catch his breath and leaned against one of the large round columns holding up the terracotta tiled roof of the long, open-sided building that stretched for blocks.

All around him, a scattering of trucks had backed up to the market and men unloaded boxes of produce, filling their stalls with sugar cane, lettuce, beets, melons, citrus, berries, apples, and nuts. His mouth watered at the sight of all that food, so close but out of his reach.

Just a few yards away, an old, thin black man struggled to get a box of melons out of the back of a rusty pickup truck. His shoulders rounded under the weight as it tilted to one side, and for a second, Tony thought he'd drop the whole box.

Tony bolted from the shadows, hopped down the steps, and ran to the truck, rescuing the box just as it slipped from the man's white knuckled grip.

"Hey!" the old man shouted.

"I got it!" Tony grimaced as he caught the heavy weight. He straightened and easily shifted the box to get a better grip. It really wasn't that heavy, but for the old man, Tony figured it might have been too much to handle. Tony knew all about doing what you had to do, no matter what. He'd failed when it had counted the most, and he swore to his grandmama's memory he'd never fail again.

The man stepped back and frowned, then he gave a nod. "Put it over there, boy." He pulled out a blue bandana and wiped his bald head with it. Despite the early morning chill, beads of glistening sweat dotted his brow.

Tony carried the crate to the raised concrete walk that separated the building from the street and placed it behind the stall.

"You need help setting up?" He turned to the old man as he brushed off his hands and gave him the most reassuring smile he could manage so's not to scare him off. Maybe he could pick up a few dollars. The unfamiliar feeling of hope burned in Tony's chest, and he swallowed it down.

The man chewed on a wad of tobacco like a cow with a cud as he stared up and down Tony's length. "You lookin' for work, boy?"

Tony nodded, afraid even to speak, wanting to do nothing to jinx this chance.

The man turned his head and spit, and Tony's hopes flew with the arc of juice that hit the pavement in an ugly brown splat.

"Two dollars an hour. That's all I can afford. Now until I'm unpacked and set up. Don't need nobody to help me sell. Should take about two, three hours." He shrugged.

"Yes, sir." Tony nodded and went to back to the truck for the next box as the old man bent to open the crate Tony had rescued. In his mind, Tony added up the money the old man would pay him. Four, maybe six dollars. Plus the four he'd picked up in that alley.

No, he'd stolen that money, plain and simple. No sense lying. God knew if you lied, his grandmama always told him, and Tony knew for sure, she'd know, too.

Shit.

Tony shook his head at the undeniable truth.

He'd have to give that money back.

*   *   *

Scott wiped down the last table and pushed the cart back into the kitchen. His shift was almost done and Willis, Tiffany's son, would be in soon to take Scott's place for the dinner and late night shift. Willis enjoyed his sleep, was a night owl, so he said, and preferred to work the late nights. Scott figured it was because the tips were better.

On week days, Scott would drop by the bank, deposit his cash and then head back to the shelter to help out there serving dinner. There was nothing else to do besides play cards or dominoes, and Scott didn't like to play. At the shelter, games frequently turned into gambling, and Scott didn't have money to give away or fight over.

Or money to be stolen.

Now, thanks to tips, nearly twenty-five dollars filled his pockets. Most of it was coins and ones, so he usually got Miss Tiffany to change it for him so he could carry it easier in his pockets, since he didn't have a wallet.

Wallets got stolen at the center. Scott kept his cash in his underwear where he could always feel it and know it was there. He rooted around in his apron, pulled out the bills, and started counting.

"Boy, come over here an' let me swap those bills out for you." Miss Tiffany stood at the cash register behind the counter, waiting for him.

"Here, I have twenty in ones, and"—he placed it on the counter, then looked down at the change—"three dollars and fifty cents in coins."

"Keep those quarters. You might want a soda." She opened the register and gave him a ten, two fives, and three ones. Scott took them, folded the bills neatly, and shoved them deep into the front of his jeans.

He didn't like having too much money on him, especially at the shelter. It was just an invitation to the others to take it.

"How about some dinner, sugar?" She grinned at him and pointed to a table. "Sit down an' let me make you something."

He smiled back and nodded. Tiffany made the best fried chicken he'd ever tasted and, even after working there for the last six months, he never tired of eating her cooking. The stuff at the shelter only passed for food. What Tiffany made? That was just below what the angels must eat in heaven.

"Can I get you some chicken?"

"Two pieces, please." Scott slid onto a chair at the counter.

"That's all?" She laughed. "Boy, you're too damned skinny for my likin'. How you ever gonna get you a boyfriend?" Without waiting for his answer, she winked, bumped the swinging door to the kitchen with her hip, and disappeared.

"I don't need…" Heat rose in his face, burning a path up to his hair, as the denial died in his mouth.

Tiffany leaned toward the gap where she pushed the hot plates through to be served and laughed. "You need a waffle, boy. No two ways about it." Then she disappeared again.

He got up, fixed a glass of iced water, and sat back down. It felt good to get off his feet, and he had a long walk back to the shelter. He glanced over his shoulder out the windows, then his gaze flicked to the clock over the counter. Almost four P.M.

It would be dark soon. He'd have to eat fast and get going. Once the business district shut down, usually at five-thirty, the streets became the playground of men like the ones who'd robbed him last night.

The clatter of plates on the aluminum counter of the pass-through and the light *ding* of the bell startled him out of his thoughts. "Order up, boy! Waffles 'n' wings! Get 'em while they're hot!"

He jumped off the stool and went around the counter for his meal, scooping up the plate and placing it in front of his chair. He ran around and sat, pausing just long enough to decide waffle or chicken first before pouring cane syrup all over the waffle and digging in. The chicken would stay hot longer.

Tiffany came out of the kitchen and leaned on the counter. Her warm gaze traveled over the planes of his face.

"Damn, I'm sure sorry they done that to you, boy." She clucked and shook her head. "Skinny white boy like you needs someone looking after you."

"I don't need anyone," he said around a mouthful of chicken. "I can take care of myself. Been on my own for years."

"Me, too. Me and Willis, ever since Katrina." Her amber eyes seemed to lose some of their spark. Then she looked around the small, nearly empty restaurant, and sighed. "I sure wish Rufus coulda seen this place. He always told me, 'Tiffany baby, you make the best fried chicken in the world. You should sell it.'"

"You do." Scott nodded as he bit into another piece of chicken. He licked his fingers and then wiped them on the paper napkins he'd pulled from the dispenser.

"Thanks, child." She leaned her elbow on the counter and stared out the window. "It's gettin' late. You best be goin'."

He swallowed the last bite of turnip greens and washed it down with the rest of the water, then slid off the stool. "Thanks, Miss Tiffany. You need anything else?"

"No, just get going. You make it home before dark, you hear?"

"Yes, ma'am." He took his plates to the sink in the kitchen, rinsed them off, and stacked them in the dishwasher.

As he passed Miss Tiffany, she grabbed his arm. "You leavin' here without givin' me my sugar?"

Heat burned in his cheeks again. "No, ma'am." He leaned over and gave her a soft kiss on her cheek. She swatted him on the arm with a dishrag and chuckled.

He scooted out the front door of the restaurant with a smile on his face, but a weight in his heart. Proud of his day's work, but sad to leave the one place where he felt welcome.

CHAPTER 4

Scott crossed the wide stretch of Canal, dodging a streetcar bearing down on him, its bell clanging a warning, and headed down Magazine. Despite the sun still being up, shadows cloaked the streets of the business district, its tall buildings blocking the last of the daylight.

Office workers scurried to their cars, to streetcars or buses, anywhere but hang around the district. Scott knew that by six, the place would be nearly deserted.

He hurried down the street, unable to shake the feeling someone was following him. Every time he paused at a street to cross, he threw a quick look over his shoulder.

People were on the street, but none of them looked like they were up to no good. He'd learned how to spot them years ago, when he first came to the city. It had been a matter of survival, and Scott knew avoiding trouble was the best way to stay out of trouble.

He turned the corner at St. Joseph. The shelter was just a few blocks away. By the darkening of the shadows, he knew the sun had set. He didn't have a watch—they got stolen—but the shelter had alarm clocks you could borrow to wake you up, if you had someplace to be. He counted himself fortunate he did; most there didn't.

Scott stopped at the entrance to the shelter to say hello to a few of the men. One of the workers, his friend, an older man named Charlie, greeted him.

"Hey, man! Where y'at?" Charlie nodded at him, his thick New Orleans drawl making Scott smile. It'd taken about a year for him to get used to hearing that soft, singsong version of the Bronx accent.

"I'm good. You?" Scott shook his head as Charlie offered a crumpled pack of no-name cigarettes.

"Makin' out just fine, man. I passed by the Mid-City Shelter today. The priests need some help. Wanna move down there for a while?" Charlie lit his own cigarette and took a deep drag.

"Naw, but thanks." Scott leaned on the handrail of the stairs. "I have a job." He couldn't keep the touch of pride out of his voice and he read the look of respect in Charlie's eyes.

"That's right. Down in the Quarter." A stream of gray smoke plumed from Charlie's nostrils as he exhaled.

Scott didn't try to correct him; he just ducked his head. From experience, he knew to keep his business to himself. If he went to Mid-City, it might be farther to walk, but it'd be a bit safer. And the Catholic priests who ran that shelter were strict and no nonsense.

"Well, if you change your mind, let me know. This shelter's getting full, and the boss wants me to see if I can shift some of the guys over to the Mid-City building."

"Yeah, I noticed some new guys hanging around." Scott hadn't liked the looks of them either. To him, they seemed a bit too interested in the comings and goings of the other men.

"Yeah, well, keep your eyes open, man. Just sayin'." Charlie flicked the butt of his cigarette into the gutter and shrugged.

"You gonna stay here or move over there?" Scott turned to go inside, and Charlie followed behind him, stopping at the door to the office.

"Guess I'll move between the two. Wherever the boss says I'm needed." He ducked inside the office and shut the door.

Scott walked over to the check-in, signed the register, and waited as Charlie, now behind the steel wire cage, handed him a padlock for the locker to store his things while he took a shower.

Scott wandered down the hall past the basketball gym. Even before Katrina, a Christian charity funded the place to house homeless men. It had showers, with lockers, and several huge dorm rooms on three floors of an old warehouse.

After showering and changing into a pair of sweats, Scott went up stairs to the second floor, carrying the clothes he'd worn that day. He'd tucked his money into his underwear for safekeeping. Walking past dozens of cots, nodding to the few men either laying or sitting on them, he arrived at his usual bunk near a window looking out on the street.

Welded to the foot of the cot's metal frame, a padlocked footlocker held the rest of his clothing and a few belongings.

He pulled back the covers, then sighed. He'd forgotten to pick up his clock.

Leaving his bundle of clothes on the cot, he trotted back downstairs, got the clock, and hurried back up.

Someone had spread his clothes over his bunk. All the guys in the dorm lounged around like nothing had happened.

Scott smiled, knowing they'd found nothing and not even blaming them for looking. He knew most of the men here had some kind of habit. They even had counselors who lead group meetings for them.

He said a silent prayer as he folded his clothes, thankful he'd never fallen into that particular hell. God knew, there'd been times when he'd been tempted to escape his reality, but he'd always managed to find the strength to resist.

Sometimes, he wasn't sure he could keep holding out.

Bunching the pillow under his head, he closed his eyes and thought of the large black man with warm chocolate eyes who'd rescued him.

Scott fell asleep thinking of strong, dark-skinned arms holding him safe.

*   *   *

Home sweet home.

Tony looked up at the spray-painted X on the four-by-eight piece of plywood covering the front door. A matching piece covered the large front window. He'd been careful not to use one of the houses where they'd found anyone dead because no way in hell could he stay there. Not in no haunted house. *Uh-uh.*

He stepped over the pile of rubble on the sidewalk and slinked down the long, narrow alley between the shotgun houses. At the rear, he checked the tiny backyard, then went up the three steps and unlocked the door. He'd found the key in one of the kitchen drawers and the only lock it opened was on the back door.

The house remained boarded up, like most of the houses in this poor neighborhood bordering the downtown area. Abandoned, just like him.

In the kitchen, most of the appliances had rusted, the floors were bare wood, but it didn't smell too bad. He took off his jacket and hung it on a coat hook near the back door, then placed the take-out bag of hamburgers on the small table he used for eating. At the sink, he turned on the water and washed his hands. The city kept the water going to the deserted neighborhoods so there would be water to fight fires. Thus, his toilet flushed and he could take a bath, but with no electricity and the boards covering the windows and doors, the place was pitch dark at night.

Most nights before going to bed, he'd sit on the back steps, in whatever light the moon cast, and listen to the sounds of the dead neighborhood. Mostly the sounds of rats scurrying and cats chasing them.

He'd tried to befriend a grey cat, but it was too wild and wouldn't come near him. Most of the time, it sat on the fence and watched him. Maybe looking for food, but if it was, the little sucker was out of luck, just like Tony.

He sat and ate the burgers, chewing slowly, savoring the taste of the still warm food, even though his stomach demanded he gobble them down. With no way of knowing when he'd eat again, he forced himself to take his time and enjoy the meal. Closing his eyes, he imagined what it might be like to have someone to eat with, like that skinny white dude.

They'd laugh and talk—about their day, about their lives before and their lives now. Make plans for the future. Maybe about leaving and going someplace where they stood a chance.

He didn't know where that was, but he'd go if someone lead the way.

When he'd taken the last bite, he gathered up the trash and put it in a plastic shopping bag, tying it in a neat bundle. Tomorrow, he'd drop it off in a Dumpster.

He didn't want to leave any evidence that someone lived here. The authorities might force him to leave, or arrest him for squatting. Parish prison didn't appeal to him.

Shaking off that thought, he went deeper into the house, where the light of the late afternoon turned to dark. In the bathroom, the light from the only working window in the house, a small transom over the tub, was enough for him to see his reflection in the mirror. He brushed his teeth and washed his face, undressed and went to his equally dark bedroom.

He'd managed to rescue a few pieces of furniture from a deserted camelback house nearby, including a bed frame and mattress, moving them during the cover of night so no one would see him.

After feeling his way along the wall, he counted the steps to the bed. He kicked off his shoes, stretched out on it, and pulled two blankets over his body to keep warm. Raised off the ground, these old houses allowed the cold air from underneath to turn the bare floors icy.

But it was better than the streets.

In the darkness, he could imagine lying next to someone, sharing the blankets and the guy's warmth.

He chuckled. Just how much heat could a skinny little white kid give off? Not much. Probably not enough to keep himself warm, much less Tony. But he'd give anything to find out.

No way would that happen. They were in two different worlds. Boy had a J-O-B, job. Stayed at the downtown shelter where there was hot water, electricity and other people to talk to. Maybe even a friend or two.

A small ripple of jealousy ran over Tony's skin, raising the temperature under the blankets. To Tony, the kid looked like the richest person he knew, and to the kid, Tony would look like poor ghetto trash. Worlds apart.

He rolled over, ran a hand down his belly, and grasped his erection. It'd been weeks since he'd jerked off, and now, here he was, balls heavy and cock thick and hard, all over some fuckin' skinny white dude.

Shit.

He spit in his hand and stroked, imagining those pale blue eyes staring up at him as Tony pounded him into the mattress. Tony closed his eyes and dreamed, until the orgasm hit him like a happy surprise and he came, pleasure pulsing through his groin with each spurt.

"Fuck." He sighed. Now he'd have to get up and wash off.

Tony climbed out of bed, one hand on the wall, and went back to the bathroom. He pissed and cleaned up, then hung the damp washcloth over the edge of the sink to dry.

He needed to go to sleep, so he could get up early and get downtown.

Just in case that kid might need him again.

CHAPTER 5

Scott thought about changing his route, going another way to avoid the guy from last night, but that's all it was, a thought. His feet took him down the same streets he'd walked for the last six months to get to work.

That didn't mean he wasn't alert, on the lookout for any movement in the shadows, or along the darkened doorways of the buildings.

Scott's breathing sped up as the same alley where he'd been jumped loomed nearer, matching his heart's staccato beat. He curled his hands into fists, ready once again to defend himself, although he'd been pretty useless in the last fight.

Eyes focused on the dark mouth of the alley, he slowed his pace, his body tensing to flee if needed.

A large figure stepped out of a doorway just before the alley.

Scott's heart did a hard leap into his throat and he had to bite his lip to keep from crying out. He braked, brought his fists up, and waited, like a boxer, to start swinging.

The man came closer, hand out, as if to give him something.

"Here. Take it." The deep voice matched the size of the man.

Scott narrowed his eyes, trying for a clearer look. This wasn't his attacker. It was the man who had rescued him, then took his money and fled.

"You took my money." At last Scott's voice kicked in, wobbling, but not cracking with the fear screaming at him to shut up and run.

"I know. Sorry." He sounded sincere, but Scott wasn't sure if he should trust him.

Scott moved to a nearby pool of light. "Come over here where I can see you."

He heard a soft sigh, then the man stepped to the light, and looked up, his face dark as the surrounding night, dreadlocks falling to his shoulders.

But those warm chocolate eyes. Scott would know them anywhere.

"Here." The man motioned with his hand again.

Scott held out his fist, uncurled it, and opened his hand, palm up.

Neatly folded bills dropped into it.

"My money?" Scott cocked his head up to look into the man's eyes. A head taller than he and about fifty pounds heavier, the guy would intimidate anyone. Still, Scott had the odd feeling he'd be safe.

"Yeah." He shrugged. "It's all there."

"Thank you." Scott didn't know what else to say. For some reason, he didn't want to embarrass the dude by checking the amount, so he just shoved the money in his pocket.

They stood there, looking at each other in the soft ring of light. Overhead, bugs bumped against the cover of the street lamp, and the distant sound of streetcar clangs filled the night with a weird sort of music.

"I have to go." Scott motioned toward the Quarter. Maybe he should take off, make a dash for it, haul ass all the way to Tiffany's. But he didn't move.

"I know." The man stepped aside to let him pass.

"'Bye." Scott dragged his gaze from the black man's and started toward Canal Street. He didn't want to go, but if he lingered, he'd be late.

The man fell into step next to him and they walked to Canal Street in silence. Scott had so many questions he wanted to ask, but didn't know where to start.

At Canal, they stopped, as if it were some sort of barrier. As if once crossed together, things would change. Scott wasn't sure what would change, but he hoped…he hoped it would be good.

"My name is Tony."

Scott turned to face the big guy. "I'm Scott." He held out his hand to shake.

The man stared at it, stared at Scott's face, then back to the hand. Then he slid his hand over Scott's, engulfing it. Black skin against white a sharp contrast. Sharp, but somehow exciting.

The man's hand was warm, dry, solid. Built like a rock, he stood over six feet, his broad shoulders straining at the old khaki jacket he wore. His dreads gave him an almost wild look, but the softness of his features and the shyness of his smile told a different story.

He towered over Scott, but Scott didn't fear him. In fact, he didn't want to let the guy's hand go, but he did, pulling it out of the tight grip holding him in place. Wondering how those large hands would feel on his body, caressing him.

"Well. Goodbye." Scott gave him a nod and crossed the street.

The man stayed on the corner, watching him. Scott could feel the dude's eyes on his back, feel their warmth, as if they were connected in some way.

He lost the feeling as he stepped into the Quarter, the warmth wicked away from his body as if he'd discarded his windbreaker and wore only his thin T-shirt.

Scott wanted that warmth back.

*   *   *

Tony touched the palm of the hand he'd held Scott with against his cheek. It was still warm, as if he'd held it to a heater or over the flame of a stove. He'd felt that gentle warmth before, a long time ago, but maybe it had just been a dream. The slim figure disappeared across Canal and down the half-lit street, on his way to Tiffany's Waffles 'n' Wings.

If he hurried he could make sure Scott got to work safe, then maybe head over to the Market and see if he could pick up some work there. There was still a lot of ground Scott had to cover, and not all of it was safe at this time of morning.

Tony followed Scott.

He still had a few dollars left from yesterday. Maybe if there was work, afterward he'd get some beignets and coffee. Maybe if he saved up some money, he could go to Tiffany's and get some wings. And a waffle with lots of butter and dark, rich cane syrup.

He licked his lips at the thought. That led him to wonder if Scott would taste like waffles, or wings or a mixture of both.

Scott, now a small, thin figure two blocks ahead of him, moved farther down Decatur Street. Tony kept him in sight, but stayed back, to keep out of sight. They passed Café Du Monde, went by the Market, crossed Esplanade Avenue and headed into the Marigny, down the blocks to the restaurant.

Scott turned into the alley.

Tony came up to the restaurant and leaned against the building to peek inside.

A good crowd this morning.

The food looked so good, smelled even better.

Tomorrow he'd definitely order himself some breakfast.

*   *   *

Scott glanced up at a movement beyond the front window. A dark shape of a man darted back, as if afraid he'd been spotted.

Tony.

Scott smiled and wiped down the next table, stacking dishes in the cart.

"Dawlin', what you smiling at?" Tiffany called to him.

He shrugged. "Nothing."

"Smile like that, well, something put it there. Something. Or some*one*." She cocked a pencil line-thin eyebrow upward.

He couldn't help but smile again and his cheeks heated.

Tiffany let out a loud whoop. "See! I knew it! You got yo'self a boyfriend."

Scott ducked his head and concentrated on a particularly large spot of syrup.

"All right. Be like that. Treat me like I ain't the only friend you got." She tsked, then rang up a customer at the register.

Scott kept his head down and continued to clean up. He pushed the cart into the kitchen, loaded the dishwasher, and swapped out his white busboy apron for his black waiter's apron.

The early morning crowd had cleared out, with only a few stragglers left, so his job would just be pouring coffee and cleaning up after them.

When he came out, Tiffany sat on a chair at a nearby table, switching into her black fuzzy slippers, the ones she wore when her feet gave her trouble.

"After-church crowd should be here soon, boy. I'm going in the back and get off these feet. Can you handle it for an hour or so?" She rubbed one foot and looked up at him.

"Yes, ma'am. I'll call you when the crowd shows." He glanced at the clock—quarter to nine on Sunday morning. Mass let out at ten-fifteen at St. Louis Cathedral.

"I got a batch of waffle mix done, and two dozen wings battered and ready to drop in the fryer. It's all in the fridge." She pushed to her feet and limped to the kitchen. "If you need me, call. Don't try to handle it on your own." She winked at him, then disappeared into the kitchen, heading for the back room where she kept a cot for the workers to rest on between shifts.

He spent the rest of the time filling sugar jars, salt and pepper shakers, and wrapping silverware in paper napkins. Occasionally, he'd glance up at the window, but he didn't see Tony again.

The smile stayed on his face until the first of the churchgoers entered, dressed in their Sunday best—hats, gloves, suits and spit-shined shoes. After he got them seated at tables and the coffee poured, he went in the back and woke up Miss Tiffany.

*   *   *

Tony waited for the old man to park the truck, then he stepped from the shadows. He stuffed his hands into his pockets to keep the man from seeing how nervous he was about asking for more work.

The old man looked him over, spit a stream of juice to the side, and gave him a quick nod. Tony grinned and met him at the back of the truck. They got the gate down, and Tony started to unload the truck.

"My name's Tony."

"I'm Roscoe." The man didn't offer more.

Tony wondered, as he unloaded the cardboard boxes and wooden crates, if Roscoe didn't have any family to help him, no sons, or nephews. 'Course, since Katrina, a lot of folks simply never came back.

E-vac-u-ees.

Everyone knew that just meant "poor black folks."

There were days when Tony envied them—the ones who got away, went off to a new city and a better life, a life with jobs, dignity, all shiny new and fresh.

Some days, he thought they were all traitors to the city. Leaving when times were hard and never coming back. Like his mama. Abandoning their pasts, their responsibilities, and their lives.

Some folks never got the choice, did they? Some, like him, had the choice, but just couldn't make himself get on that bus. He didn't deserve to leave. Didn't deserve to have a fresh start, a new life.

His brothers and sister didn't get that chance, so why should he?

CHAPTER 6

Tony was waiting for him when he got off his shift. Leaning against the building, he gave Scott a nod, then fell into step beside him.

"Work okay?"

"Yes." Scott smiled, wondering where this was going. Wondering where he wanted it to go.

"I worked today." Tony grinned at him.

"That's great! Where?"

"The market. I unloaded produce."

"That's a good job." Scott shot a glance at him. "You look pretty strong. Throwing those boxes around must be easy for you."

Tony ducked his head, and although he couldn't see it, Scott bet Tony blushed at the compliment.

"Yeah. I guess. 'Bout all I'm good for, anyway."

Scott stopped. Tony took another step, then stopped, too.

"Don't do that."

"Do what?" Tony cocked his head at him.

"Run yourself down. It's bad enough we're treated badly by others. We don't need to do it to ourselves." Scott didn't mean to sound as mad as he felt, but by the way Tony took a step back, he figured he'd come across that way.

"Okay." Tony nodded, eyes wide.

"Okay." Scott relaxed. "Anyway, any job is a good job." He started walking again, and Tony fell in beside him.

"Yeah."

They walked in silence to Canal Street. Scott didn't realize how much he missed just hanging with someone. Well, someone as young as him. Charlie was nice and had looked out for him, but he was in his late thirties. The other men at the shelter weren't his age; most of them in their forties, fifties and even older. Some just looked older from the booze and the drugs.

"Well…" Scott didn't know if Tony planned to walk him all the way home or not. It was kind of weird, but kind of nice. And sweet.

"It's almost dark." Tony looked up at the sky.

So he knew the business district wasn't safe after dark. After all, he'd been waiting to jump someone, hadn't he? Or had he just been down there looking for someone to rescue? Scott doubted that.

He crossed the large intersection. "Were you going to jump me the other night?"

Tony chewed on his bottom lip. "Yeah. I…I didn't have no money."

"So why did you stop that guy? Mad he got to me before you did?"

"Naw. I coulda had you first. I just let you pass." Tony moved his fingers like they were walking.

"Why?"

Tony halted, looked at the ground, and whispered, "You smelled nice."

Scott stared at the big man. "What? I smelled nice?" He burst out laughing. All he'd needed to stay safe was to take a bath more often?

Tony's brows drew together and his lips tightened. "Don't laugh!" he shouted.

Scott stopped and sobered. "You're right. I wasn't laughing at you. I was laughing at the merits of good hygiene."

"Oh." Tony's hands relaxed and he pushed the dreads out of his face. "Okay."

"Thanks." Scott took off again down the block.

"Well, you did. Still do," Tony muttered, and Scott's heart did a little flutter.

The shelter steps were a few yards away. The walk had been quick with someone to talk to, even though there hadn't really been that much talking.

"This where you stay?" Tony pointed at the sign hanging over the sidewalk.

"Yeah. It's not bad."

Tony thrust his hands in his pockets and stared at his feet. "I have a place."

"You do? Where?" Scott hadn't heard of another shelter nearby, except the one in Mid-City.

"A house. Down on St. Josephine."

Scott thought about where it would be located. "On the other side of the bridge?"

"Yeah, near the old St. Thomas projects."

The federal government shut down the housing projects after the flood and never re-opened them. They stood empty and boarded up, and the neighborhoods around them weren't much better.

"That's great." Scott didn't know what else to say. The sun had retreated behind the buildings, and they had reached the shelter. Charlie stood on the steps, giving Tony and him looks Scott couldn't decipher. "Well, I gotta go now."

Tony looked up at him, need and hunger burning in his eyes. Time dragged as they stared into each other's eyes. Scott knew something important might happen, or the moment might pass and they'd go their separate ways.

"Want to stay with me?" Tony blurted out.

Scott blinked. "What?"

Tony looked up, then down, then shuffled his feet. "Nothin'. See you." He spun around and headed down the block.

Scott's heart stopped, then started in his chest as he watched Tony's slumped shoulders, before his gaze dropped to the firm ass filling out the worn jeans. Without thinking, he ran after Tony, caught him by the arm, and pulled him to a stop.

"Yeah. I do." Scott looked up into chocolate eyes, swimming in pain and tears.

"Huh?" Tony looked down at him, head tilted to the side.

"I want to stay with you. It'll be farther to get to work, but I can take the bus."

"The bus costs almost a dollar." Tony rolled his eyes, as if he couldn't believe Scott would spend the money to live farther away with him.

"I don't care." Scott squeezed Tony's arm. "I don't care."

Tony glanced back at the shelter. "They got hot water here, I bet."

"Yeah."

"I only got cold water."

"If I want a hot bath, I can come here and get it. You can, too, you know."

Tony's eyes widened. "Really?"

"Hell, yeah. You just sign in, get a padlock for your stuff, and hit the showers. And you can have a hot meal, too."

"Oh." He sighed. "I don't have any power."

Scott shrugged. "Okay. No lights."

His rescuer stared at him, still unbelieving.

Scott laughed. "Anything else you want to warn me about?"

Tony bit his lip and nodded.

"Well? What is it? 'Cause if it's roaches, man, we got the big flying ones and the nasty little ones at the shelter. And I seen a few rats, too."

"There's only one mattress."

"Oh." Scott thought about that and his body heated. "Okay."

"Okay?" Tony blinked, then smiled. "Really?"

"Really."

"You trust me?"

Scott sighed. He moved his hand down Tony's arm and the strong muscles beneath his touch flexed. "You could've jumped me a dozen times, I figure. Dragged me into any alley in town and ..." He coughed. "Well, yeah, I trust you."

"Okay."

"Do you trust me?" Scott slipped his fingers between Tony's fingers, the large hand swallowing his.

Tony's mouth twisted, then he laughed, as if that were the funniest thing Scott could have said.

"What's so funny?"

"Asking if I trusted you."

"How is that funny? Don't think I can hurt a big guy like you?" Scott put his hands on his hips and threw his shoulders back.

Tony reached out, took Scott by the back of the neck, and pulled him to his chest. Scott used his arms to resist, but they couldn't stand against the power coiled in Tony's arms. They slammed together, and the force nearly knocked the breath from Scott. Tony stared down into his eyes, and Scott lost his breath anyway.

"I figure you could kill me, if you wanted to." And by the way Tony's gaze searched his, Scott knew he wasn't talking about taking Tony's life. There were other ways to destroy a man, to leave him broken and dead inside.

"I won't hurt you, Tony," Scott whispered into Tony's chest. He inhaled, his chest filling with the unique smell of Tony, slightly musky, slightly sweaty, and just slightly sweet.

"I'll never hurt you, Scott." Tony ran a finger down the side of Scott's cheek, and Scott shuddered.

No matter what might happen in the future, in that moment, with his face buried in Tony's neck, Scott believed him. At least, he wanted to believe him. Desperately.

And that shocked the hell out of him.

CHAPTER 7

"Who's your friend, Scott?" Charlie glared at Tony, barring his way across the steps.

Tony glared back. "None of your business, mister." His hands clenched as he faced Charlie. He didn't like this bastard and he really didn't like the way he looked at Scott.

"Relax, Charlie. He's a friend. We both need a hot shower and some food." Scott pointed at Tony as he climbed the steps.

The man narrowed his eyes, but stood aside. Tony wondered if Charlie was more to Scott than just a friend and he didn't like the kick in the gut that came with that.

Charlie went inside, through a door and appeared at a counter. He placed two padlocks on the counter and shoved them toward Scott. "He needs to sign in if he's staying." His tone of voice made it crystal clear to Tony that Charlie didn't like the idea. "We're sort of full, you know."

"I know. It's just for the shower and dinner." Scott smiled and took the locks. "Come on, Tony. I'll show you the way."

They went down the hall, then veered to the right, past the gym. Scott went through a swinging door marked Men's Showers, and Tony found himself in a large locker room. Rows of tall metal lockers lined the walls and between them stretched long wooden benches.

"Pick a locker, stow your stuff, and lock it. Put the key on the string around your neck while you get cleaned up. Towels are on the shelf over there. Shampoo and soap are in the dispensers on the shower wall." He pointed to stacks of thin white towels.

They each took a towel, got undressed, and wrapped the towels around their waists. Although the urge to look ate at him, Tony didn't peek at Scott and he didn't think Scott peeked either.

After they stored their stuff, they stepped into separate stalls hung with grey plastic curtains for privacy. Tony pulled off his towel and hung it on a hook, then turned on the taps. Hot water sprayed from the overhead nozzle and he jumped as tiny pinpricks of fire assaulted his skin. At first, it was too hot to stand, but he relaxed into it and eventually turned around so it beat over his back.

The dispensers on the wall had shampoo and liquid soap. He pumped out a handful and rubbed it all over his body. He'd taken plenty of baths in cold water, but there was nothing like a hot shower to wash all the grime, sweat, and stink off.

Once clean, he lathered up his dreads, gave them a rub, and then rinsed off the shampoo.

With his body cleaner than it'd been in a long time, he just felt better.

In the stall next to him, the water turned off as Scott finished. Tony did a final rinse, sorry to see the hot shower come to an end, and turned off the taps. He dried off with the towel, then wrapped it around his waist and stepped out.

Scott stood waiting for him.

"That was da bomb!" Tony grinned. "Been a long time since I had a hot bath."

"Well, anytime you want one, we can come back."

"Good to know."

They sat side by side on the bench to get dressed. Tony hated to put his dirty clothes on over his clean body, but he had no choice. He could change once he got home.

They pulled their jeans on, and Tony ventured a sidelong glance at Scott.

Damn, the boy was skinny. His ribs showed, not bad, but enough, and Tony could see every bump on his spine. What he needed was some fattening up. Lots and lots of Tiffany's waffles and wings should do the trick, not the kind of food they served here, he bet. That couldn't put meat on a rat.

Tony hadn't had a hot meal in a while, if you didn't count hamburgers or the hot dogs they sold at the gas stations two for a dollar. Sometimes, they had a special and you could get a candy bar with that.

Scott could use a few dozen candy bars.

They shrugged on their shirts.

"Let's go up to my bunk and get my stuff."

Tony followed Scott up the stairs to the second floor and into a large room. About two dozen cots, half of them filled, lined up in two rows.

First thing he noticed when he entered was how most of the men sat up, their gazes on him, sizing him up, and it was obvious, they didn't like what they saw.

Tough shit.

He put on his most bad-ass face and strutted down the aisle, every inch of his body radiating a "don't fuck with me" attitude.

"Stop that…you're scaring everyone," Scott whispered, but then he winked.

Tony shrugged. "Just settin' some ground rules, that's all."

"Right." Scott rolled his eyes.

"Don't be rollin' your eyes at me, boy." Tony winked back.

"Right." Scott stopped at a bunk, knelt, and unlocked the padlock on the locker. He opened it, pulled out a backpack, and stuffed everything from the locker into it. Then he stood, shut the lid, and turned to Tony. "Let's go down and get some food, then we'll head to your place."

Tony smiled. "Food sounds good." He rubbed his belly and it growled. Looking up, he caught Scott grinning at him.

"I'm hungry, too."

They went back down to the cafeteria and shuffled down the serving line, pushing their trays ahead of them as the servers filled their plates. Scott led Tony to a table and they sat.

The food was hot, plentiful, and really not that bad.

But it was no waffles and wings, that's for damn sure. Still, he was grateful to sit down in the well-lit room and eat with Scott. They ate in silence, stealing glances at each other.

Despite wanting it to be worse than what he had to offer, the shelter really wasn't that bad. Tony wondered if Scott now thought he'd made a mistake saying he'd leave this place and go live with him in a rundown shack.

"You don't have to come with me, you know." Tony stared into his tomato sauce-covered spaghetti.

"I know."

"You can change your mind."

Scott put his fork down. "Look, if I change my mind, I'll let you know, okay?"

"Okay."

They ate more spaghetti, forks scraping to gather the last of the pasta.

"Still want to leave?" Tony asked around his last bite of bread.

"Yeah."

"Just checkin'." Tony smiled, as Scott laughed and shook his head.

A tray slammed down on the table, shaking their plastic glasses of iced tea. Charlie dropped onto the bench next to Scott, glaring at Tony as if he'd just killed someone. Trying to look all dangerous and threatening. Trying to…

What the fuck?

Muthafucka thought he could scare Tony off? No fucking way. Scott was *his*. The urge to slam his fist down and declare "Mine!" nearly spilled out, but he kept control.

"Charlie? What's going on?" Scott sat back, brows raised.

"I heard you were leaving. I'm just worried about you, that's all."

"No reason. I'm fine."

Charlie's gaze darted to Tony, and Tony met him with narrowed eyes. Charlie held Tony's stare, refusing to back down, but when he spoke, it was to Scott.

"You don't have to do this, you know. Leave the shelter. Not if you don't want to. Not if someone's forcing you." Now Charlie's uneasy glare turned to outright hatred.

Tony flicked his gaze to Scott and a shiver of fear raced through him. What if Scott changed his mind? What if Scott wanted to stay here with Charlie?

Scott took another mouthful of pasta, chewed, swallowed, then said, "No one's forcing me to do anything. Tony's my friend. He's got a place so I'm going to try it out, that's all."

"Well, if you need help, you know where I am." Charlie gave a final glare, then stood and stormed out, leaving his tray and food behind.

Tony exhaled. "Damn, man, did that fool lose his fucking mind?"

"Seems so." Scott's lips twisted as he stared after Charlie, the regret on his face plain as day to Tony.

Tony put his head down and stared at his empty plate. "He's pissed 'cause he wants you."

"What?" Scott's head spun around, his long black hair whipping with the motion.

"Uh-huh. I could tell. I seen it in his eyes, man. Fool wants you bad."

Scott stared at the door to the cafeteria, still swinging from Charlie's exit.

"He's a nice guy, but I don't want him." He looked up and met Tony's gaze, but didn't say anything else.

Tony didn't press for more, afraid Scott might say he didn't want Tony either.

They finished with a piece of yellow cake covered in a thin chocolate frosting, then bused their trays and left the cafeteria.

They passed the office and went out the door.

"Scott?" Charlie leaned on the railing to the steps, smoking another cigarette.

"Yeah?" Scott paused.

He held out a card. "It's got the number here. If you need anything, okay?" This time, there was only concern in Charlie's eyes. "Anything. I mean it."

"Thanks, Charlie." Scott nodded, slipped the card into his backpack, tossed it over one shoulder, and trotted down the steps. He turned back and waved to Charlie. "See you around!"

Charlie looked like he was about to cry.

Goddamn muthafucka.

Tony grinned at Charlie, then slipped his arm around Scott's shoulders as they walked away from the shelter.

"You know Charlie can see you, right?"

"Uh-huh." Tony chuckled.

"You are so bad-ass."

"Yeah, you right!"

Scott laughed and bumped Tony with his shoulder. "How far?"

"Other side of the bridge"—Tony pointed to the bridges spanning the Mississippi River—"then about ten more blocks."

"That's not too far. Where's the nearest bus?"

"On Tchoupitoulas, just a few blocks over."

"Cool. I can ride it up to Poydras, cut across behind the casino, and still go down Decatur."

"And if you get a transfer, you can take the riverfront trolley. Brings you all the way to Esplanade."

Scott laughed. "Sure, I can do that in the morning, but maybe in the

117

afternoon, I'll walk back."

"I'll walk with you," Tony volunteered.

"No need. I can manage."

"Well, if I'm working at the market, I can just hang around until then."

"Like you did today?"

"Yeah."

"Did you follow me after you took my money?"

"Yeah."

"How come?" Scotty glanced at Tony.

He shrugged. "Don't know." And it was the truth because he didn't know why he followed Scott, not the first time. Anyway, if he said something it'd only sound silly.

Scott bumped him with his hip. "Maybe you saw something you liked?"

"Maybe." Tony looked down at his feet, watching them as he walked.

Scott grinned.

Tony looked up, caught the grin, and rolled his eyes. "Shut up."

"I didn't say anything." Scott held out his hands as he proclaimed his innocence.

"Well, just don't be rollin' no eyes at me, that's all."

Scott looked up. Above them, the wide spans of the two side-by-side bridges soared, blocking the night sky from his sight. "Those are some bridges."

"Sure is. I used to have folks on the West Bank, but they're gone now." Tony pointed across the river, then dropped his arm, regretting he'd brought it up.

"Where's the rest of your family?"

"Gone." He didn't want to talk about them, not now, and ruin the mood he was in, the warm feeling he wore, like a blanket around him.

"Where?"

"Just gone, okay?" Tony shouted.

Scott held out his hands, moving them in a "calm down" motion. "Okay, okay. Forget I asked."

Tony simmered. He shouldn't have shouted, but he really didn't want to talk about them. If Scott knew the truth, he'd leave, Tony was sure about that. And now, more than anything, Tony didn't want to be alone.

"Just a few more blocks." Tony looked around and sighed. It'd been a long day and he couldn't wait to get home with Scott.

CHAPTER 8

The first thing Scott noticed as they stood under a streetlight was that this was the last light he could see for…well, it seemed like forever. They stood on one side of the street, and on the other, an eerie landscape stretched in front of them.

"Damn, Tony, it's dark." Scott strained to see, but the world's lights had gone out. He looked up at the sky, and the stars looked as if he could touch them, they were so clear and bright.

A cat yowled. In a vacant lot down the block, something skittered over rubble, and a small dark shape dashed across the street.

"Cats?" Scott clung to Tony's hand.

"And rats." Tony shrugged. "Cats come out in the day; the rats at night. Mostly."

Scott shivered. "I don't like rats." He took a step closer to Tony, making Tony feel about ten feet tall. He wrapped his arm around Scott.

"I got a cat."

"Really?"

"Well, he's wild, but he visits me in my backyard."

"You got a backyard?"

"Yeah. It's small."

"Cool."

They stood there a little longer, eyes adjusting to the dark. "Let's go. It's just down the block."

They stepped off the curb and crossed into darkness.

Scott let Tony lead him down the street. On either side, narrow houses stood empty. Without realizing why, he lowered his voice. "No one lives here, do they?"

"No. Just me, I think. Never saw no one else, but then I try not to let anyone see me."

As his eyes adjusted enough for Scott to see, more details of the homes they passed emerged. Sheets of plywood covered doors and windows. A few of the front doors had been busted open, black rectangles in less black squares. Everything was empty.

Lifeless.

This small part of the city hadn't flooded, but had been vacated, yet no one had come back to claim it.

"Where are all the people who lived here?" Scott whispered.

"Gone. Evacuated."

"But there's no flood damage."

"Naw, it didn't flood here. Still, most of these houses had real poor people living in them. Guess they found something better wherever they went." He shrugged.

"Why didn't you leave?"

Tony tensed, dropped his arm from Scott's shoulders, and clamped his mouth shut tight.

Scott felt Tony's body react to the question. He stopped and touched Tony's arm. "Sorry. I forgot. No talk about family."

They walked on in silence.

Almost to the end of the block, a large pile of rubble lay across the sidewalk. Tony hopped on top, held out his hand, and helped Scott over it. Then, still clutching Scott's hand, he pulled him through a small broken gate.

"This is it."

Scott stared up at the narrow shotgun. Plywood covered the front door and window.

"How do we get in?"

"'Round back. Come on." He tugged, and Scott followed.

They went to the side of the house and slipped into a black tunnel. On one side, the wooden boards of the house and on the other a chain link fence. Scott ran his hand over the wood, letting it guide him in the dark.

Tony stopped at the end, peered around the back of the house, then sighed. "All clear."

Scott leaned forward and whispered, "From what?"

"Just checkin'. Seein' if anyone been here, that's all."

"Right." Scott didn't understand, but this was Tony's place, and he knew what to do, so Scott went along with it.

They went up a few concrete steps to a back door. Tony fished in his pocket and came out with a key. He unlocked the door and pushed it open.

They went inside, and Tony left the door open.

What little light came from the doorway showed Scott they stood in a small kitchen. A smell filled his nostrils, damp mixed with mildew, mixed with age. It wasn't a stink so much as an air.

"Not bad." Scott nodded. In the near dark, he saw the flash of Tony's smile, and his heart did another little flip.

"Thanks." He grabbed Scott's hand and placed it, palm flat, against the wall. "No lights. You got to feel your way to the back."

They edged along the long hall that ran down one side of the house from back door to front door. They came to an open door, and Tony pointed. "Bathroom."

Scott peered in. Dim light from a high window gave the room an almost illuminated glow. It looked clean. A claw-footed tub stood against the wall, a pedestal sink at one end, the toilet at the other.

"Great. I need to pee." Scott stepped in and went to the toilet, not bothering to close the door. He unzipped, pulled out his dick, and pissed, leaning forward to make sure he didn't miss.

Tony waited, leaning against the wall in the hall.

Scott zipped up, flushed, and then came back to Tony's side. "You?"

"Yeah." Tony went in, same song and dance, then zipped, flushed and came back out. "Bedroom's through here."

He led, hand feeling his way along the wall, as Scott followed. The three-sided rooms opened onto the hall with no wall to close them off. Tony switched his hand to the other wall, and Scott did the same and they moved deeper into the room.

Tony stopped. "Here's the bed."

"Great. I'm bushed."

Tony stepped aside. "You want to get in first?"

"Sure." Scott dropped his backpack on the floor, put his hand out, found the bed, and sat. He pulled off his shoes. "How many blankets do you have?"

"Two, but they're thick. I keep my socks on." Tony shrugged off his jacket and spread it out on the bed, like an extra blanket. Scott did the same.

"Okay." Scott, socks on, stood, pulled the blankets back, and slipped into the bed, rolling over to the far side of the doublewide mattress. It creaked as Tony sat, then creaked as he stood, then creaked as he climbed in under the covers.

The heat under the blankets shot up ten degrees, or so it seemed to Scott. The big man's body radiated warmth. Tony rolled over on his side to face Scott.

Scott rolled over to face Tony.

Neither said a word, but Tony's deep breathing sent a shiver through Scott. He'd been with men before, had always known he liked boys. When he first came to the city, he'd traded his body to men for shelter, food, and cash and sworn he'd never do that again. Those times may have involved Scott's body, but never his heart.

With Tony, there was a difference. Scott wanted Tony. Wanted him to touch him, caress him, to feel his big, rough hands on his skin. To feel his lips, his kisses. Under his jeans, Scott's cock came to life, pressing harder as it grew.

Scott reached for Tony's hand and threaded their fingers together on the mattress between their bodies. They lay that way for a long time, just staring at each other in the darkness and breathing in each other's scent.

Tony didn't move, but his breathing changed, from deep and slow to shallow and rapid. Something else changed in the dark. The level of heat under the blanket almost roasted Scott's already on-fire body.

Scott wondered if Tony was as hard as he was. How big his dick was, how it would look, feel, taste.

Wondered if he made a move, would Tony welcome it or reject him. If Tony offered only friendship or more. God, he wanted more. Wanted to belong to someone. Wanted someone to care about him as much as he cared about him.

Scott reached out in the dark, his hand breaking the invisible barrier between them, and touched Tony's face.

Tony sighed.

Scott shuddered at the sweet sound. He ran his hand over Tony's cheek, across his forehead, back down to his chin, then his fingertips outlined Tony's lips. They parted, and Scott slipped the tip of his finger into Tony's mouth.

Tony sucked it in, fast and hard, his tongue dancing around it, driving Scott crazy. Then with a sharp nip, he released Scott and pulled away.

Scott, breathing hard, heart beating so fast it felt more like a vibration than a beat, pulled Tony on top of him with the hand holding Tony's hand.

Tony rolled over without the slightest hesitation.

That was a good sign.

The weight of the bigger man pressed Scott into the mattress, and Scott felt grounded, secure, desired.

Tony cradled Scott's head in his hands as Tony's forehead rested against Scott's.

"Fuck, Scott," Tony whispered, his voice shaky with either fear or need, Scott couldn't tell.

He stretched up and found Tony's mouth with his.

Tony gasped, pulling back slightly, then returned to Scott, his lips brushing softly over Scott's. Scott's cock stiffened, uncomfortable in his jeans. He shifted, slid a hand down, and adjusted himself.

His hand brushed Tony's hand, doing the same thing to his jeans.

Scott laughed. "Guess we should take off our pants, huh?"

"Yeah." They broke apart as both of them wiggled out of their jeans. The pants were dropped over the edge of the bed and hit the floor, then the two young men rolled back to the center of the bed.

They resumed touching each other's faces, kissing softly, tasting, exploring, building the desire and heat between them. Tentative, afraid of rushing, afraid of frightening Tony off, Scott kept his hands above Tony's waist and under his shirt, although his own body screamed for Tony's searching hands to delve lower and discover what waited for him, just below Scott's navel.

Scott pushed Tony's shirt up and pulled it off. He kissed warm skin, soft and scented of male, moving his lips lower, over rounded shoulder, down firm chest, until he'd reached the wide flat disk of Tony's nipple. Flicking it with his tongue, Scott pulled soft moans from Tony until Tony shifted under the blankets and the nipple drew to a hard point.

Scott took Tony's hand and guided it south. Tony's fingers bumped along Scott's ribs and over the sharp angle of his hip, as Scott led it straight to the place that ached the most.

Tony brushed Scott's cock with the back of his hand, and Scott inhaled, his breath caught on the power of just that glancing touch. With each touch, each jostle, waves of arousal beat against his groin. He arched toward Tony and moaned.

Tony kissed Scott, smiling against his lips.

Made bold, Tony took Scott's shaft in his hand.

"Oh, God." Scott shuddered at the feel of heat, rough skin, and eagerness wrapping his flesh.

Tony pulled up, dragging his hand along the tender skin, and Scott cried out.

Scott reached for Tony, trailing his hand down all those hard chest muscles, past springy pubic hair, and wrapping it around a thick shaft.

He shuddered again as Tony whispered, "Scott."

Scott claimed Tony's mouth as he stroked Tony's cock.

Chest to chest, cock to cock, they humped and stroked, moaned and gasped, bringing pleasure to each other, taking each other to the very edge with bites and kisses and suckled tongues. Their hands merged, rubbing cock against cock, pulling and thrusting through that tight ring, until they exploded over the edge of the cliff.

The stars shooting behind their eyelids illuminated each other, laying bare their naked need.

CHAPTER 9

Scott woke in the dark without a single clue what time it was.

"Tony, wake up." He shook Tony's arm as he sat up.

"Huh? What?" Tony sat up, his head whipping around, eyes wide and staring.

"I have to go to work and I don't know what time it is? Shit!" Scott slapped his head and fell back on the bed.

"Oh, yeah, man. Forgot about that." Tony scratched his chest.

"At the shelter we had alarm clocks."

"I got a watch in my jeans." Tony rolled to the side and came back up with his pants. He dug in the pocket and pulled something out, then handed it to Scott and flopped back, rolling over onto his belly and burying his face in his pillow.

In the dark, Scott could feel the round face of the watch, but only one side had a strap. He held it up to his face and squinted.

"This is no good. I can't see a thing, man." Scott complained. "If I'm late again, Miss Tiffany will have my ass in a sling."

Tony sighed. "Here, give it." He took the watch, pressed a button, and the dial glowed. Then he pushed it back into Scott's hands.

"Cool!" Scott hit the button, the face lit. "Three A.M." He exhaled, relieved he had plenty of time.

"Do we have to get up now?" Tony's muffled voice came from the side of the bed.

"You don't, but I need to get up in a little bit."

"Good." Tony reached out, grabbed Scott and pulled him to his side.

Scott curled against Tony as those strong arms wrapped around him. Tony sniffled into his neck, his breath puffing warm against Scott's skin.

"Mmmm, you smell good, Scott." Tony licked a line from Scott's neck to his shoulder, and Scott shuddered.

Scott backed up closer to Tony, pressing his butt against Tony's crotch. A thick, hard cock speared its way into the crack of Scott's ass, and Scott rubbed up and down on it.

"Shit, boy, you gonna make me come." Tony groaned. "How much time you say we got?"

"Enough." Scott bumped back again.

Tony moved his hips back and forth, sliding his cock along the valley between the firm globes of Scott's bottom, and then reached around and took hold of Scott's dick.

"God, that feels so good." Scott sighed with contentment.

They took their time, rubbing and stroking, Tony's kisses traveling over Scott's shoulders and neck, his tongue searching Scott's ear, his jaw, until Scott shifted, turned his face toward Tony, and their lips met.

Scott opened for Tony's tongue. Tony filled the opening, delving deeper and deeper into Scott's mouth, touching teeth, sucking tongue, exploring the roof of his mouth. And all the time, jerking Scott off as he thrust along Scott's seam.

The pace picked up, and Tony shifted, his cock dropping and now spearing between Scott's thighs, the head of the thick dick pushing past Scott's balls. Scott clamped his legs tighter as Tony's thrusting sped up. The slapping of Scott's sac against the head of Tony's cock made a sort of music, along with their moans and sighs.

Tony did all the right things to Scott. He let go of Scott's cock, spit into his hand, then took a new grasp of the hard hot flesh. This time, his stroking matched the pumping of his cock through Scott's legs, and together, their arousal ramped upward, each hard stroke pushing them higher.

"Gonna come, Scott." Tony's harsh breathing sounded so loud in Scott's ear.

"Me, too, Tony, me, too." Getting it from his balls as they pulled and stretched with each thrust, and from Tony's hand as he jerked him off, rough hands in a tight circle, Scott hung on the edge.

"Here it comes…oh, fuck!" Scott froze and shuddered as he came.

Tony cried out, and Scott felt the swell and pulse of Tony's orgasm under his balls. They shuddered, then Tony wrapped his arms around Scott and pulled him so tight Scott thought he might not breathe.

"Shit, that was fucking good," Tony muttered.

Scott laughed. "Yeah, you right!"

They lay there for a few minutes, then Scott tapped Tony on the arm. "Gotta get going. We need to clean up first."

With a weary sigh, Tony sat up and threw back the blanket. "Guess we need to get a clock, huh?" He grabbed his jeans from the floor.

"Yeah. I'll get one today." Scott picked up his pants, got out of bed, following Tony as he led the way to the bathroom.

They cleaned up, changed clothes and headed to the kitchen. Tony opened the back door, and Scott stopped and looked out on the small backyard.

A cat sat on the fence, amber eyes staring at them.

"That him?"

Tony looked past him. "Yeah, that's him. I call him Top Cat."

"Good name."

"He's wild as shit. Lives off the mice and rats."

"That's good. Keeps them away from here."

Tony nudged Scott. "Let's go."

Scott went down the stairs as Tony locked up and shoved the key in his pocket.

They walked down the alley to the front of the house, checked the street, then climbed over the rubble, crossed the street and headed to the bus stop.

On Tchoupitoulas, they only had to wait about fifteen minutes for the bus. It lumbered to a stop, the doors opened, and Tony and Scott got on. Scott paid their fares and they headed to the middle of the bus and sat.

Way in the back, an old white guy leaned against a window of the bus, but he and Tony and Scott were the only riders all the way to Poydras.

*   *   *

"Well, thanks for walking me to work." Scott shifted his feet as he stood at the entrance to the alley. "Why don't you come in and have some breakfast. My treat."

Tony looked into the window, licked his lips, and grinned. "Really?"

"Sure. Best wings and waffles in town." Scott's voice took on a tempting tone.

"You cook them?"

"Naw, Miss Tiffany does the cooking. I clean up, wait tables, and pour coffee." Scott shrugged.

Tony looked inside, his hands fidgeting with the zipper of his jacket. "I don't know."

"Come on. Come with me and I'll introduce you to Miss Tiffany." Scott grabbed his hand and pulled Tony down the alley.

They came to a screen door, and Scott opened it. "Come on in."

Tony stepped inside, hands thrust in his pockets.

"Miss Tiffany?" Scott called out.

Tiffany came out of the pantry, carrying a large box of coffee filters. "Hey, Scotty, how you makin'?" She stopped when she saw Tony. "Who's this fine young man?" Her eyebrows went up and she looked him up and down.

"This is Tony. He's my friend." Scott smiled and bit his bottom lip, praying Tiffany wouldn't mind that he'd brought Tony to the back door.

"Welcome, Tony. Any friend of Scott's a friend of mine."

"Is it all right if Tony sits out front and has some breakfast?"

Tiffany put down the filters and ripped open the box. "Of course, long as someone's paying."

"Great!" Scott dug in his pocket and pulled out some money as he shepherded Tony toward the swinging door to the kitchen. "Here, take this. It should be enough."

"I got my own money, Scott." Tony pushed it back and set his jaw.

"I know, but I said it was on me. You can buy me dinner tonight, okay?" Scott looked into Tony's face, then smiled.

"Okay. Dinner's on me." Tony nodded and went through the door.

"Just sit anywhere. I'll be out in a bit." Scott closed the door and turned to get the bus cart.

Tiffany stood in the center of the kitchen, hands on her ample hips, grinning bigger than a bear. "That's your somethin' special, right? Makin' you all smilin' and grinnin' and happy?"

Fire raced up Scott's face to the roots of his hair. "Well, yeah, I guess."

"You guess? Boy, I can see it in your eyes. See it in his eyes, too." She chuckled and went back to making the next pot of coffee.

Scott got his apron on and pushed the cart out of the kitchen before she said anything else. Behind him, he heard her making kissing sounds and he thought his face would burst into flames.

*   *   *

Tony looked up from a menu and laughed, then he ducked his head and pretended to study it. And, oh, man, the menu looked so good, with pictures of the food right on it. He knew exactly what he wanted.

A waffle. Golden brown, with extra butter, and plenty of rich, dark cane syrup.

And two wings.

And a cup of coffee.

He licked his lips in anticipation of the meal he'd been dreaming of since the first morning he'd met Scott.

Scott finished cleaning off the tables and pushed the cart into the kitchen, then came back out with a black apron on to take his order.

"A number one, please." Tony grinned up at his lover.

"Coffee?" Scott asked, pencil poised over the order pad.

"Yes. With cream."

"Got it." He tucked the pencil behind his ear, took the menu, and went behind the counter, stuck the sheet on the order wheel and spun it around for Tiffany.

"Order up!" Scott called out.

Tony watched as Tiffany came to the window, took down the paper, gave him a wink, and disappeared. It made him feel as if he were a part of some secret, part of the place itself.

He was so thankful Miss Tiffany had treated him nice, not like he was ghetto trash. Maybe if she knew how Scott and he had met, it'd be another story. He sobered, not wanting that to happen ever. She looked a little like his grandmother, the kind of woman who would brook no foolishness and demanded honesty.

Scott moved around the place, taking orders, filling coffee, as Tony watched him. Scott had a smile on his face and a good word for everyone, and it filled Tony with pride that this was his man. How in the world he ever deserved someone like Scott, he'd never figure out.

His coffee arrived, with a small metal pot of cream. "Thanks, Scott. It smells so good." He inhaled and then dumped four sugars in, and nearly half the cream.

"Like it sweet?" Scott laughed.

"Sure do." Tony winked at him, and Scott blushed. It looked good on him, and it tickled Tony that he could make Scott turn that wonderful shade of pink.

"Order out!" Tiffany rang the bell.

Scott went to the window, got the platter and brought it over to Tony. He sat it on the table and stood back. "Best waffles and wings in town."

"Mm-mm-mm! I can't wait!" Tony smeared the butter all over the waffle, then poured the syrup, nearly drowning the golden waffle.

"Man, you do like it sweet! Want some waffle with your syrup?" He chuckled.

Tony took a bit and rolled his eyes. Then he chewed, making soft moans that sent Tiffany, who'd come out of the kitchen, into gales of laughter.

"I loves a man who loves my cookin', child."

All he could do was nod, his mouth full of waffle.

Scott moved off, working the room, and Tony grinned up at Tiffany, swallowed, then said, "I think I died and went to heaven, Miss Tiffany!"

"Good Lord, boy! You sure know how to sweet talk a woman, you sure do."

"A guy, too," Scott muttered, just loud enough for Tony to hear.

Tony didn't bother answering. He finished the waffle and picked up the first wing, tore it apart, and took a bite. "Damn, Miss Tiffany, you put your foot in these wings!" She burst into laughter, shaking her head at him.

For the next five minutes, he didn't say a single word.

But that didn't mean he didn't make any noise, not if you counted the moans of delight.

CHAPTER 10

"Scott, get over here!" Jimmy called out.

Scott went over to the table of regulars from the club. "What's up?"

"You tell us." Jimmy raised a perfectly tweezed eyebrow.

"About?"

"Tall, dark and de-li-cious, of course." Jimmy put his hands on his hips and jerked his head at Tony.

"Oh." Scott smiled.

"Oh? That's all you got to say about him?" Bob chimed in. "Uh-huh, you have to dish."

"So you came over to the dark side, dawlin'?" Peter, who had mocha-colored skin, pursed his lips and nodded in approval.

Scott's face went up in flames at the teasing. He cleared his throat and shrugged.

Across the room, Tony got up, went to the register and paid.

"So, bring him over here and introduce us." Jimmy pulled out a compact and checked himself out in it, then snapped it shut.

"Down, Celine," Derek drawled. "That's Scott's man."

"Lordy, that man's muscles have got muscles." Jimmy pretended to swoon.

Scott laughed. "Okay, okay." He turned to Tony. "Hey, Tony."

*   *   *

Tony looked up, stuffed the change into his pocket and then

131

sauntered over to Scott. As he reached the table, he took in the four guys eyeing his man and slung an arm around Scott, staking his claim.

"What's up?" He tried to sound cool, but his heart was beating like the bass drum in a jazz band.

"These are my friends. This is Jimmy, Bob, Derek and Peter. They work at the Cage aux Follies club on Bourbon Street."

"Hi." Tony nodded. "How you guys makin'?"

"Not as good as you, Tony." Jimmy grinned.

Tony pulled Scott closer and grinned back. "What can I say?"

Jimmy got serious and leaned forward. "Listen Tony. Scott's special, to us and to Miss Tiffany. What are your intentions?"

"Intentions?" Tony cocked his head at the guy. What the hell did he mean by that?

"You know…how you plan on treating him? If you hurt him, we're not going to be happy. We may look like a bunch of fags, but we can still kick your ass."

"Whoa! Whoa!" Tony held out his arms trying to calm them down. They obviously cared about his man; he couldn't fault them for that. "Look, I'll tell you what I promised Scott. I swore I'd never hurt him, and I meant that."

Jimmy's narrowed eyes relaxed and he nodded. "Fair enough. Take good care of him, Tony."

Tony grinned. Seemed he'd passed the test. "I plan on it."

"Hey, I'm standing right here!" Scott huffed.

"Yeah, you right!" Tony gave him a kiss on the cheek and let him go. "Gotta go to work, baby." Damn, it felt good to say that, even better that it was true. If he did anything from now on, it would only be to make Scott proud of him.

"Okay. See you after work." Scott smiled at him and damned if Tony's dick didn't want to stand up and wave back.

Before everyone saw his hard-on, he waved goodbye and headed out the door. He hustled down the street, cut over to the market and sat on the steps waiting for the trucks to show up. He was early, but he didn't care.

A truck pulled up, but it wasn't Roscoe. Tony got an idea, jumped up and jogged over to the truck. "Five bucks to unload your produce."

The guy getting out of the cab gave him a hard look. "You were working with Roscoe, right?"

"Yeah. But he's not here yet." Tony stuck his hands in his pockets and waited.

"Sure." The man walked around and dropped the tailgate. "Five bucks."

Tony grinned and held out his hand for the man to shake on the deal. He did, and Tony got to work.

Just as Roscoe pulled up, he finished the last of the crates. He had time to wipe the sweat off his brow and take the five-dollar bill the man gave him, before hustling over to the other truck.

"See you're working already." Roscoe spit his tobacco juice on the ground, in what Tony hoped was approval.

"Yeah, got here early." He waited until Roscoe opened the back of the truck.

"What you waiting for, son?" The old man gave him a nod, and Tony grabbed the first of the boxes. "What he pay you?"

"Five dollars to unload."

"Good deal. I'll match that."

Tony nodded. It was a good deal. He could move faster, get the job done sooner and collect almost as much money guaranteed, instead of two bucks an hour.

As he unloaded, Roscoe put his produce out on the stand.

"Hey, I was thinking, how about two bucks to break down your boxes, toss them in the Dumpster, and load the crates back on the truck at the end of the day?" Tony might be pushing it, but he wanted to make some money while he could.

Roscoe chewed his tobacco, thinking, Tony figured. Then he nodded. "Deal."

"Great!"

When he finished with Roscoe, he walked around to some of the other vendors who were working alone. He asked a few, including the first guy, if he could break down their boxes and reload. A few agreed to the deal.

The rest of the time, he hung out, helped where he could in the stalls, and at the end of the afternoon, he began breaking down Roscoe's boxes and hauling them off, then moved on to the others.

By the time he was ready to meet Scott at Tiffany's, he had nearly twenty bucks in his pocket and a feeling that put him on top of the world.

Roscoe called over to him, "Hey, Tony! Come here. I got something for you."

Tony trotted over to his truck. "What's up?"

"Here. Take this. I had some stuff left." Roscoe shoved a brown paper bag at him. Tony took it and looked inside. Apples, oranges and bananas filled the sack.

"Whoa! This is great! Thanks, Roscoe." He looked up at the old man.

"Well, go on. Git! I'm sure you got somewhere you need to be."

"Yessir!"

"See you tomorrow, boy." Roscoe headed for the cab of the truck.

Tony waved at him, tucked the bag under his arm, and started toward the restaurant to pick up his boyfriend.

Man, he liked the way that sounded. 'Course, they'd never said anything, made anything official or nothing, but still, Scott had come to live with him, hadn't he?

He reached Tiffany's, and Scott came down the alley. "Hey, Tony!"

Tony's heart did a little flip at the big smile and warmth in Scott's pale blue eyes.

"Hey, man. Look what I got." He showed Scott the bag.

Scott peered inside and reached in. "An apple!" He took a bite. "Delicious, my favorite. Thanks."

"I made a lot of money today." Tony almost busted with pride.

"Great. I did okay, too. Hey, on our way home, let's stop at the drug store on Canal and pick up a few things."

They started walking down Decatur toward Canal, just strolling side by side, chatting about their day. When they reached Central Grocery, Tony stopped.

"Hey, my treat for dinner, right?"

"Yeah."

"How about we split a muffaletta?" Tony motioned to the door.

"Sounds great!" They went inside, stood in line and ordered. In no time, the guys behind the high wooden counter built the large round sandwich, ladled on the olive salad, wrapped up to go and put in a bag. Tony added two sodas from the machine, paid, and Scott carried it out.

"Where you want to eat?" Scott asked.

"How about in the square? The riverfront will be too cold."

So they walked down to Jackson Square, found a bench in the sun, sat, and spread open the paper-wrapped sandwich, cut in quarters, between them. They each ate half, along with another apple for Scott, and a banana for Tony.

Tony sat back as he took a long drink from his soda, staring at his man, at the landscaped square, and figured, Man, it just didn't get any better than this.

*   *   *

Scott wandered down the aisle and found the clocks. He picked out one with an illuminated dial that worked on batteries. It had an alarm and a snooze button. Then he moved over one aisle and found two flashlights, complete with batteries, and put those in the basket slung over his arm.

Tony came around the corner and dumped six candy bars in.

"Whoa! Sweet tooth attack!" Scott chuckled.

Tony just shrugged. "You done?"

"Almost. Come on." Scott led the way to one of the last aisles and stopped in front of a shelf filled with condoms. He glanced at Tony, who stared at him wide-eyed.

"Figured we might need some." Scott kept his voice low, so no one would hear them.

Tony just nodded. Scott wasn't sure if fear or excitement burned in his lover's eyes, but no matter which it was, it turned him on.

Scott moved over a bit, searching for what else he'd need, and pulled a tube of lube off the rack. He tossed it in the basket and grinned up at Tony, who nearly choked, as his head whipped around to see if anyone had seen Scott's selection.

"Relax." Scott rolled his eyes. "No one cares, Tony."

They went to the counter and checked out. Scott paid for the clock, flashlights and sex stuff, and Tony paid for the candy bars. They took the plastic bag, grabbed another one for the bag of fruit Tony still held and left.

Tony and Scott walked down Canal Street toward the Tchoupitoulas bus stop. They caught the bus and made it home just as it got dark.

*   *   *

After two quick icy showers, they dried off, and with a wordless understanding between them, crawled into bed naked. Scott set the alarm, put the clock on the floor on his side of the bed, and rolled over to face Tony.

The room's darkness deepened as full night came on, and Tony's face disappeared, less than a foot from him.

He liked this, lying in the dark, feeling the weight of Tony next to him and the sound of his breathing, knowing they were sharing this time together. It wasn't scary, but comforting.

"Where you from, Scott?" The question came out of the dark.

For a moment, it startled Scott. He thought that since Tony had refused to talk about family, this was an odd question. Unless Tony wanted to talk about family, but didn't know how to start.

Scott figured it was up to him to get the ball rolling.

"From a little town up in St. Tammy parish. You wouldn't have heard of it. Anyway, I never knew my dad. We were real poor. My mom got sick and died when I was eight. No one claimed me, so I went to a group home. Stayed there until I was sixteen, then I ran away. I never finished high school."

"I did." Scott heard the touch of pride in Tony's voice. "You come here then?"

"Not at first. Mostly I hung around town. But by then I knew I was gay, and I'd already had more beat downs over that, so I knew I couldn't stay. I'd always heard about New Orleans, and the French Quarter and gays, so I thought I'd come here."

"Sorry about your mom, man. So you came here about what, three years ago?"

Scott laughed. "My timing sucks. I got here the June before Katrina hit. I'd been living on the streets. That's where I met Charlie. He was the one who talked me into coming to the shelter."

"Oh." Scott felt a ripple of something pour off Tony. Probably jealousy, but there was no need for that. Charlie was too old.

"Yeah, well. Just before the hurricane hit, they bused us to Baton Rouge, to a shelter there. We stayed there until December, then they bused us back."

"You didn't want to stay?"

"Naw, Baton Rouge was okay, you know, but I wanted to be here." Scott shrugged. "There's just something about this city, you know. It's the place, the food, the atmosphere, and the people. Great people, like Tiffany, the guys from the club, and you."

Although he couldn't see it, he could tell Tony was grinning.

"Anyway, I've been here ever since. End of story." Scott let it hang out there, the invitation to share, but without asking.

"I lived here all my life. Grew up in the Ninth Ward."

"That was where the levee broke, right?"

"Right." Tony shuddered, and Scott reached out to stroke his arm, soothing his lover. "My mama was just no good. My grandmama took care of us kids until she died."

"How many kids?" Scott figured that was a safe question.

"Me, the two boys, D'orel and D'enzel and Baby Girl."

"Were the boys twins?"

"No, just real close in age. They looked alike 'cause they had the same daddy. Not the same as my daddy or Baby Girl's. They were light-skinned like Mama and Grandmama. Baby Girl and me, we're dark."

"Oh." Scott didn't want to say too much, just wanted to give Tony room to talk. He slid his hand down, found Tony's hand, and wove their fingers together.

"I *promised* I'd look out for them. Promised Mama when she left us and promised my Grandmama before she died." There was an edge in Tony's voice that cut Scott's heart.

"Your mom left? When?"

"Two days before Katrina. She and her pimp booked it, man." There was a lot of anger in Tony's soft voice. "Left me in charge."

"You were what—seventeen?"

"Eighteen."

"You were really still a kid, Tony."

"I was in *charge*, man. The man of the house." Tony bit out the words, hard and sharp. "They were *my* responsibility. *Mine*." Tony trembled.

Scott kept quiet.

Tony took a deep breath and, for a moment, Scott wasn't sure he'd continue.

"The levee broke at night. We were sleeping, me in the front room on the sofa, the boys and Baby Girl in the back on the beds. The water hit the house so hard, the whole thing shook. I think it shifted off the piers, and the windows blew in. Fuck, before I knew it, there was water up to my neck coming through the windows and the front door, and furniture swirling around." He took another shuddering deep breath, and Scott braced himself for what he knew was coming.

"I never got to them. I *couldn't*, man. The water was rushing around, things were breaking, and next thing I knew, I was floating outside the house and down the block. Shit, I wound up on a roof top." A strangled sob broke the quiet. "I couldn't see a damn thing. I couldn't even see my house. I called for them for hours, 'til I couldn't make a sound, but I couldn't find them, Scott. I couldn't find them."

Another sob that broke Scott's heart.

"No way you could, baby. Not with the water." Scott pulled Tony into his arms and petted his back with long, soothing strokes. "It's not your fault. You did your best. No one could've saved them."

The big man sobbed into Scott's neck, letting out all the fear, the grief, the guilt he must have been feeling for so long.

When he quieted, Tony continued, "Two days later, the National Guard pulled me off the roof in a boat. I was supposed to get on a bus and go to Houston. New life. Fresh start." He shook his head into Scott's chest. "But I *couldn't* go. I couldn't leave *them*. I'd left them inside, and they died, and I couldn't just leave them and have a life when they didn't. See?" He raised his head, staring at Scott in the darkness.

"I know. I understand, Tony." Scott sniffled, his own tears burning tracks down his face.

They held each other for a long time.

CHAPTER 11

Sometime in the night, Tony's arms wrapped around Scott and pulled him to him. Tony rolled over, bringing Scott on top of him. Naked, warm under the blankets, their bodies responded like the healthy young men they were.

Tony arched up into Scott, a hard pressure stabbing Scott's belly. Scott pressed back, returning the gesture. Tony's hands ran up and down his back.

"Damn, you're skinny, baby boy."

"Thought you liked that. And what's with the 'baby boy'?"

"Well, you're my baby, aren't you?"

Scott laughed. "I guess I am." He figured if Tony had loved his little sister and called her Baby Girl, maybe, just maybe, that meant he loved Scott, too.

"Besides, you need a little fat on you. If you eat those candy bars I bought you…"

"Those are for me?"

"Yeah."

"Thanks."

"Okay." Tony chuckled, then caressed Scott's ass. "But your ass is fine, man."

"Glad you like it."

Tony squeezed each cheek, pulling them open, his fingertips brushing just barely into the crevice. Scott moaned. Right, he'd bought something just for this.

He reached over the bed, felt around for the longer of the two boxes, touched the box of condoms, smiled, then located the lube. He tore it open and handed it to Tony.

"Here, we're going to need this."

"What is it?" Tony took it from him.

"Lube. I want you inside me."

Scott rode the shudder of Tony's body. "Damn, man."

For a moment, Scott thought he'd made a mistake. "That's okay, isn't it? You want to fuck me, don't you?" he whispered.

"Oh, yeah, baby boy. So much." Tony's breath puffed on his neck, then the man reached up, took Scott's head in his hands and brought him down for a kiss.

They kissed for a long time, dueling with their tongues, their bodies rubbing and pushing against each other. If they kept this up, Scott would come too soon. He wanted to come with Tony inside him. For once, he wanted to really enjoy, not just tolerate, having sex with another man.

He came up for air. "Lube, now."

"Fuck, I dropped it. I can't see a damn thing." Tony scrambled for the tube, his hands searching for it on the bed.

"Shit! I forgot the flashlight." Scott reached under his pillow and retrieved the flashlight he'd stashed there and turned it on.

"Yeah!" Scott laughed as they both blinked in the hard light until their eyes adjusted. He put it back on the floor next to the bed, on end, the light shining up to hit the ceiling, throwing a soft halo of illumination onto the bed.

"Here it is." Tony popped the top and squirted some on his fingers. His free hand grabbed Scott's cheek again and pulled it to the side as his other hand slipped between.

Scott shivered. "It's cold."

"Sorry."

It soon warmed, and Scott pushed back into Tony's fingers as they stroked up and down his valley. Damn it felt so good, his hands down there, his fingertips brushing over his hole. With each swipe, Scott pushed up as they passed over, trying to get Tony to delve a little deeper.

"You want it?" Tony asked, his voice not much more than a growl.

"Yeah, please. Put your finger in." Scott needed to feel that finger in him, needed to have some part of Tony inside.

Tony pressed against his opening. Scott pushed back, and Tony's fingertip slid inside.

"Oh, God." Scott sighed.

Tony groaned, arching into Scott as he pushed deeper, pulled out, and thrust in again. Shameless, Scott worked himself on Tony's finger. He knew what it felt like when someone hit his prostate, and now he angled his hips for it, unsure if Tony would know where to find it.

Tony's finger slid over it and sparks shot off behind Scott's lids. His eyes flew open and he looked down at his lover. Tony, eyes wide open, stared back at him.

"God, you're so beautiful, all sexed up," Tony whispered. "I love when you make that little noise." He crooked his finger over the gland again, and Scott mewled. Guess he did know after all.

"That's the one. Oh, baby boy, shit, I want inside you."

Scott nodded. "Condom," he gasped, barely able to speak except for grunts, groans and kitten-like cries.

"You do it. I don't want to stop." Tony's cock felt like a thick steel rod against his belly, demanding more.

Scott leaned over, grabbed the condom box, opened it and pulled one out. After ripping the packet open with his teeth, he paused and looked down at Tony's dick. He'd never seen it and now, he couldn't seem to get his fill. Thick, darker than Tony's dark skin, the rim a lighter ring, the bulbous head dripping pre-cum, just took his breath away.

That was going in his ass.

He shuddered with desire and need, unafraid. He'd been fucked before, so this was nothing new, except this time he was so turned on, this time it was his lover, a man who cared about him. His boyfriend. And that made all the difference in the world to Scott.

He balanced the rubber on the tip and unfurled it, covering Tony's length. He scooped up lube and smeared it on, then worked the slick over his own cock. God, it needed to be touched, too.

His entire body had never felt like this before, needing to be fucked and touched, and he wanted to be kissed and bitten and handled by Tony. All by Tony. Only Tony.

"Hold it for me." Scott leaned forward, as Tony positioned himself, pressing the head of his cock against Scott's opening.

Scott settled down onto the head, the pressure almost too painful. He relaxed, then Tony thrust up with a cry, and entered him.

"Oh, God!" Scott cried out, as the pain ripped through him. "Fuck, you're big!"

"Yeah, you right! The better to fuck you with." Tony laughed, groaned, then withdrew, his length sliding out, returning only to impale Scott again.

"Yessss."

Tony pushed up, Scott lowered himself, and they began an easy rhythm. Scott rode up and down on his knees, Tony lifted his hips with his feet planted near his own ass. Scott ran his hands over Tony's chest, plucking at the dark nipples, feeling the contours of Tony's body, loving the way the fine sheen of sweat made Tony's skin shine like polished ebony.

"Touch me, Tony," Scott whispered. "I need you to touch my dick." His shaft stood against his belly, aching, dripping long steams of pre-cum onto Tony's body. Scott ran his finger through it and then tasted it. Not as strong as cum, but tasty.

Tony slicked up his hands again and took hold of Scott. His oiled hands slid up and down the shaft, a tight circle, squeezing hard at the bottom, then softer at the top, jerking Scott off as he fucked him.

It was the hottest thing Scott had ever experienced and he wanted it to last forever, but when Tony shifted and his dick scraped over Scott's gland, Scott nearly came.

"Gonna come soon." Scott panted, leaning forward to find that angle again. Tony picked up the pace, slamming into Scott. "Harder."

Tony pumped, the muscles in this thighs, belly and arms standing out, his cock breaching Scott with each thrust, going so deep, and hitting his sweet spot each and every fucking time.

His body on fire, every nerve sensitive and aware, the shaft of his cock sent waves of ecstasy through his body to his balls. They slammed up tight, and the clenching of the muscles in his groin told him he was moments away from coming.

"Gonna come," he shouted.

"Fuck, yeah. Do it, baby boy. Come on me. Give it to me, baby boy." Tony's hand was a blur as he jerked Scott's dick, his hips like pistons, pumping into him, driving him up the wall and with a heart-lurching burst, Scott exploded.

Sprays of white semen jetted out, arching over Tony's belly, to paint his chest, hard white against soft black, and Scott shuddered, his orgasm dragging out the pleasure with each spurt, until Tony had drained him, and his dick went limp in Tony's sweet hand.

"So good," Scott whispered.

Tony let him go, grabbed his hips, and grinned. "Hold on, baby boy.

I'm going to fuck you 'til I come."

Scott nodded, leaned back, and let Tony have his body to use anyway he needed. His lover's eyes narrowed to slits, his teeth caught his bottom lip, and he grunted with each slamming thrust.

Scott rode him, letting Tony push and pull him, knowing he'd have bruises where Tony's fingers clamped on him, and not caring. Fuck, he'd show anyone his marks, proud of his lover, proud of how he turned Tony on, and how he'd satisfied his man.

Tony cried out, thrust up so hard and deep Scott thought he'd rip in two, and froze, filling the condom with his cum. The look on Tony's face was so beautiful Scott wanted to cry.

He'd done that. Given Tony that pleasure. Made his face look like an angel.

Both men shuddered, then Tony's dick slipped from Scott, and Scott collapsed on top of him, his cum spread between them, and neither of them caring.

Once they could move, Scott slid off Tony and they rolled to face each other.

"Hey, I was thinking." Tony touched Scott's face with a single finger, tracing his jaw to his ear.

"About?"

"Think one day we can get a real place?"

"We have a place." Scott tilted his head, not sure what Tony was talking about.

"No, I mean a *real* place. An apartment. With hot water, electricity, and furniture. You know—a home." The desperation in Tony's eyes read so clear to Scott. He understood that longing completely.

"Yeah, I do." He nodded. "I think, with your money and mine, we could get a little place. I've got some money saved."

"Money? Saved, how?"

"In a bank." Scott smiled.

"How'd you do that?"

"All you need is twenty-five dollars and an ID."

"Really? I got that. I got a driver's license." Tony grinned.

"You do? Hey, maybe we could even get a car?"

"One day." Tony chuckled. "You so crazy, baby boy." He kissed Scott softly. "Let's work on the apartment first, okay?"

"Okay."

"Think on Monday, I can open a savings account?"

"Sure. I don't see why not."

They were quiet for a while, then Scott reached over and turned off the flashlight, plunging them into warm, familiar darkness. Tony surrounded him, in the air, in the bed, his scent, his heat. Scott wasn't sure if what he felt right now was it, but he couldn't keep it inside any longer.

"Hey, Tony?"

"Yeah."

"I love you."

Silence.

Scott's stomach rolled over.

"I love you, too, baby boy."

They reached for each other in the dark, finding their hearts, and losing them to each other, to the cocoon of safety they shared, and to the city that care forgot.

"Know what I'm thinking?" Tony whispered.

"No, what?"

"We should get breakfast at Tiffany's. You know, to celebrate."

"Sounds good. I'll pay." Scott knew Tony had more pride than money.

"Okay. But I'm getting dinner."

"Deal."

Tony pulled him close, wrapping a leg over Scott's legs, claiming him, surrounding him, loving him.

"You're the best thing that's ever happened to me, baby boy."

Scott blinked away the tears and buried his head in Tony's neck, holding on so tight he could barely breathe.

"I need you, Tony."

Tony kissed him, smiling against Scott's lips. "I knew you did."

MY HEROES HAVE ALWAYS BEEN COWBOYS

CHAPTER 1

Simon Tai stared at the rack of shimmering sequin-covered gowns and shuddered. There was no way in hell he was going to wear one of those to the costume party, invitation be damned.

This might be New Orleans, and he might be gay, but he wasn't *that* gay.

For a minute, he thought about not attending his boss Francis's fifth anniversary party, but that would be suicidal. At least, career-wise. Although, if Simon had to wear one of those dresses, he might just slit his own wrists.

Besides, in this failing economy, the prospects of finding another job in his field that paid as well, much less anywhere in New Orleans, were slim to none.

Simon was no fool. It'd taken him a month to land his position as manager of Francis's small but highly rated French Quarter hotel, and Simon wasn't going to piss it away, not even if it meant putting on high heels and a tiara.

He glanced again at the invitation clutched in his sweating hands.

Stag or Drag. Seriously? As Francis had explained to him, stag meant dressing straight, and didn't mean going alone to the party. Then Francis had just winked and said, "You can figure out what drag means, can't you?"

Simon sighed. He hadn't even had a choice. Francis had seen to that by designating *Drag* on the inside of the gold leafed invitation. Simon was so not a "drag"; he was much more of a "stag." He saw himself as a young buck, assuredly male, and definitely horny. Sure, it had been ages since he'd last rutted, but still.

Well, that was Francis, God bless his little queenly soul.

Francis was the gayest man Simon knew, and in the French Quarter that was saying a lot. But he was also the sweetest guy, a shrewd businessman, and over the last year, had become not just an employer but a good friend.

Facing the fact there was no way he would slight Francis, Simon shoved the invite into the back pocket of his slacks and forced himself to look through the dresses.

How the hell was he supposed to know what size to get?

Of course, he'd flatter himself thinking his size surely had to be in the single digits. He took a dress down, size eight, and looked it over. No way would his shoulders fit.

Maybe something sleeveless? Off the shoulder?

Oh, my God. He couldn't believe he was even having those thoughts. This surely had to be some lower level of gay hell.

"What are you looking for?" A deep rumbling voice came from behind him, right next to his ear. Simon's knees wobbled and he shoved the black velvet empire gown he'd held up against him back on the rack, but he missed the rod with the hook of the hanger and the dress fell to the floor.

"Shit." Simon bent to pick it up.

"Let me get that for you." The voice purred.

"No. It's okay. I've got it."

Simon's hand and the voice's hand touched as they reached for the hanger, and Simon jumped back, bumping his ass into the man's crotch, then flew forward, nearly losing his balance.

"Sorry." Warmth spread across his cheeks.

Jesus, could he be anymore klutzy?

"It's okay." The voice chuckled.

Simon turned and stared up into the eyes of the voice. Deep blue eyes. Brown eyelashes. Prominent nose. Thin lips. Short cropped brown hair. Simon knew he should get to the man's body, stop staring at his face, but it was such a nice face. And he was half a head taller than Simon, the perfect height.

Perfect.

"Yes?" The man tilted his head, one eyebrow cocked upward.

"I'm looking for a dress." Jesus, did he just utter those words? He may have been gay, but he'd never had the least interest or desire to dress in women's clothing and pretend he was a woman.

"For yourself?" As the guy hung up the gown, his steady gaze bored into Simon.

He lost brain function, then, as if someone had pull-started his mind like a lawn mower, Simon began his explanation, a speech he'd barely planned, much less practiced.

"It's for a party. For my boss. No, not *for* him. For me. Wait, the party's not for me. I mean, I have to *wear* it to a party. A costume party," Simon stammered as he reached for the invitation and then shoved it into the man's hands, offering proof it wasn't really his fault, and that he *never* shopped here, much less had *ever* shopped for women's clothing.

"I see." The fellow took the invite, opened it, then smiled.

Oh, my God, he's gorgeous.

Simon tapped the card stock. "It's my boss's idea. He's British and thought it would be a lark, as he says." Simon giggled. "He called it a fancy dress party."

Oh, shit. Did he just giggle?

If the guy had wondered if Simon was gay, that just answered his question.

"Fancy dress, huh?" No giggle from Mr. Gorgeous.

Simon looked at the floor, willing the ground to open.

Where the hell was a hole when you needed one to fall into? Like cops, there was never one around.

Simon looked up as the man handed back the invitation.

*   *   *

Charles struggled to keep his face straight. This was too easy. The poor man was practically dying of embarrassment, and Charles knew he should stop yanking the guy's chain, but he couldn't help himself.

The guy was just so fucking cute.

"So what's the problem?" Charles leaned against the counter, dead serious.

"Well. I've never..." He waved his hand at the rack of gowns.

"Never?"

"Dressed up. In an evening gown. In any dress, actually," the poor man stuttered. "I'm not a queen," he declared.

Charles didn't doubt him for a minute. To the unpracticed eye, he looked straight, but Charles had unfailing gaydar and all his blips, beeps and sweeps had gone off when he'd spotted the handsome Asian.

"But you are gay, right?"

The man licked his lips, and Charles watched the soft, wet pink tip of tongue make its way around before slipping back inside, mesmerizing Charles.

"Is it that obvious?" He looked down and then up at Charles from under thick black lashes, and Charles's dick responded with a hard jerk against his corduroys.

"No. A wild guess, that's all," Charles assured. Thank God because he didn't want to be wrong about this one.

With a sigh of relief, the man smiled at Charles, and Charles upgraded his "cute" to "adorable." Charles had a thing for adorable men and it'd been a long time since he'd met anyone who embodied that word. He'd always been attracted to Asian men, but had never dated any. No way was he going to let this two-for-one opportunity go by.

A plan formed in Charles's mind. A wicked, devious, delicious plan.

"What's your size?" *Impersonating a salesperson must be a crime somewhere, right?* But only if he got caught.

"I have no idea." The guy shook his head, panic showing in his dark brown eyes.

"Don't worry. These gowns aren't right for you." Charles couldn't help but lean closer. The light fresh scent of the man's aftershave reminded Charles of the ocean.

"They aren't?" He looked relieved.

"No. You need something else." Charles turned and scanned the racks of costumes around the shop. "Something more…earthy."

As soon as he'd seen the invitation clutched in the guy's hand, Charles had approached, hoping to start a conversation. It was the same invitation Charles had left sitting on his table at home.

This was too perfect. His invitation declared him *Stag*. And he'd already set his mind on the costume he wanted.

A cowboy.

He'd always wanted to be a cowboy, had loved everything about them, from their silent, steady ways, to their rugged good looks, to their sexy swagger. If Charles could go back in time, be anything in the world, he'd choose to be a cowboy of the Old West.

Since he couldn't really be one, he might as well dress up as one.

And what fun would playing cowboy be without an Indian?

He headed over to a rack on the far wall. "This is just right for you." Taking down the tan leather and beaded costume, he held it out to show the guy.

With an authority that he pulled right out of his ass, he declared, "You'd be the perfect Pocahontas."

*   *   *

Simon walked over, maneuvering around the racks, to take a closer look at the costume. It was a long dress, nearly to his ankles, with fringe and beadwork down the sides, long sleeves and a wide bead-covered collar at the neck. It came with a black braided wig and a feathered band.

"I don't know." Squinting, he tried to picture himself in it.

It would certainly cover him, leaving only the bottom part of his legs exposed. And he could wear boots or maybe he'd find a pair of moccasins.

But the wig? He'd never thought about wearing a wig.

"I tell you, this is what you want. A man like you wouldn't be comfortable in one of those formal gowns, would you?" He gave Simon a killer smile, melting any doubts Simon had left.

"No, I wouldn't." Simon reached out and took the costume. "Will this fit me?"

"What's not to fit? It's basically a straight sheath. If it's wide enough for your shoulders, it'll be wide enough for your hips."

That sounded reasonable. And besides, it was getting late. The store would close soon and he needed to make a decision. The party was tomorrow night and he'd already wasted too much time this week trying to avoid the entire mess.

"Okay, I'll take it." Simon nodded and gave the guy a smile.

"Perfect." There went that purr again. He could purr in Simon's ear all day long, all night long, for that matter.

"Just take it up to the register and they'll ring you up." He jerked his head to the front of the store.

"Thanks." Simon nodded and made his way through the racks to the counter.

"I'd like to get this." He handed the costume to the cashier.

"Of course. Was anyone helping you?" she asked, not batting an eye that a man was buying a woman's dress. You have to love the Quarter, especially if you're gay.

"Yes. A young man." Simon strained to see to the back of the shop to point out the guy. "Huh. I don't see him." He shrugged, bummed not to get another opportunity with the guy. Wrap *him* up. I'll take him to go, Simon thought.

Why was it that all the gorgeous guys were straight?

She looked to the rear, too. "Must've gone in the back."

She rang Simon up, bagged up the costume, and handed it to him. "If you need anything else, come back and see us for all your costume needs."

Simon thanked her, waved, and left the shop.

This outfit was so much better than one of those spangled, revealing evening gowns he'd look ridiculous wearing, not to mention how in the world he'd create breasts to fill it out. He would have had to buy high heels, fancy jewelry, maybe even a feather boa or stole and this was already setting him back enough money.

And since it was really a costume, he could wear it for Mardi Gras next year.

If he had to dress as a woman, why not a Native American princess?

CHAPTER 2

Charles watched his Pocahontas leave, then picked out tan leather chaps and a matching vest and took them to the counter. He already had a hat and a pair of boots.

"This is all." He placed them down.

"Cowboy, huh?" She smiled up at him. "You'll make a killer cowboy. Good guy or bad guy?" She winked, flirting with him like mad.

Playing along, he leaned closer. "I'm always good." He winked.

She practically squealed as she licked her lips. Then she rang him up and bagged the clothes. Pulling a business card from the stack, she wrote down a phone number.

"Call me if you need anything at all." She put it in the bag.

"Will do." He gave her a nod and sauntered out of the shop. As he strolled down Royal Street, he opened the bag, took out the card, and tossed it in the first wrought iron trash can he came to.

He could have asked for the guy's number, but he wanted his plan to play out. It would be so much more fun that way.

And now that he thought about it, he'd definitely be going as an outlaw. He could just picture his face on a Wanted poster.

Charles Mabry

Wanted

Dead or Alive

Now, he just had to find a pair of six-shooters and holster to complete the ensemble.

153

And maybe a mask.

*   *   *

"You *have* to help me, Sara," Simon begged his sister. "I have no idea what I'm doing and I've never put on makeup before in my life." He paced the length of his small apartment on Burgundy Street in the Fouberg Marigny, just outside the French Quarter.

"Simon, really. You're gay." She sighed. He could just see her rolling her eyes.

"Gay doesn't mean I'm a wannabe woman. It just means I'm a guy who likes other guys."

"I know. You never were into that stuff, even when we were teens." She gave a long-suffering sigh. "What's the point of having a gay brother if he doesn't want to put on make-up or swap clothes?"

"So, not only am I a disappointment to our *parents* because I'm gay, I've failed as a gay *brother* because I'm not gay enough?"

"You've never been a disappointment to me, Simon," she reassured him. "You know I've just always wanted a big sister." She laughed.

"Sara." He growled at her teasing. "Are you going to help me or not?"

"Of course. I can tell this means a lot to you. Just meet me at the drug store on Canal and Carrolton. We can pick out the stuff you need there."

"Great. See you there in thirty."

"Thirty." She hung up.

Simon snatched up his car keys and headed out the door. He locked it, then clomped down the dark stairs to the bottom and opened the door to the street. Stepping out, he checked in both directions, then locked the door and went to his car.

Even though the Marigny was relatively safe, it was best to be cautious. Muggings and purse snatchings still happened. Hurricane Katrina hadn't washed away the crime.

He pulled away from the precious parking space in front of his house and drove to meet his little sister.

*   *   *

"Honestly, you need overall foundation." Sara held up a bottle of makeup.

"Does that go all over my face?" Simon whispered. The last thing he wanted was to be overhead discussing makeup at the same place he bought his condoms and lube.

"Yes, then you apply the powder and blush." She pointed to the other packages on the wall.

"No. That's too much crap on my face. I fought off zits in high school; I'm not doing it again." He shook his head. "Look, I'm going as a Native American, not as the female lead in the *Mikado*."

"Too bad because you'd be perfect. Why didn't you just go as a geisha?"

"Hell, no! For one thing, we're Korean, not Japanese. Being gay is bad enough, but if Dad found out I went Japanese, he'd stroke out. For another, wear all that white makeup and that god-awful wig? I'd rather die. No, this is the lesser of two evils. Besides, isn't that just what everyone will expect?"

She put it back on the shelf. "You're right. Indian it is. Okay, I've got it." She snatched several items off the rack—eyeliner, lipstick, mascara.

"Seriously?" He plucked the mascara out of her hand.

"You'll need it. Besides, you have gorgeous lashes, thick and full. They'll need emphasis."

"Oh, God, I don't want emphasis. I just want to make it through this party alive and with my dignity intact."

She pried the mascara from his fingers. "It's waterproof. Even if things go bad, it won't run."

Simon groaned. *Tears?* She expected that before the night was over, he'd be in tears? Come to think of it, so did he.

"Okay. Keep the mascara."

She nodded and dropped it into the small basket slung over her arm. "Now, for the Indian part of this get up." She led him through the store to the aisle with kid's toys.

"What are we doing here?"

"You're going to be an Indian. You'll need a bow and arrow." She shrugged as she cruised down the aisle. "*Voila!*" She held up a miniature bow and arrow set.

"You're not serious, are you?" He looked at it. It had rubber suction cups on the tips of the arrows and brightly colored feathers at the end. The bow looked as if were wood, but by the weight of it, he could tell it was plastic.

"You just have to carry it, not actually shoot anyone."

"Only myself," he muttered as she put the package in her basket.

"Now, war paint." She moved farther down the aisle.

"War paint? You thinking I'm going to get into a fight? I may be Asian, but I don't know the first thing about martial arts. You're the one who can kill a man six different ways with your pinky." He smirked at her.

"You could've discovered ancient Asian fighting secrets, too, if you'd gotten off your ass and stopped playing those video games when we were kids." She elbowed him in the ribs and he grunted.

"Please, Sara, focus. What else do I need?"

"Well, I think that if you're not going to wear foundation or blush, this will give the impression you're an Indian." She picked up a package of Halloween makeup. It had black, white, red, blue, green, and yellow pots of cream, an applicator brush, and a sponge.

"The long dress and feather headband won't give me away?"

She glared at him. "Look. Do you want my help or not?"

"I want your help." He sighed.

"Good. Then quit whining. Let's check out." She spun around and stormed off to the front of the store with her basket.

Thank God she hadn't made him carry it.

At the counter, she checked out, and he forked over his credit card to pay.

The cashier gave him a puzzled look when she took the bow and arrow out to ring it up.

"It's for my nephew," Sara lied.

The teenager nodded, popped her gum, and bagged it up.

Once outside the store, Sara handed the plastic bag of goodies to him. "You're on your own now, Big Chief." With a flutter of her fingers goodbye, she skipped to her car and got in.

Simon sighed and went to his car, got in and tossed the bag on the passenger seat.

He should go home, try on the costume and see how it looked. Plan his makeup. How he'd wear the bow and arrow. If he'd wear the bow and arrow.

Instead, he drove to the nearest snowball stand, stood in line, and ordered a large vanilla orchid snowball with condensed cream on top. Then he drove to Bayou St. John and parked.

Simon strolled over to his favorite bench across from City Park and sat. As he ate his snowball, he thought of anything else but putting on that outfit and becoming an Indian princess.

HEARTS OF NEW ORLEANS

CHAPTER 3

Charles stood in front of his full-length mirror and struck a pose. His eyes narrowed as he glared at his opponents. He was John Wayne facing off a pack of desperados.

"Do you feel lucky?" he drawled, raising one eyebrow.

No, wait. That was Clint Eastwood.

He shrugged, slapped his hand to the holster, and pulled the toy pistol. It tumbled out of his hand, did a few summersaults, and fell to the floor. He sighed, bent, and retrieved it. He put it back in the holster and tried it again, this time a bit slower.

He slapped leather and the gun slid out, still in his hand.

Bang!

Bang! Bang!

Got 'em right between the eyes.

He raised the gun barrel to his lips and blew away imagined smoke, then shoved it back into the holster.

"No one accuses me of cheatin' at poker. No one." He pushed the cowboy hat back on his head and gave a sharp nod.

Charles laughed. He made a pretty good cowboy, if he did say so himself.

He studied his look in the mirror. He hadn't shaved in two days, giving the stubble on his chin a rough, yet sexy look.

Damn, he loved the leather chaps. They wrapped his legs like a pair of gloves, leaving just the crotch of his jeans exposed. His gaze focused on the impression of his semi-hard cock.

Okay, he got off on dressing up as a cowboy. It had been his fantasy forever.

"Guilty as charged, Sheriff."

Now he just had to decide whether to wear a shirt under the vest, or go without one. He peeled off the vest and his shirt, then slipped back into the vest.

Definitely without.

The vest gave a sexy glimpse of his smooth chest, hard pecs, and with the low rider jeans and the chaps, a few hairless inches of skin showed below his navel. Thank God he had an innie and not an outie and thank God he'd been faithful about going to the gym and working out.

Of course, if he'd been a real cowboy, his muscles would have been honed by hard work, chasing cattle, bustin' broncs, and riding the range, not lifting free weights and running on a treadmill.

Forget the range; he wanted to ride his Pocahontas.

He rubbed his hand over his jeans and the touch merely made him harder.

God, he'd been sporting a boner ever since meeting the guy in the costume shop yesterday. And in a few hours, if Charles's plan went well, he'd get the chance to do that very thing.

He made a note to thank Francis for inviting him. Charles had only met the hotel owner a few months ago when he'd gone there to talk him into ordering wine from his small distributing company, but Francis had been so open and friendly, Charles had taken to dropping by whenever he'd been in the Quarter.

Now he wondered how Pocahontas knew Francis. An employee maybe? Another casual acquaintance?

Oh, hell. What if he were Francis's lover?

Now there was a faux pas, if ever he'd seen one.

He'd have to play it safe until he found out what their relationship was, or he'd risk putting his business with Francis in jeopardy.

But outlaws were risk takers. They loved action and danger and living on the edge. If he wanted to be a cowboy, he'd have to break out of his safe zone and take up residence in the wild, wild west.

He picked up the black mask and slipped it on. Only his eyes, mouth and chin showed. Pocahontas would never recognize him. Not until he removed the mask and revealed himself.

Perfect.

*   *   *

Simon stared at his clean, just shaved face in the mirror above the sink in his bathroom. On the countertop he'd spread out all the makeup he'd bought the day before.

After staring at the costume all afternoon as it hung on his door, he'd sucked it up and put it on. Amazingly, it fit his shoulders perfectly, falling to a soft drape over his narrow hips, with plenty of room to spare.

Damn. No excuses left. He'd have to go to the party now.

All he had to do was to fix his face and put on the wig.

Simon picked up the eyeliner and tore open the package. He removed the cap and stared at it. It looked just like a marker.

He ran it over the back of his hand, marking his skin with a black line. He smudged it with his fingertip. The line softened, but the color remained dark and intense.

Taking a deep breath and holding it, Simon brought the pen to his left eye and slowly drew it along the rim just above his lashes. When he got to the end, he stopped and sat back. Frowned.

Something didn't look right. It was crooked in the middle.

He drew the line again, making it thicker.

Not quite right.

This time, he ran the liner over the last mark, creating a wide band of black around his upper lid, and then extended it out beyond the corner of his eye.

Wow. That was it.

He inhaled and worked on the right eye, then underneath each eye, to form a thick bar of black encasing his eyes, spreading out to the side in a bold slash.

It was dramatic, intense and his eyes popped out at him.

Shit. He looked *good*.

Simon closed up the liner and took out the mascara, to make his lashes even fuller and more lush than normal.

Waterproof, huh? Bring it on, Tammy Faye.

He leaned forward, mouth open, tongue out, and stroked the brush over his already dark eyelashes, coating them in Midnight Black, doubting whether it would make any difference at all.

Wow. Quelle différence! No wonder women wore this crap.

He applied a second coat.

Damn.

He sat back and stared at his face.

It was good, but he hadn't gone far enough, all the way to the edge and over.

He ripped into the package of Halloween makeup and, ignoring the applicator, dipped his fingertip into the red pot, and ran it over his cheekbone, making a bold stripe of war paint. Then he repeated it on the other side.

Now, he glanced at the beadwork on the collar of his dress. Which color would go with his dark eyes? Red. Blue. Green. White.

He wiped off his finger, dipped it into the green and slashed it across his cheek beneath the red streak.

A stranger looked back at him.

But the effect still wasn't complete.

He held up the tube of lipstick Sara had picked out and pulled off the top, then rotated the stick up until a bright red tongue peeked out. Then, taking another deep breath, he opened his mouth and ran the lipstick over his full bottom lip.

The silky crème glided over his lip. Simon felt sensual. Naughty.

Aroused.

Imitating what he'd seen women do thousands of times in his life, he followed the outline of his upper lip, then smacked his lips together to spread the color.

Goddamn, he looked…hot.

A blend between Goth and Native American.

After wiping off his fingertips, he sat back and stared at his image.

This was unreal.

He was Simon, but not Simon.

Simon enhanced.

Simon different.

Simon released.

He stared at his face. He looked like those younger men he'd seen at some of the gay clubs downtown. Twinks. They weren't afraid to wear makeup to enhance their looks. To declare who they are and what they want.

And he'd be the first to admit he'd found those daring young men exciting. Would he excite other men, men like himself? Placid men, content with who they thought they were? Would they long for a touch from him, to steal a kiss, a have a chance to capture such beauty for a night?

A chance at *him*?

Simon picked up the wig and brushed back his bangs with one

hand. He slipped the wig on and adjusted it. A thick fringe of black bangs brushed his eyebrows, and two long braids tied off with tan leather strips ending in multicolored beads hung down his chest. A jaunty imitation eagle feather stuck up out of the headband.

He straightened and took in the image in front of him.

Goth Native American.

Simon complete.

CHAPTER 4

Charles pulled on his boots and tugged his jeans down over them. Standing up, he gave his reflection a last look as he rethought his decision to go without a shirt.

If anyone had doubted whether he was straight, this outfit would clear up any confusion. Tonight, he'd be among friends, gays and straights, who'd accept him anyway he chose to present himself.

Maybe that's what gave him the courage to play dress up.

He'd never flaunted his body, never been so open about his sexuality. He'd hidden behind a facade of respectability and looking straight most of his life. Even when he hit the clubs, he dressed conservatively.

Sure, he'd noticed the other men there, men without a care in the world, half-naked, their firm, young, sweat-covered bodies, hair stylishly mussed, eyes dark with liner and promises, lips full and red, as they danced to the beat of driving bass rhythms.

Charles closed his eyes and groaned.

He adjusted his stiff cock in his jeans. He had to stop thinking shit like that or else everyone at the party would know what he was thinking the minute he stepped through the door.

The leather chaps and his tightest jeans left nothing to the imagination.

Maybe he should shoot one off before he went. Just to take the edge away and the bulge out of his jeans.

He stared at the evidence of arousal outlined like a steel rod.

What the hell? So what if everyone knew he was primed and ready. He was supposed to be an outlaw, right? And they lived on the edge.

Charles put on the hat, snugging it low on his forehead, and pulled his mask down around his neck. He'd put it on when he got to the hotel, when he'd truly become the cowboy. He picked up the holster and stuffed it into a small gym bag.

He was ready. More than ready.

He left his uptown camelback house, locking the front door behind him, then trotted down the steps, through the small front yard, and out the gate. It swung shut, just missing him as he hit the remote and slid into the driver's seat of his black Mustang.

The sun was setting and it'd be night soon. Time for the bad boys to make an appearance, to come out and play.

He was an outlaw cowboy going into town on his trusty steed and looking for trouble. There were broncs to bust, cattle to rustle, and lawmen to elude.

And a certain Native American princess to capture.

*   *   *

Simon sat on the edge of his bed and stepped into the soft slippers he'd bought on Canal Street. They were the closest he could come to moccasins. And they were definitely comfortable.

He stood and looked down at them.

There was a noticeable bulge right at his crotch that blocked the view of his feet. It totally ruined the line of the dress.

Damn, he'd have to do something about that. *Maybe wear a cup?*

Digging in the drawer of his dresser, way in the back behind the socks that didn't have mates but he'd never thrown out, his hand touched something soft.

He pulled it out and held it up.

A black leather jockstrap?

Simon laughed. He hadn't seen that thing in years. A lover had bought it for him and had insisted he wear it before they had sex. The lover was long gone, but his gift had kept on giving.

He hoisted up the dress, slipped off his briefs and stepped into what was basically a leather man-thong. Too tight, the thin string rode up the crack of his ass, the full cup just barely cradling his package, pressing it against his body, reminding him that he wore it.

He glanced up at the mirror over his dresser, swiveled to the side and checked the profile. Not completely flat, but at least his cock was under control. Twisting, he checked out his ass. The black leather strips ran around his waist, met in the middle, and then disappeared like a river running below ground.

Damn, it looked hot.

He dropped the dress and smiled at his secret.

No one would know he was wearing it. It felt naughty and wicked. The black leather went with the whole outfit and definitely with his new look.

What would he look like in just the thong, black wig, and makeup?

Would he look wanton and decadent or cheap and whorish?

Either way, it would be a win-win scenario.

Who knows? Maybe he'd find someone who got turned on by black eyeliner, braids, and leather thongs?

Now that would really be one strange, wild man.

A man he'd love to meet.

Well, at least for tonight. Just for the party, of course.

Simon had no intention of *ever* doing this again. *Ever*.

No matter how hot he looked.

He just wasn't *that* kind of gay.

*   *   *

Simon hurried the three blocks from the parking garage on Iberville to Burgundy, then three blocks down Burgundy to the Chateau Francois. He shouldn't have been worried about being seen. No one batted an eye at a Native American man/woman dressed in full costume, war paint streaked across her/his face. And it wasn't even Mardi Gras.

Only in New Orleans.

Simon smiled as he came through the door and strode to the front desk.

"Hello, Carrie. Is everything going well?"

Carrie, the night manager, looked up and blinked. Then her head cocked to one side and she narrowed her eyes at him.

"I'm hearing my boss Simon's voice, but I'm seeing an Indian princess."

"Not Indian. We prefer to be called Native American."

"Oh, my God, Simon, you're gorgeous," she crooned as her eyes widened.

"Thanks." He gave her a twisted smile. "I did it for Francis."

"Right. All for Francis." Okay, she didn't believe him at all. "You have no intention of picking anyone up in there, do you?"

Simon rolled his eyes. "Carrie, is everything under control?" He didn't plan letting Carrie in on any intentions he might or might not have, especially when he didn't have a clue himself.

"Everything's fine, Simon." She nodded to the grand ballroom. "The party's started, Francis is in his glory, and all's right with the world." She leaned over the desk and whispered, "Make sure you act as if you can't tell it's him behind that Diana Ross wig."

"Diana Ross? Of The Supremes?" he asked.

She nodded. "Right. He's the fourth Supreme, the tall, skinny white one."

He gave her a wave and turned to check out the lobby.

The decorations for the anniversary party gave the hotel a festive air. Exquisite flower arrangements covered every tabletop and tasteful signage announcing the event sat beneath each one. All had been designed by Francis. He'd been working on the party for months and seen to every detail personally.

It really did look beautiful.

Simon took a deep breath and crossed the lobby's parquet wood floor to the ballroom's massive carved doors. He did a quick check in the large, gold leafed French mirror on the wall. Makeup still in place and still looking good. But his scalp itched under the cheap wig. He scratched, then straightened the braids so they hung even on both sides.

He put his hand on the knob and turned it, took a deep breath, and then pushed through the door.

Inside, the ballroom glittered. Francis had outdone himself this time.

Long buffet tables, draped with black linens and pushed against the maroon fleur-de-lis flocked golden walls, held piles of cheese, seafood, canapés, and sandwiches. On the other side, two bartenders in tuxedos held court at a miniature bar, preparing drinks as fast as their clients could order.

Strewn all around the large room, groupings of furniture—tables, chairs, settees, couches, and ottomans—were set out for the comfort of Francis's guests. Most of them, those who weren't at the buffet tables loading up on boiled shrimp or mini-muffelettas, were lounging on said furniture.

In the corner near the door, a jazz quartet played Dixieland, giving the party a festive atmosphere, yet not so loud you couldn't hold a conversation.

And there, in the middle of it all, Francis held court, dressed in a silver evening gown, Diana Ross wig, diamond chandelier earrings to die for, and three-inch heels.

Simon would have been more shocked to see him in a tuxedo or dressed as a pirate.

After closing the door behind him, he made his way through the crowd to greet his host for the evening.

"Hello, Francis. For a minute, I barely recognized you," Simon said, getting his obligatory kissing up out of the way. He wondered if Francis's expensive wig itched as much as his did.

"And who is this gorgeous thing?" Francis stared at him. "Simon, is that you?" He seemed to be genuinely surprised.

"Yes."

Francis opened his mouth, then shut it. He swallowed and gave Simon a smoldering look. "Good God, if I knew you looked that hot in drag, I'd have made you come to work every day dressed as a woman." He fanned himself with an evening gloved hand as Simon gave him a quick kiss on the cheek.

"Thanks, I think." Simon frowned and looked around. "But no thanks for sending me the drag invite. I hope you've gotten your laughs."

"Laughs? No, dearest, I just wanted to push a few people out the door, so to speak."

"I'm already out of the closet, Francis. I'm not sure what door you mean."

"Why, the door of respectability, the door of ordinary, the door of mundane!" Francis winked at him and then turned his attention to a younger man, dressed as a caveman, who'd sidled up with a glass of champagne. "Thanks, darling." Francis took it and sipped.

Simon waited for the introduction as the caveman checked him out. And then leered at him, appreciation showing in his eyes. Simon couldn't help but feel flattered.

"Simon, this is Dan. Dan, this is Simon, the hotel's premiere manager." Francis made the intros between sips.

"Simon, pleased to meet you." Dan stepped forward, but instead of a handshake, he kissed Simon on the cheek. "You're gorgeous," he whispered on a breath in Simon's ear.

"So I've been told." Simon smiled back, unsure if Dan was a friend of Francis's or a *friend* of Francis's. Either way, Simon wasn't interested in the strong grunting types and he didn't plan on being hit over the head and dragged to Dan's cave by his braids.

Dan smiled, then turned his attention back to Francis, slipping his arm around Francis's trim waist, laying claim. Francis kissed his cheek and grinned at Simon.

"Mingle, dearest. Mingle." He waved his hands at Simon to shoo him away.

Simon turned away and headed to the buffet tables.

Might as well get something to eat.

*   *   *

Charles spotted him the moment he stepped through the door. His breath froze. It couldn't be anyone else but his Pocahontas. And he was more beautiful, more exotic, than Charles even imagined.

Any cowboy with a lick of sense would have fallen for him in a heartbeat. His princess was regal, taller than most women, but not as tall as Charles. Broad shoulders, but not too broad, straight backed, narrow hipped, and high cheekbones painted in streaks of color to emphasize them.

He couldn't take his gaze off his maiden's dark lined eyes. The look shot past striking and blasted its way straight to his dick. All he could think about when he looked at the man was taking him. Raising up that dress and burying his cock deep inside that sweet little ass. Kissing those deep red lips.

He moved farther behind a sofa in the corner and rubbed his erection, trying to shift it in his jeans. *What the fuck.* He'd already decided not to care about who saw what.

Tracking his princess, Charles watched as the man said hello to Francis, and then was devoured by Francis's latest boy toy, the caveman.

Charles growled. The Indian princess was his.

CHAPTER 5

Simon loaded his plate with shrimp, mini oyster quiche and a few olives. After scanning the room for a vacant seat with a nearby table, he moved toward one. Concentrating so hard on reaching the open spot before anyone else, he never saw the cowboy until he stood, hands on his hips, blocking Simon's way.

"Howdy." The cowboy stared at him. He wore a black mask.

Simon stared back. Tall, lean, and well built, the vest the man wore covered a broad hairless chest. Tight jeans and leather chaps. *Very* tight jeans. With a very predominate bulge. Very thick. Very long.

Oh, my.

Simon gulped and dragged his gaze from the cowboy's crotch.

The man's blue eyes devoured him from behind the mask, and his square, rugged jaw and thin lips were all Simon could make out.

"Hello." Simon couldn't think what else to say except, "Take me, I'm yours."

"My name is Charles." The man didn't make a move, just stood there. Behind him, a woman, a real woman, dressed as a Greek goddess, took Simon's chair. Oh, well.

"Charles? Not Billy the Kid? Jesse James? Black Bart?" Simon teased, as he rattled off the names of all the cowboys he could think of.

"No. Just Charles." He smiled and showed perfect white teeth.

"I'm Simon."

"Not Running Flower? Dances With Wolves? Desert Blossom?" the cowboy countered.

"No. Just Simon." If the guy would tell him who he wanted Simon to be, he'd be it. Good God, he'd never seen such a sexy man since…well, since yesterday when he bought his costume.

"Hello, Simon."

"Hello, Charles."

They stood there, staring at each other, unable to do more than bask in each other's gazes. It was the oddest, yet most exciting moment for Simon in a long time.

His cock twitched in the thong, reminding him that it existed and needed tending.

What would it be like to have a masked man suck him off?

"Well, do I have to pull my pistol and take you at gunpoint or are you coming along quietly?" The cowboy's lips twisted in a sexy smile, one side rising higher than the other, his hungry blue eyes searching Simon's brown ones.

Simon couldn't help but glance down at Charles's crotch again. "By pistol, do you mean the one in the holster, or the one in your pants?" Then he shot his gaze up and nailed the cowboy with it.

"I'll use the one in the holster if I need to, but I'd rather use the other one."

"I think I'd rather you use it, too." Simon swallowed. Okay, he'd never been so bold before. He liked being bold. Just say what you were thinking. Or do what you wanted.

"Me, too." The cowboy glanced around, then motioned with a jerk of his head to two empty seats on a couch in a dark corner. "Seat?"

"Don't mind if I do." Simon headed toward it, Charles following. Simon hoped Charles was checking out his ass.

When Charles put his hand on Simon's waist to help guide him around some people, a thrill raced through him, landing in his dick. Then Charles let him go. Simon wanted more touching.

They reached the small couch, and Simon sat, placing his plate of goodies on the Moroccan mother of pearl inlaid table. Charles sat next to him and threw his arm across the back of the dark green velvet couch.

Simon settled back and turned toward the cowboy, almost nestling under Charles's shoulder.

"This is nice." Simon looked up into Charles's face, giving him a closer inspection. "Do I know you?"

"Yes. We've met before."

"Have we?" Simon searched his memory. If he'd met someone this gorgeous, he'd remember it, wouldn't he?

Charles leaned in. "We have. But I don't know anything about you."

"Me?" Simon giggled. Damn, why did he keep doing that? "I'm just Simon."

"You're so much more than just Simon." Charles gaze swept over him. "You're incredible. You're the most irresistible man I've met in ages."

"Irresistible?" Simon squeaked out.

"Adorable." That sideways smile appeared again, and this time, Charles ran his finger along Simon's jaw.

Simon shivered and closed his eyes, letting the building arousal fill him. Oh, this man was dangerous. Simon decided he liked dangerous.

"Adorable?" Simon whispered. He opened his eyes.

Charles leaned in for a kiss.

He waited, watching as Charles's eyes closed, his lips parted slightly, and the warm weight of Charles's hand rested on his thigh.

Simon's eyes crossed as Charles's mouth drew closer, closer, then Simon gave in, closed his eyes, and their lips touched. Charles's mouth was hard, yet pliant, his lips smooth, and Simon let the way they pressed against his lips be all he knew, all he could feel.

Charles ran his tongue over the crease of Simon's mouth, asking for entry.

Simon allowed him inside. Charles's tongue swept in, gently probing, tasting, then withdrew, and Charles broke their kiss.

Simon shuddered.

The world shrank down to the two of them, sitting on the sofa in a dark corner, holding each other, blue eyes staring into brown.

"God, you turn me on," Charles whispered.

"Really?" Simon giggled.

Charles took Simon's hand and placed it on his crotch.

Undeniable evidence.

"You were like that before, when we first met tonight." Simon didn't remove his hand and didn't apologize for noticing.

"I've been watching you since you came in." Charles covered Simon's hand with his and pressed. "In fact, I've been hard just knowing I'd see you here tonight."

Simon gasped. "How did you know I'd be here? Did Francis tell you?" His gaze darted to the center of the room, but Francis and his caveman had vacated the center spotlight.

"No, he didn't tell me. I told you, we've met before."

"But I don't remember telling anyone about the party."

"You showed me your invitation." Charles grinned.

"I showed you—" Simon cut himself off as realization dawned. "The guy from the costume shop." He reached up to remove the mask, but Charles caught his wrist in a firm hold.

"Not yet."

Simon took his hand down. "Not yet?"

"No, not yet. For now, tonight, I want to be the cowboy, the outlaw."

"And what do you want me to be?"

"A beautiful Indian princess whom I've captured." He bit his bottom lip.

Simon leaned back and exhaled. "And do your plans for this princess include ravishing her?"

"Not against her will. I may be an outlaw, but I have some honor." He placed a hand over his heart, under the leather vest.

Simon slid his hand on top of Charles's and his fingertips brushed a hard nipple. Charles shuddered, arching into his palm.

"I'd go willingly to your bedroll, cowboy." Simon smiled. "In fact, I think I can arrange a suitable place to bunk for the night."

"Your teepee?"

"No, somewhere close, though."

Simon stood, tugging Charles's hand. Charles got to his feet, and Simon pulled him toward the doors of the ballroom, away from the crowd and out of the party.

To find a place where a cowboy could capture an Indian princess.

CHAPTER 6

Charles couldn't believe it...his plan had worked. It was destiny. Fate. Kismet.

He'd never felt like this before, that everything was right. The stars-in-alignment sort of right. The once-in-a-lifetime right.

He'd lost his mind...that was it. He was not a romantic, not the kind of man who fell head over heels in love, who got all giddy and goofy over anyone. At least, he hadn't until now.

Now, he was all those things.

And it was all Simon's fault.

Simon. He liked the name. *Simon and Charles. Charles and Simon.*

Good God, if he didn't get a grip, he'd be carving their names in trees, doodling their names all over the placemats in restaurants, writing home to his mother in Baton Rouge to tell her he'd finally met the one.

He followed Simon, still no last name, through the crowd. Near the door, Francis had taken up guard, presumably to stop anyone from leaving. From what Charles could see, there was no need because everyone was having a great time. People talked, danced, drank and ate, and in New Orleans, those were the hallmarks of a successful party.

"Simon!" Francis put out a gloved hand just like a Supreme doing "Stop In The Name of Love." Where do you think you're going?"

Simon pulled Charles behind him, hiding their linked hands.

Charles leaned past Simon and grinned. "Hi, Francis. Great party. Happy anniversary."

"Hello, Charles!" Francis beamed at him, then his gaze slid from Charles to Simon, then back, then down to Simon's hand behind his back. Realization, then joy, bloomed in Francis's eyes. "Oh, my."

"What?" Simon tensed, and Charles gave his hand a gentle squeeze.

"It's perfect, just perfect! My wine distributor and my head manager. It's too delicious, my dears."

"Oh." Simon seemed embarrassed, and Charles lost a bit of his grin. Then, Simon shrugged. "He had a gun."

"I can see that, dear." Francis stared pointedly at Charles's crotch. "A big one, too. Lucky thing." Then he turned his attention to Charles. "Now, I don't want him hurt. You must return him unharmed, or I'll have to send a posse after you." Francis laughed.

"Don't worry your pretty little head, ma'am." He touched his hat respectfully. "I'm thinking there won't be any complaints come the morning." Charles put his hand on Simon's waist, bringing him back against his body, where he nestled his cock between the cheeks of Simon's ass.

Simon groaned just loud enough for Charles to hear.

"Just see that he's kept warm, happy, and satisfied." Francis wiggled his fingers at them and moved away, opening their escape path to the doors.

Simon looked back over his shoulder at Charles. "So? Will you?"

"Keep you warm, happy, and satisfied? It's my solemn intention," he drawled. Oh, yeah, he couldn't wait to see *that* particular look on his Indian's face.

"Good. I haven't felt that way in forever." Simon faced him, looked into his eyes, and Charles felt the pull straight down his body to his cock.

"Me either." He ran his hand down Simon's side, cupped his ass, and gave it a hard squeeze.

Simon gasped, then his eyelids fluttered. "Let's go. If you don't stop that, I may have to be carried the rest of the way."

"If I need to carry you, so be it." He gave Simon a small nod and touched his fingers to his hat. "I'm a gentleman cowboy."

"Nice. But I think I'd like a desperado tonight." Simon's dark eyes glittered, and he spun around and led Charles through the large door and into the lobby.

The door shut behind them, muffling the sounds of the party.

He didn't know what Simon had planned, but this was a hotel, he was the manager, and Charles was sure Simon would think of something.

*   *   *

Simon stalked up to the front desk and leaned on it.

"What's available?" He tapped the marble countertop with his fingers. It was a Saturday night in the French Quarter, but he knew they'd have rooms open for the party. Francis would have thought of everything, including retaining a few rooms for those party guests unable or unwilling to make the trip home.

Carrie's gaze danced from his face to the taller man standing behind him, then back to his. She grinned and punched in a few numbers into the computer.

"One-oh-one and one-fifteen might be best." She gave him a knowing nod.

Francis had insisted on using the European way of calling the first floor the ground floor and the second floor the first. The second floor held their best suites, those with balconies facing the street, but Simon knew one-fifteen faced the private courtyard and had a whirlpool bath.

"One-fifteen." He held out his hand for the card key. Behind him, Charles leaned into his back, pressing what could only be that long, thick dick of his into Simon's ass. He shuddered at the burning lust and hard need that coursed through his body. The cowboy bit his ear, and Simon rolled his eyes and drummed his fingers on the counter.

She punched out the card, swiped it, then handed it to him. "Anything else, sir?" She grinned at him now.

"I'll call if I need anything."

She snapped to attention, practically saluting. "I'll be here. Enjoy your stay at Chateau Francois, *monsieur.*"

Simon turned away and dragged Charles by the hand to the elevator. He pressed the brass call button, and the old-fashioned wrought iron machinery creaked its way to the lobby from the second floor. It reminded him of the one in the *Rocky Horror Picture Show* and, although Francis had denied it, Simon always believed that had been Francis's inspiration.

Now, as Charles stepped up behind him, pulling Simon tight to his body, all thoughts and questions evaporated like water drops on asphalt in August. All he knew was the pounding of his blood, the thud of his heartbeat and the ache of his dick as Charles's touch swamped his brain.

174

He cursed silently as the elevator took its sweet time getting to the bottom floor. He wanted to groan as it reached their level, halted, then the doors slid open to invite them inside.

Charles shoved him from behind, and he stumbled into the cage. Charles continued in, pinning him against the iron bars.

"Fuck, I want you," Charles whispered in his ear.

Simon wrapped his hands around the cool metal bars as Charles hit the button, the doors closed and the elevator jerked, ascending to the next floor.

Before Simon could catch his breath, Charles had returned, his hot body smashed against Simon's as he ground his erection into Simon's ass, teasing him with the riding he promised.

And God knew, Simon wanted the cowboy to ride him. Hard and fast and all night long.

It'd been ages since he'd had more than a just quick jerk off or blow job, so he was more than ready to be fucked. Then he wanted to fuck his cowboy. They could take turns doing each other until Francis banged on the door and threw them out of the hotel.

How long would his cowboy stay?

The elevator stopped and the doors opened.

Charles grabbed him and spun him around. Simon looked up into the masked man's eyes and his knees weakened.

Hunger.

Lust.

Thank God, Charles wanted him as badly as he wanted Charles.

Simon pushed Charles aside. "This way." He jogged down the hall, Charles like a spaniel at his heels, until he reached the room. With a quick swipe of the card in the lock, the light turned green and Simon pushed down on the handle and opened the door.

Charles followed him in, and as it closed, Charles pinned him to the wall with his body. Simon pushed back, rubbing their erections together.

"I want you." Charles smashed his mouth down on Simon's and demanded entrance.

Moaning, Simon opened for him. Charles's tongue thrust in, plundering the cave of Simon's mouth, tasting, touching, stroking, driving Simon's arousal higher. His cock was a hard, straining rod in that stupid man-thong, and moist drops of pre-cum dotted his belly.

Charles broke the kiss. "You will be mine, princess."

Simon gulped down air and stared into lust-filled eyes. "But the princess has a secret, cowboy."

"A secret?" Something flared in Charles's eyes.

Simon reached up and jerked off his wig, tossing it across the room.

"Your Indian princess is a prince." He scrubbed his hand over his short hair, leaving it standing up in thick spikes. He'd wanted out of the false braids all night, and now he wasn't sure if this would ruin it for Charles or not, but he took the chance.

Charles groaned. Then he leaned forward, buried his hands in Simon's short, black hair, fisted it, and forced his head back to expose his throat.

"A prince. Even better. I've always wanted to fuck a prince." He growled as he nipped along the muscles of Simon's neck, then licked over the same path.

Simon's legs nearly gave out.

"I want to taste you." Charles slid down Simon's body to kneel at his feet. He palmed Simon's erection.

Simon slowly pulled up his dress, exposing his shins, his knees, his thighs, then at last, his groin.

"Holy fuck!" Charles sat back on his heels. "Oh, my God," he whispered.

Simon stared down at the top of the cowboy's hat, unable to see what was happening with his lover. Was that reaction good or bad? Simon tensed.

Then Charles reached up, grabbed the brim of his hat, and tossed it away to join Simon's wig on the floor. He looked up, his eyes dancing with arousal, and licked his lips.

"You are my prince."

Simon melted.

CHAPTER 7

Charles had never seen anything so hot as Simon's hard dick thrusting up and out of the black leather pouch that failed to contain it. This was like his own personal porn, with his now-prince in the starring role.

Leaning forward, he licked the underneath of Simon's exposed shaft using the flat of his tongue until he reached the plump, dark head, tasting the pre-cum dripping from it. Lightly salty, a paler version of what he knew Simon's cum would be like, Charles lapped it up and swirled his tongue around the cap.

Simon's head hit the door with a thud, his hands buried themselves in Charles's hair, and he moaned. "Oh, fuck."

"That'll be later, prince." Charles reached up, hooked his fingers in the thin straps holding the leather thong up and pulled it down to puddle on the floor around Simon's feet.

Simon's cock sprang free, slapping against his belly.

Charles sighed. He pushed Simon's legs apart, then cupped the firm sac and rolled the two sweet nuts in the palm of his hand. His prince groaned, his fingers flexed, and his knees bent as he braced himself against the wall.

Charles looked up at his prize, his own cock pressing painfully against the zipper of his jeans. He undid his holster and the twin guns fell to the floor, unbuckled the chaps, and, at last, he unzipped and freed himself from the denim. Wrapping his hand around his shaft, he stroked once, twice, then let it go. Any more and he'd come on the floor.

He wanted to come in Simon's ass.

But first, he wanted to taste Simon. Take him in his mouth and make his prince cry out and beg to be fucked.

Holding onto the shaft of the perfectly placed prick in front of him, he opened his mouth and greedily swallowed it down.

Simon crowed and jerked.

The thick cock hit the back of Charles's throat and he swallowed, massaging the stiff shaft he'd captured.

"Please."

Charles sucked hard as he pulled off, then surged back down, repeating the act until Simon's hands in his hair tightened painfully.

"Now, cowboy. Now!" Simon pulled him off with a pop.

He surged to his feet and took Simon's mouth in a claiming kiss that declared, "This mouth is mine." Reaching around, he grabbed Simon's ass and pulled it tighter to him, rubbing their erections together.

They broke apart, gasping for breath, staring into each other's eyes.

"Charles," Simon whispered. "Bed."

Charles stepped back, took Simon by the hand and led him to the king-size bed in the center of the small room. He didn't bother to look at his surroundings, but somewhere in the back of his brain, it registered that the bed had to be an antique. The iron head and footboards had a patina of age that he doubted had been faked.

Simon stood at the side of the bed, waiting.

"Let me undress you." Charles pulled the long dress off his prince, exposing every inch of skin to his gaze. "Get on the bed."

He climbed up, and Charles watched as the most perfect ass he'd ever seen presented itself to him. Shuddering, he stroked himself, needing the touch of a hand, even his own.

"Fuck, you're beautiful, my prince."

His lover turned, lay back on the mass of pillows, his legs splayed open and inviting, his cock flat against his belly, his thickly black lined eyelids half lowered, barely hiding the longing, lust and heat of his gaze.

His prize, waiting for a plundering.

*　　　*　　　*

His cowboy stared at him, his lust-filled gaze sweeping over

Simon's body, heating it with every slowly passing moment. He'd never felt so wanton, so sexy and so desired.

"Drop 'em, cowboy," Simon ordered.

His cowboy toed off his boots, shucked out of his jeans and vest, and stood next to the bed naked except for his mask. The man had the body of an athlete, tall, slender yet built, with a light tan to his skin. His cock stood proud above a nest of neatly trimmed brown curls.

Simon took a deep breath, held it, and then let it go in a slow exhale filled with longing through parted lips. The cowboy's gaze focused like a tight beam tracking his every move, first on his face, then as Simon slid his hand over his belly, touched his nipple, then down again to cup his own balls. He didn't think the man took a single breath.

"God, I wish you could see yourself. See how fucking hot you look, spread out for me." Charles's Adam's apple bobbed as he swallowed.

"Not half as hot as you in that mask, outlaw."

"Am I going to need my six-shooter?"

A thrill raced through Simon. "Yes."

Charles grinned, then stepped away from the bed, scooped up one of his pistols and returned. "I want to warn you. I'm armed and I know how to use it."

"Show me."

Charles spun the gun around his finger, the silver blurring with the motion, then stopped, pointing the hot orange plastic tip at Simon.

"Pretty good, outlaw."

"Been practicing."

"I'll just bet you have. What do you intend to do with me now?"

"I won't hurt you, unless you ask." Charles's eyebrow rose, the gun never wavering.

Simon reached up and grabbed the bars of the headboard. The cold of the old metal chilled his heated palms, sending a shiver through him. Then he stretched his legs out toward the sides of the bed.

"I'm afraid you have me at a disadvantage, outlaw."

"Indeed." Charles nodded and took a step closer.

Simon looked up from under his thick lashes and ran his tongue over his painted lips. As Charles let out a soft groan, Simon's dick ached for more of the cowboy's touch.

"I'm at your mercy."

"You are." Charles nodded again

"Will you show me mercy?" Simon licked his lips again, just to hear Charles moan.

"No mercy." The outlaw shook his head.

"I won't be taken easily. An Indian prince knows how to fight."

"You don't have a bow and arrow or a knife."

"I have other weapons." Simon flexed his arms, making the muscles in his biceps bulge and arched his back off the bed, thighs tightening and belly taut.

Charles gaped at him, and Simon thought he'd come at just the look on the man's face.

"I can see you're not a man to underestimate, prince." He moved forward, kneeling on the bed, the gun still pointed at Simon, and ran his hand over the top of Simon's foot. Simon shivered.

"But I still have the advantage and a few weapons of my own." He continued to glide his fingertips along Simon's skin, up to his knee, where he swirled around the kneecap, then up his thigh.

"I wouldn't have expected any less from a desperado like you."

"I'm wanted, you know?" Charles gave a rakish smile.

"Indeed?"

"In several states."

"What crime did you commit?"

"Crimes." Charles's fingers dipped down to skim the tender flesh of Simon's inner thigh.

Simon gasped. "Crimes?"

"Let's just say, I'm not above taking liberties, or for that matter, taking what I want when I see it."

"Do you see anything you want here in this room?"

"Why, yes, I do." His fingers ran along the seam of hip and thigh, avoiding Simon's balls and cock.

"I don't have any money."

"Not money."

"I don't have any jewelry."

"Not jewels, either." Charles's finger ran around the outside of Simon's nest of black curls, the sensation sending electric sparks to Simon's balls.

He arched his back, dug his heels into the bed, and raised his ass off the mattress as he hissed, but he refused to ask for anything. He wanted his cowboy to take what he wanted. At gunpoint, if necessary, and if Simon had anything to do with it, he'd make sure it would be necessary.

"I don't own any land or livestock."

"Got land. Got my mustang and that's all I need." Charles

continued on, his fingertips raking upward to Simon's navel, circling it, dipping inside, then moving higher.

"Is that *all* you need?"

When he circled Simon's nipple, Simon cried out. "Damn you, masked man!"

Both men burst into laughter. Simon caught his breath, caught Charles's gaze and caught the giggles. He'd never had so much fun or been so turned on. Who knew all it would take was a toy gun, a mask and some eyeliner?

Charles hung his head, hands on knees, snorted, then straightened and sobered up. He raised the gun again. "Not *all* I need, my captive."

Simon pulled harder on the headboard, trying to think of his next line. "I have nothing but…my body."

Charles leered at him. "And a fine body it is, I must say. But after tonight, prince, it will belong to me."

"Yours?"

"For the taking. To do with as I wish." Charles reached out and flicked Simon's nipple with his finger.

The sting rocketed through Simon and once again he rode the crest of arousal. A new spate of pre-cum oozed from his slit. Any lessening of his hard-on had been reversed by the touch of his cowboy.

"And if I refuse?" Simon wanted to refuse, wanted to be taken, forced to give up his body to the masked stranger.

"When I'm through with you, you'll refuse me nothing." Charles tweaked his other nipple, and Simon moaned through his clenched teeth.

CHAPTER 8

Charles leaned down, unable to resist tasting the naked man stretched out in front of him. With a slow swipe of his tongue, he licked the hard point of Simon's nipple. Simon sucked in a hard breath and arched into his mouth.

Salt from the man's body flavored the tip of Charles's tongue. He savored the taste, longing to learn all the flavors of Simon's body.

True, Charles wanted to bring his captive prince to the heights of pleasure, but he wanted to do it in his own time. He licked the other nipple, earning another sharp hiss. Simon's cock leaked like a faucet, its swollen cap now nearly purple with blood, and the thick vein decorating the underside of his shaft stood out in high relief like a sculpture. The tight, wrinkled ball sac, two shades darker than his skin, had snuggled up to Simon's body, full of juice and ready to unload.

Trailing his tongue over his lover's body, Charles mapped the changing landscape, the small hills and valleys, the taut peaks and the smooth expanses of Simon's nearly hairless chest. Only a small sparse patch of black hairs sprouted in the center of the man's chest, then nothing until the small ebony nest around his shaft.

Each and every inch of skin Charles tasted was delicious. He'd never had such a sexy lover, someone who turned him on effortlessly, without guile or practiced methods. What he experienced here with this man was unlike anything he'd ever done.

This ought to be against the law.

In some states, it was.

He didn't care. He was an outlaw, a desperado, used to taking what he wanted, the consequences and laws be damned. Charles grinned, looked up and locked gazes with his prince, who watched him with his plump bottom lip caught between his teeth.

Sexy as hell.

Charles's own prick, heavy and engorged, dragged across the covers of the bed, leaving a trail of his arousal. He leaned across Simon, letting his oozing cock mark his captive as it dragged over hot, flushed skin.

The sensation of the tip of his dick sliding over Simon's heated flesh almost set him off, but losing his load now wouldn't be right. A cowboy should show some restraint, shouldn't he?

Only until he was ready to let go, ride his lover full tilt, and empty both barrels into his target.

Simon arched up to press against his cock, moaning. "Are you going to fuck me?"

"Not yet, my pretty prince."

Charles lowered his mouth to nuzzle those balls, inhaling the scent of his Indian. Musky, warm, the smell of pre-cum, sex and longing filled his nostrils and he couldn't resist taking a lick over that plump cock head.

"Cowboy," Simon warned with a growl. His heels dug into the bed as he raised his ass off the covers in an unspoken demand for more.

Charles obliged him. After all, he'd asked so prettily.

*   *   *

Simon thought the top of his head would blow off if Charles didn't suck him, and it took everything he had to keep his hands clamped tight around the headboard's bars. He'd had to lock them down, forget about them, or else the urge to run his hands over his lover's body would overpower him.

And he wanted to be tortured a little more before he exploded.

"More?" Charles raised one eyebrow. "My prince begs for me?"

Simon huffed out a breath. "No." An Indian prince would never give in so easily, no matter how hot the fire burned or how tightly Charles restrained him.

"Shall I stop or take what I want?"

There it was, the ultimate question. Simon only had to think for a moment about his answer, what little thinking he could do with all the blood in his body circling his groin. "Take it, if you dare."

Charles leaned forward, tossed the pistol to the floor, wrapped his hand around Simon's shaft and licked it like a lollipop. "Oh, I dare."

Then he swallowed it down.

"Oh, God!" Simon shouted as warm wetness surrounded his flesh. He'd never had such an erotic encounter. Blowjobs, sure. Some guy from a bar on his knees, or one of his friends with benefits jerking each other off, but nothing as powerful as this.

As he tried to thrust into his cowboy's mouth, trying to get as much as possible down that fantastic throat, Simon bucked up and down.

Charles clamped his hand on Simon's hip and leaned down, pressing him into the mattress. "Don't move."

The force of it took Simon's breath away. Charles was strong. Bigger than he was, taller and oh, my God, he loved that feeling.

For the first time he could remember, he wanted someone to manhandle him.

Wanted it rough and hard and desperate.

He bucked again, testing his limits.

Again, Charles leaned into him, pinning him to the bed with his body and arms, all the time sucking him off, each downward plunge deeper than the last. In a quick move, he shifted and threw one leg over Simon's leg to stop it from moving.

A mixture of fear and excitement pulsed through Simon as he became even more immobile and as Charles wreaked more havoc on his body. He was helpless to stop the assault.

Not that he wanted to. *Fuck, no.*

The man could give head like no one he'd ever been with, and Simon knew this act could become an addiction. For the first time since they'd met, he wondered if there would be more than just this night. Would his masked man want another night or even more than fantastic sex?

No, he needed to put that stupid thought out of his head, relax and enjoy what was happening here and now.

This kind of adventure didn't happen every day.

At least not to him.

*　　*　　*

Charles loved overpowering his prince. He'd never been so dominant, or so rough with a lover, or had so much fun. Normally he topped, but what he was doing now went beyond his usual fare. There hadn't been much passion in his previous couplings; they were either brief, rushed, nameless encounters, or slow and languid afternoons spent with a few longtime but casual lovers. He'd found something new with Simon—passion, fervor, and a burning need sending every nerve ending in his body into maximum overload.

Playing out his fantasies seemed to be just the thing to set him on fire and illuminate what had been missing in his life. It was a good life, filled with some good friends, fine wine, and no deep emotional attachments, but next to what he now experienced with Simon, it paled and laid bare the truth.

He hadn't really been living until now.

Charles rolled farther onto his lover and pushed his legs apart, spreading the Indian's thighs wide enough to accommodate him.

"It's time, prince." He growled, wrapping his hand around the base of Simon's prick.

"Time?" Simon swallowed, his eyes wide, sweat beading on his brow.

"To come for me."

"I won't." Simon's eyelids shuttered and his face flushed.

"I control you."

"No, you don't." He shook his head.

"I say when you come." Charles pumped up and down, dragging his fist over the skin of Simon's dick, making his lover shudder in pleasure.

"No."

"Yes." He increased his speed, leaned down and lapped at the drops that dribbled from the angry red slit.

"Oh, God…" Simon moaned. He tried to move, but Charles held him down with one hand and the weight of his body as he worked the stiff, turgid flesh.

"You're going to come now."

Moving lower, Charles licked the ball sac, drawn close to Simon's body, then sucked one into his mouth, pulling it away hard, then let it go.

Simon cried out, "Charles!" He came, shooting fountains of white over Charles's hand, splattering his belly and tangling in the hair around the base of his dick.

CHAPTER 9

Simon let go of the headboard and fell back onto the bed, limp, unable to move a muscle, his body still tingling as he came down from one of the hardest orgasms of his life. He shuddered. It was all he could do for the moment.

He opened his eyes and looked down at Charles, kneeling between his legs.

His outlaw.

"Damn you, masked man." He sighed, unable even to laugh.

Charles chuckled. "Have I pleased my prince?"

Simon nodded and waved a weak hand. Oh, hell, yeah, he was pleased.

"I'll take that for a yes."

Simon smiled and rolled his eyes. "Cowboys. Think you run the West, don't you?"

Charles looked him over, lust still burning in his eyes. "We do."

Simon snorted. "We Native Americans were here long before you were, you know?" Simon wondered if his war paint was still intact or if he'd smudged it. Thank God, the mascara was waterproof or his sweat might have made it run.

Looking like Tammy Faye after a twenty-four hour telethon would not be sexy.

But asking if his make-up was running wasn't sexy either. How did women manage it?

He decided if Charles didn't mention it, he should forget about it.

"Now you've had your way with me, am I free?"

"Free?" Charles shook his head. "'Fraid not. I've only just begun. When I get through with you, you're going to be broke to the saddle."

"Do you expect me to buck like a bronco? I hope you don't plan on using spurs." Simon raised an eyebrow. Just what did Charles want from him? The answer to that question sent a ripple of excitement rolling through him like a pebble dropped in a pond.

"No. I expect to ride you until…" He trailed off, as if he'd changed his mind.

Simon tensed. "Until?"

Charles stared into his eyes and, for a long moment, they searched his. Then, he leaned forward, his hands on either side of Simon's head and looked down, it seemed, into the depths of Simon's soul.

"Until you say you're mine."

Simon's lips parted in a soundless gasp, only for Charles to take them in a demanding kiss. He nipped, sucked, and teased Simon's bottom lip, drawing a whimper from him as he wrapped his hands in Simon's hair and tried to keep them together.

Simon pushed the cowboy away with a Herculean effort, but wanted nothing more than to linger in the man's kisses.

"I belong to no man," he declared and looked up at Charles from half lowered eyelids, hoping like hell he looked sexy and not like some crying clown who'd escaped from the circus.

"You *will* belong to me. I *will* have you." The cowboy licked the seam of his lips.

Simon turned his head to avoid the next kiss. "You can take my body, but you'll never take my soul." God, could Scarlett have delivered that line with any more drama?

"I don't want your soul." He nuzzled into Simon's throat, his warm breath puffing on heated skin, sending more shivers down Simon's body. He licked a line from the dent beneath Simon's Adam's apple up to the tender spot below his ear.

He closed his eyes, enjoying the sensations the cowboy aroused in him.

"What *do* you want?" Simon held his breath.

Charles rested his forehead against Simon's. He took Simon's hands in his, entwining their fingers in a tight clasp and lowered his body to completely cover Simon's. "I want your heart."

Oh, my God. How could he stand up to those words? They blew everything Simon believed away. That there was no such thing as love at first sight. No destined lovers. No soul mates. All the things he'd once thought had been created by romantics through the ages to make people like him—the ones who'd never experienced it—feel somehow *less*.

From the moment he'd laid eyes on Charles at the costume shop, he'd felt a pull toward him. Not just sexual. Yeah, there'd been plenty of that, but he'd thought he'd really like to get to know Charles, that he'd like this person.

And tonight, even though he had no idea who was truly behind that mask, Simon had been drawn to the man, let him take over, kiss him in a crowded room, and even shamelessly arranged for a room at the hotel where he worked.

Shit. Even his boss Francis knew. And had approved.

But giving his heart to a stranger?

Why should that be so hard? He'd already given Charles his body. If Simon ran true to form, his heart wouldn't be far behind. And he'd learned from those few times heartbreak always followed, hadn't he?

"You can't *take* my heart. You'll have to earn that, cowboy." He stared up into Charles's eyes.

A slow, sexy grin broke over the desperado's face.

"I think I'm up to the challenge." He kissed Simon again, taking his time, each soft touch filled with tenderness, filled with…

No, Simon wasn't going to let his imagination and longing get the best of him.

Instead, he just melted into the kiss. It was utterly, completely, totally wonderful. If this was what happened when he wore eyeliner, he promised to wear it more often.

Simon pulled away and studied Charles. "What do you plan on doing?"

"Well, first thing, my prince, is to make love to you." Charles kissed the tip of his nose.

"Make love?" Simon whispered. Even though he didn't have much experience in the true love department, he'd had enough to know the difference between fucking and making love.

Charles nuzzled his throat and sighed. "Yeah. Make love. Just like you deserve."

God, that sounded so good. If it were only true.

"Do desperados ever fall in love?" Simon held his breath, thinking he'd gone too far. This whole game had gone too far, but he didn't want to turn back now.

"I reckon they do." Charles nodded. "What about Native American princes?"

"It's been known to happen." Simon swallowed. "Once in a blue moon."

"Well, prince, I don't know what color the moon is tonight, but I do know that what's happening right now is special and rare." He kissed Simon, lingering over his lips, tongue and mouth.

"I think a desperado might say just about anything to get what he wanted, wouldn't he?" Simon spoke against those tempting, teasing lips.

"He might." Charles nodded, that sexy grin slipping over his face again.

Simon wove his fingers in Charles's hair and pulled him down for a deeper kiss. When they came up for air, both gasping, lips swollen and wet from their efforts, he laughed. "For now, I think I'll wait and see just how convincing you can be, outlaw."

"That's all I'm asking."

"All?"

"Well, no, not all." Charles grinned, then fell on Simon, pinning him to the mattress and plundering his mouth like a starving man.

Oh, hell, yeah, this was the stuff of wet dreams. Fantasy come to life.

Right now, he didn't care if he ever woke up. Waking would be in the morning, when daylight ushered in reality.

For now, he was all about playing the game.

CHAPTER 10

Charles kissed his prince again. God, the man had no idea how sexy he looked with that thick bar of black across his eyes, his short ebony hair spiked up in a just-been-fucked look, and the little shy smile that danced on his lips.

He'd promised to make love to Simon and he fully intended to give it all he had. Sure, he'd been with other men, even been in love once or twice when he was younger, but it had never been like this.

Charles wanted to unwrap Simon, unfold all the layers inside the man, and learn what made Simon, Simon.

His Indian prince.

He supported his body on his hands and lifted off Simon, then rolled to the side. From here, he could touch, suck and kiss every precious inch of skin. He licked Simon's nipple, bringing it to a peak, and then latched onto it and sucked hard.

Simon moaned and arched upward.

The way he responded to Charles was just so fucking hot. He could barely keep from coming. With a quick stroke or two on his dick, he satisfied his need to be touched. If he let Simon touch him or suck him, he'd lose the last of his meager control.

Dragging his tongue over slightly sweaty skin, he tasted Simon. *Delicious.* He kept going, his goal the thick thatch of black hair that surrounded Simon's choice cock.

Once there, he'd suck it, then use his fingers to prep Simon, make him writhe and beg and call out Charles's name. That's what he wanted to hear, that soft pant and the throaty way Simon gasped when he came.

Just the memory of it sent shivers down his spine, straight to his balls.

He reached the nest of ebony curls and paused. Simon's cock stretched as he watched. It grew, thickening, rising up to present itself to Charles's lips.

No sense in refusing a perfectly good offer.

Charles held out his hand to lick it, get something slick between his skin and Simon's flesh.

"Check the bathroom."

"What?" Charles looked up at his lover.

"In the drawers. The room comes fully stocked for all our customers'…uh…needs." Simon blushed.

"Don't move," Charles ordered as he got off the bed.

"What? And risk being shot?" Simon chuckled.

Charles gave him a quick frown, then darted into the bathroom.

It was gorgeous. Old World decadence. Gold leaf and flocking in the same fleur-de-lis pattern covered the ballroom's walls. In the center of the room sat a gleaming white claw foot tub fashioned to look antique. He peered inside.

Whirlpool jets.

He groaned and filed it away for later. They'd need to clean up and he was positive they could both use a soak by then.

"What's taking so long?" Simon called from the bedroom, just a touch of petulance in his voice.

"This place is gorgeous."

"I know. Francis did a great job with the hotel. Really turned it around."

"Where's the stuff?" He twisted around, looking for what he needed.

"Try the drawers under the sink."

Charles went to the sink. It had been a carved mahogany buffet in another life, but now hosted twin under-mounted sinks with marble tops and gold-plated faucets. A basket sitting between the sinks held toiletries and towels. He pulled open the top drawer of the cabinet.

Good God. He'd hit the mother lode. Two boxes of condoms and two bottles of lube nestled inside. He plucked out the condom box, opened it, and took several out. After putting it back, he inspected the lube.

One bottle of *His* and one bottle of *Hers*.

191

"Charles," Simon called, "did you find it?"

He took the *His* and the condoms and hurried back to his impatient lover.

"Damn, you weren't kidding when you said the place was prepared." He held up his treasures.

"How many condoms did you take?" Simon's eyes gleamed; Charles hoped, with excitement, not disbelief.

"As many as I think I might need." He tossed them on the bed with a touch of arrogance.

Simon picked up a few. "Six?" He raised an eyebrow at his cowboy. "I think you're writing a check your body can't cash, outlaw."

"Oh, I can cash it, so don't you worry your purty little head about it." As hard as his dick was, Charles figured that by morning he'd just about use these up. He might even need one or two more.

He climbed on the bed and moved to kneel between Simon's legs.

"I also got some lube. It says, 'Guaranteed to make your man tingle.'" He flipped open the bottle and poured some on his fingers and rubbed them together. "Are you ready to tingle?"

*   *   *

Simon nodded as he pushed up on his elbows to watch Charles take Simon's shaft in hand and stroke it, spreading the slick over his heated flesh. His dick throbbed, but before he could take more than a few breathes, he felt something different. A hint of warmth. It grew warmer and the skin on his shaft fucking *tingled*.

He moaned.

"Guess that means it's working." Charles chuckled.

Slipping back down on his back, Simon closed his eyes and focused on Charles's hands. Damn, the man knew how he liked to be touched. How did he do that?

"So good, cowboy." Simon sighed and stretched, working himself into the bed and spreading his legs even wider. God, he was a slut.

The tingling continued, intensified. The more Charles worked his dick, the more he pushed and pulled, rubbed and scraped, the better it felt. Simon's balls grew unbearably heavy.

"You need to try this, too," Simon panted out.

"All in good time, my prince," Charles said.

Still pumping, Charles slipped his fingers over Simon's balls and massaged them with the lube. Warmth spread over his sac, and it

192

tightened in response. His dick hardened, a sweet ache settling in his groin.

"No fair. That stuff would give a limp fish wood."

"All's fair in love and war." Charles worked it into the tender skin between his balls and his back door. "I wonder what it would feel like…"

Charles quickly added more to his fingers without missing a beat of jerking Simon off and dabbed it onto Simon's opening.

This time, the warmth was immediate, the tingling intense. Simon wasn't sure if they were supposed to use it internally.

"Are you sure about this stuff? Is it safe?" He raised his head to look into Charles's eyes.

Charles picked up the bottle again and scanned it. "Yep. Perfectly safe."

Simon sighed and let his head fall back as his lover worked the lube around his tight entry. Teasing, Charles let his finger brush over it, only to withdraw. It drove Simon crazy. He wanted Charles's finger to penetrate him. Wanted him to work his prostate.

God, he needed fucking.

*   *   *

"Oh, God, I need to be inside you," Charles whispered. He pushed his finger past the ring of muscles guarding Simon's sweet ass, surrounding the digit with heat and pressure. His lover was tight and Charles knew he wouldn't be able to last long once his cock was inside his prince.

Simon growled and pushed back. Charles worked his finger in and out, pressing on his gland, making Simon cry out. As he finger fucked Simon, Charles experimented with the man's reactions to what he was doing to him.

The faster he went, the harder Simon pushed back.

If he nailed his gland, Simon arched his back and hissed.

When he combined sucking Simon's prick with finger fucking him, he reduced Simon to a writhing ball of helpless man, on the verge of orgasm.

"Not yet," he ordered. "Wait until I'm inside. I want you to come on my cock."

Simon nodded, his bottom lip caught between his teeth with the effort. "Hurry."

Charles nodded and pulled out his finger, snatched up a condom and ripped into it. Faster than he'd ever done it, he rolled it on, then slicked it with more of the lube.

"Do I need to go slow? How long has it been?" He gazed into Simon's eyes.

"Not long enough." Simon shook his head, then his eyes narrowed. "If you go slow, I swear I'll get off this bed and go home."

Charles saw the truth burning in his eyes. Simon wanted to be taken and taken hard. Charles's prick swelled with that knowledge and pride, and he fully intended on giving his prince what he wanted.

"You want it fast, Simon?" He brushed the tip of his cock along the crease of Simon's ass.

"Yes." Simon hooked his arms under his knees and pulled them up, displaying his pink pucker to Charles.

"You want it hard?" Charles positioned himself at the opening.

"Yes!" Simon whimpered.

Charles took Simon's hips in his hands and pushed inside, stretching the ring, diving deep into that scorching hot tunnel.

Simon cried out, "Charles!"

He froze. "You okay?"

Simon nodded. "Fine."

"Put your legs around my waist." He guided them into position, then he leaned forward on his hands. He looked down into Simon's face, his eyes wide and dark with arousal, his lips still red and those heavily lined and lidded eyes staring up at him.

Charles couldn't help himself. He shifted his weight and ran his fingertips over Simon's face. "God, you're gorgeous. Did I tell you that?"

"No. Maybe. Am I?" Simon gave him a soft smile.

"You are." He lowered his head and planted a soft kiss on Simon's lips.

"Can I take off your mask now?"

"Yeah. I reckon there's no need for it now." He'd gotten what he'd lusted for so why not lose it? He slipped it off and tossed it aside.

Simon reached up and traced his face with his fingertips, over his brow, cheeks and down his nose. The touch sent shivers through Charles.

"I like this. You have beautiful eyes." Simon smiled.

"Aw, shucks, prince." He winked. "I ain't nothing special."

"You are to me." His lover sighed. "Fuck me, cowboy." And

194

slapped Charles on the ass.

"Shit!" Charles cried out. The cheek of his ass stung, but it was such a good pain, so erotic that instead of hurting it made him harder. "As my prince commands."

Charles pulled out slowly, and Simon shuddered. Then he slammed home, nearly taking Simon's hips off the bed with the force of it.

"Oh, God, yes!" Simon's hands twisted in the covers.

Charles shafted his ass hard, setting a steady rhythm and speed, each thrust hitting against the gland. Beads of sweat popped out on Charles's forehead and back, matched by similar drops on Simon's chest.

He gave himself over to the act, their bodies interlocked in the most primal way, rocking back and forth, in and out, doing the age old dance of lovers.

Simon reached up and wrapped his hands around Charles's neck and his heels dug into the backs of Charles's thighs, as if Simon wanted to crawl inside, lose himself in Charles's body.

And Charles wanted to be buried inside Simon. Deep, deep inside. So deep he'd never find his way out. Not that he wanted out. He'd be perfectly content to repeat this performance anytime Simon wanted.

For the first time in a very long time, he wanted more than just sexual relief.

More than getting off or killing time.

He wanted a man.

One man.

Simon.

CHAPTER 11

All Simon knew was right now in this moment. He rocked in the hold of Charles's strong arms, his body receiving his lover, opening his very being to this man.

Charles angled his hips and thrust, brushing hard against Simon's prostate.

"Oh, God!" His balls slammed against his body, the strength of his orgasm gathering there, building. Charles struck again. And again.

Simon exploded, pleasure ripping through him, spilling over his belly, splashing across one nipple, trails of white on the landscape of his body.

As his channel convulsed around the thick cock trapped there, Simon felt it swell. Charles cried out his name, froze, and then shuddered, his head tossed back.

God, Charles was gorgeous when he came. Simon thought he'd never get tired of seeing the look of agonized pleasure on Charles's face. No other expression could be mistaken for it, and he was the one privy to it. Had been the cause of it.

And before the night was out, he'd see it several more times if he had anything to do with it.

Charles eased out of him, pulled off the condom, and got out of bed to dispose of it in the bathroom. He returned with a cocky walk.

"That your gunslinger strut?" Simon asked as he pushed a pillow under his head. He took his time checking out Charles's body, not at all shy about not hiding his interest.

"No. It's my I-just-fucked-a-prince strut." Charles did a little dance, hopping up and down on one foot like he was doing a war dance.

"That's not how it goes." Simon laughed.

"Sure it is. I just made it up." Charles halted his dance, and hands on his hips, stared at Simon.

"Looks like you're trying to make it rain."

"Well, only if it's raining men!" Charles held up his hands and waved them. "Hallelujah!" He winked at Simon.

Simon giggled. "I never knew cowboys could be so funny."

Charles sobered. "Cowboys are *never* funny. They're clever. They're sarcastic. They're even relevant. But they're *never* funny."

"No?"

"No. Funny is what you call one of them there tenderfoots. Not a hardened, dyed-in-the-wool, raised-in-the-saddle outlaw like me." He climbed onto the bed and flopped down next to Simon, then rose up on his elbow to glare down at him.

"Okay. Okay." Simon warded him off with his hands. "You're just a wise-ass, bad-ass outlaw."

"Damn straight." Charles nodded once. "And don't you forget it."

"I won't." Simon bit back another giggle. "It's just that…well, I was thinking."

"Yes?" Charles cocked one eyebrow.

Simon held up his hands. "Now that I'm free, I'd capture myself a cowboy." He twisted, turned, and faster than he thought he could move, he straddled Charles's waist.

He took Charles's hands in his and pushed them down on either side of his head.

"Like this." He bent over and nibbled along the edge of Charles's jaw.

Charles groaned. "Damn. Ambushed." He lifted his chin to give Simon more access to his throat.

Simon laved his way down, his lover's pulse throbbing under his tongue. He'd just come, but damn if he wasn't getting hard again. He traced a line along Charles's collarbone, to his chest, then down to his dark brown nipple.

With the very tip of his tongue, Simon circled it, then blew a soft puff of breath across the wide flat disc. It wrinkled and drew to a tight point.

Charles groaned.

"Now, you're *my* prisoner," Simon whispered against Charles's skin.

"I'm terrified." Charles chuckled.

"You should be." Simon narrowed his eyes. "What I have planned for you no man has survived."

"Scalpin'?"

Simon took Charles's hair in his fist, tugged on it as if testing it, then shook his head. "No."

"Skinnin'?"

Simon ran his tongue across Charles's chest to the other nipple and licked it. "No." Charles caught his breath and held it even as he arched into Simon's mouth.

"What could be worse than that?" Charles gasped.

Simon let him go and stared into his eyes. "Torture by a thousand bites."

Charles shuddered. "Bites?"

"Indian love bites." Simon nipped his chest, and Charles hissed. "No man can stand up against them."

"I'm not just any man, prince."

"I can see that, but I don't think you will."

"And if I don't?"

"If you survive?" Simon sat back, letting his fingers take his tongue's place on Charles's body, moving over the skin in a constant glide.

"What will I win?"

"Me." Simon flicked his finger against Charles's nipple, earning a flinch and hiss from his captive. "My body. For as long as you'd care to have it."

Charles's brows shot upward and he licked his lips like a hungry man watching dinner come out of the oven. "A worthy prize. One a man, especially this man, would do anything to win."

"So." Simon sat back and gave Charles what he hoped was a smoldering look. He wanted his cowboy quaking with anticipation. "Are you ready to begin?"

"Do your worst." Charles jerked his chin up, looking so sure of himself.

Simon wasn't sure at all. He'd talked big, but he wasn't positive if what he'd planned to do to his lover would be enough to drive him over the edge. Or that he couldn't take it.

He'd never tried to torture anyone, with or without sex. Well, not torture maybe, but make them cry Uncle.

"If it's too much, if you need me to stop, if you want to give in, just say the word." Simon leaned down and bit him on the shoulder.

Charles hissed. "What word?"

"Two words really." Simon put his lips next to Charles's. "I surrender."

Charles laughed. "Surrender? Desperados *never* surrender. They go out with their guns blazing."

"Guns?" Simon looked around the bed and shrugged. In his best Mexican accent, he said, "I don' see no steenkin' guns."

*   *   *

Charles groaned. At the awful joke and his own carelessness.

Talk about getting caught with your pants down.

He'd abandoned his guns when they'd stripped to bare skin. He shivered as he stared into Simon's determined eyes. He reckoned losing might be as good as winning.

Might. If it weren't for the prize.

Simon's body. For as long as he wanted it.

Hell, that might just be a very long time.

How much time did they have in the room? Checkout was usually at eleven in hotels. Eleven a.m or eleven p.m. It didn't matter which because it wouldn't be enough time.

"I'm tough as nails, prince. Bring it on," he dared.

Simon smiled, leaned down, and nipped Charles's ear. A gentle bite, nothing he couldn't deal with. Another bite. Still soft. It tickled really. If this was the best he could do, Simon would be his in no time. Another tiny nibble as Simon worked his way up Charles's ear, each soft bite raising bumps on Charles's skin as he fought from shivering.

Okay, maybe not so easy. His dick stirred.

A quick lick to soothe, then Simon switched to his other ear. Grabbing onto Charles's earlobe, he bit, then suckled it. Charles's eyes rolled as Simon's warm, sweet breath panted in his ear.

He grabbed the sheets and held on.

Simon nipped his throat in controlled small bites. He hadn't been joking about the thousand bites. If his lover kept this up, dozens of bruises would cover Charles's body by the end.

His cock stiffened, renewed, at the thought of his body marked by his lover.

He groaned as Simon paused where neck met shoulder and clamped on as he sucked up another hickey. His cock jerked to painful fullness, begging to be touched.

He humped air.

Simon ignored him. He released Charles and resumed the tiny bites as he made his way over Charles's shoulder. To his upper arm. He stretched it out and nipped down the tender skin on the underside of his arm. Charles gasped with pleasure, more turned on than he ever thought he'd be.

Maybe this would be harder than he thought.

Maybe he'd underestimated the prince.

Maybe he'd break, surrender, and give himself to the Indian instead.

Would Simon want to keep him longer? Or when the time came to leave the room, would they just get dressed and go their separate ways?

Simon bit his chest, bringing Charles's attention back to the near torture Simon inflicted on his body.

"God," he gasped as Simon latched onto one of his nipples, raking his teeth over it, bringing its already hard point to unbearable arousal. God, his dick throbbed, screaming, "What about me? Someone suck me!"

Charles thrust his hips into the air, trying to draw attention to his cock, but Simon ignored him. And it.

How could he ignore it? Didn't he ache, too?

Simon moved deliberately over his belly, taking nips and bites as he traveled, ever so slowly, down Charles's aroused and aching body.

He ground his teeth together, ensuring no sound, not even a growl, could escape.

Simon attacked his ribs and the side of his belly with light, tickling teeth.

Charles burst out laughing. Damn it, he'd always been ticklish there.

A smug grin spread over his lover's beautiful face.

"Bastard. No fair," he got out.

"All's fair in love and war." Simon licked along his side, and Charles howled.

"Lowdown..." He laughed. Bite. "No good..." Lick. Giggle. "Cheatin'..."

Simon nibbled his way right to Charles's navel, caught a thin piece of skin between his teeth and pulled.

"Ow!" That didn't tickle.

The pain, unbelievably erotic, flew to his cock like a bee to the hive.

His lover let it go and soothed it with a soft swipe of hot tongue. Charles shuddered. His dick thickened and stood straight up as if begging for attention. If it could have, it would have waved at Simon and called out, "Me! Me! Bite me!"

Simon raised his head from Charles's body, gazed into his eyes, and licked his lips. "Surrender?"

"Never!" Charles shouted.

"Never is a hard word." Simon shrugged. "Have it your way, cowboy."

He lowered his head and bit into Charles's hip. Sharp. Unexpected. Intensely erotic. He sucked up another mark, each pull of his mouth dragging Charles's balls tighter to his body.

Simon let go, swirled his tongue over the mark, then lunged and took possession of his other hip, his hands still pressing Charles into the bed.

Charles cried out as he shot his load in a hard rush of pleasure. Fists clenched, back arched, he marked his own body with hot cum.

CHAPTER 12

Fountains of white ejaculate pulsed out of Charles's beautiful prick and splattered across his belly. It was so fucking hot Simon could barely stand it.

He'd been hard as steel ever since he'd started the biting and now he fucking throbbed. His own cock demanded to be stroked and to unload.

Simon knelt between Charles's legs, sat back on his calves, grabbed his shaft, and pumped. Once, twice, and on the third quick slide over the sensitive head he came, shooting jism directly on Charles's spent dick.

The streaks of his cum on his lover's body shook him to the core. He'd marked his man in more than one way, and it'd been glorious.

He wasn't finished, though.

Not until the cowboy surrendered to the Indian prince.

Using his arms to brace his body, he held himself suspended over Charles, refusing to abandon his position of dominance, knowing if he gave his cowboy a chance, he'd turn the tables on him.

"Damn, that was good," Simon whispered. He took Charles's bottom lip in his teeth and worried it. Charles moaned.

"Surrender?" he asked.

"Never."

"Good."

Simon shifted, grabbed the edge of the sheet, and wiped Charles clean. "I'll get a wet cloth later," he promised. For now, he wanted to continue his game.

"Oh, no, you don't!" Charles tensed, then surged forward, grabbed Simon by the shoulders and threw him over, landing on top of his back.

"Now, who's captive?" he growled in Simon's ear. Charles mashed Simon's face into the mattress.

"Shit."

"Say it. Say 'I'm the captive.'"

"Bite me," Simon muttered.

"Don't mind if I do."

Charles bit him on the shoulder and sucked hard. Simon squirmed beneath him, his cock filling.

Again? What was he, sixteen? What was it about Charles that got him so excited, so aroused, so damn hard?

He pushed into the mattress, the sensitive head of his dick rubbing against the soft six-hundred-count Egyptian cotton sheets, but he found no relief.

"Hold still, my prince."

"So you can bite me again?" He struggled, but Charles had him pinned and, God forgive him, he loved it.

"Yeah. You like it, don't you?" He bit Simon's other shoulder, near the back of his neck, and shivers shot through Simon.

Hell, yeah, he liked this. Too much. The weight of Charles on his back, the strength of Charles's hands as they gripped his wrists, the heat from his breath on the back of his neck. His cock hardened, pressing into the mattress. He had to bite his lip to keep from crying out, "Yes!"

"No answer?" Charles chuckled. "Perhaps I'll let you up when I hear those two words from *you*."

Simon shook his head, afraid even to speak, afraid if he did, he'd just beg the outlaw to fuck him again. Take what he wanted. God, he was shameless and a slut.

"I think I know what you want." Charles moved. A sharp sting from a bite on Simon's ass sent his breath exploding out of him in a whoosh.

"Hey!" He hadn't expected that, but he should have. He should expect anything from a desperado.

"Hmm. I like the way you taste, prince." Charles took another bite of his ass; this time sucking up what Simon knew would be a big, beautiful lover's mark.

Simon writhed on the bed, Charles clinging to one cheek of his butt like a terrier on a rat.

Then Charles released him, and Simon groaned.

The sound of a condom packet ripping open and then the squirt of lube told him the outlaw wasn't done with him. *Thank God.*

"Spread 'em!" Charles ordered with a hard slap to Simon's thigh. It stung and his flesh quivered. His dick ached. His hole convulsed in anticipation of its imminent breaching.

Charles knelt between Simon's legs now.

He had no choice. His body wouldn't refuse, no matter what his mind tried to tell it. Control and determination gave way to raw, primal hunger and the need to surrender.

Simon obeyed without a sound.

Charles pushed his lube-covered fingers between the cheeks of Simon's ass and slicked him up, lingering on his opening, teasing it. Simon pushed into the touch, eager to be penetrated.

"Just relax, my prince."

A finger entered him, and he sighed with the pleasure. Charles held still while Simon fucked the digit, until he whimpered his need for something bigger and longer.

Something thicker than just one finger.

Charles's cock.

Simon shuddered. "Please." He couldn't help himself. His lover had him so worked up, so aroused, he thought he'd blow his load, wasting it on the bed.

Charles grabbed him by the hips and lifted him to his hands and knees. He placed the flared head of his cock against Simon and pushed in.

Charles echoed Simon's groan and they both held still.

"Damn, I love how you feel. You're so damn tight," Charles whispered. "Like a vise. Don't let go."

"Never." Simon squeezed his muscles around the thick rod buried in his ass.

Charles inhaled and blew his breath out in a slow exhale. Preparing. Simon waited. Time stretched.

The first withdrawal slid from his body like silk against velvet. When it slammed back inside it had become velvet over steel.

Simon cried out; the pleasure was so intense, so heady, bordering on pain. Delicious, delirious, delightful pain.

His lover shafted him, hard and fast, rocking his body with each thrust. Simon lowered his head to the bed, canted his ass just right, and Charles's hard dick swiped across his gland.

As Charles claimed his channel, a shudder raced through Simon, followed by the next, and the next, each building in his balls, pushing him with each stroke toward his release. He closed his eyes, bit his bottom lip, and tried to hold it off, to extend the ecstasy of this fucking for as long as he could manage it, but his outlaw was relentless and brutal in his taking.

Simon's body, strung so tight he thought he'd break, raced toward the edge of the chasm, hung there, battered by the steel shaft incessantly fucking him, until Charles removed his hand from Simon's hip and took possession of Simon's cock.

Stretched over Simon's back, Charles stroked him. It was the straw that broke the camel's back, the last hurtful word in an argument, the final angel dancing on the head of a pin.

It was more than Simon could take.

"I surrender!" Simon cried out as he spilled, each pulse painting the sheets, until there was nothing left to give and everything left to take.

Charles groaned, thrust once, twice, then emptied into the condom. He collapsed on Simon and they slid to the mattress, tangled in each other's arms and legs, semen and sweat.

"I surrender, too," Charles whispered in Simon's ear before giving it a gentle nip, then a tender kiss.

His lover's warm breath on the back of his neck was the last thing Simon remembered before falling asleep.

*   *   *

The phone was ringing.

Simon sighed and rolled toward the noise, but something halted his body halfway there. He opened one eye and peered through the dim light of the room.

Morning.

A heavy arm draped over his chest.

His ass tingled and his dick was hard.

A soft snort sounded from behind him on the bed.

Simon smiled.

Charles.

He'd captured an outlaw last night. Brought him here to this room and he'd had the best sex of his life. And the most fun. An unexpected meeting, a chance encounter, a heated look from cool blue eyes behind a black mask.

The ringing stopped. A moment later, the red message blinked.

Simon slipped from under his lover's arm and sat on the edge of the bed. He ran his hand over his face, then stood and went to the bathroom.

After taking a piss, he checked his face in the mirror.

Smudged black bars still masked his eyes. No tracks down his cheeks from his mascara. Damn, that stuff really did work. His lips were no longer deep red, though.

He turned on the water, opened a bar of soap and worked it into a lather, then washed his face. What was left of his makeup came off, and when he patted his face dry and looked up, the Indian prince had disappeared and Simon Tai stood there.

Plain, ordinary Simon.

He sighed.

Time to face the morning. And Charles.

He turned and left, padding across the room back to the bed and stared down at his lover. Well, his lover last night. Maybe even this morning, if he played his cards right and if Charles was still interested.

He picked up Charles's mask draped over the clock. Damn, was it really ten a.m.?

The red light blinked.

He picked up the phone, put down the mask, and hit the message button.

"Simon? It's Francis. I hate to disturb you, sweetheart, but the room is booked for today. Check out is at eleven and if you and Charles are up to it, lunch is on me in the dining room at eleven-thirty. TTFN!"

Simon groaned. So much for a round of morning sex.

He sat on the bed and stared around the room. His buckskin dress sat in a pile on the floor and his wig lay in one corner. A pair of pistols and their holster were next to the bed and Charles's boots peeked out from under the vest and chaps.

A strong hand reached for him, wrapped around his arm and pulled him back down.

"Good morning." Charles smiled at him before landing a perfect kiss on his lips.

"'Morning." Simon sighed. "They need the room by eleven."

"What time is it?" Charles scrubbed his face with the palms of his hands.

"Just after ten."

"Shit. That late?" He flopped back on the bed, taking Simon with him, seeming not to want to let Simon go.

Why did that make him so happy? It was stupid, really.

Simon rolled onto his side. "You can have the first shower, if you want."

"I want. Especially if you're in there with me." He gave Simon a wicked grin.

"We don't have much time."

"I don't need much time." Charles threw back the covers, revealing his stiff prick.

"Morning wood." Simon sniffed.

"Simon wood." He swatted the thick rod and it bounced back as if eager to get to work.

Simon laughed and rolled his eyes. "Whatever."

Charles swung his legs over the edge of the bed as he sat up. "Last one there is a rotten egg!" He slapped Simon on the ass and bolted.

Simon followed in hot pursuit, but Charles beat him there.

"No fair!" Simon panted as he clung to the doorway of the bathroom.

Charles leaned over the claw foot tub and turned on the faucets. "All's fair, baby."

He put his hands on his hips and cocked his head. "Baby? What happened to prince?"

"I like baby. Suits you."

"I am not a baby." Simon shook his head as he tested the water. *Perfect.*

"Sure you are." No sense arguing about it, so Simon let it go. Besides, he kind of liked the endearment.

They got in and pulled the shower curtain around the oblong shower rod, blocking out the world. Simon took the soap, lathered up and began to wash.

Charles took the soap from him. "Let me. I know just what I want cleaned."

He ran the bar over Simon's chest, down to his belly, then with one hand, covered Simon's hard cock with foamy soap.

Simon groaned and thrust his hips into the tight grip. "God, Charles, I love when you touch me."

"I love it, too." Charles took down the showerhead and used it to rinse the lather off. "Perfect. Clean as a whistle."

Simon smiled down at him. "You know how to whistle, don't you?"

"Sure. You just put your lips together and blow." Charles delivered the line like a pro. Then he went to his knees, took Simon's shaft in his hand and, like a pro, sucked Simon's cock to the back of his throat.

Simon cried out and buried his hands in Charles's wet hair to hold himself upright and steady.

Charles worked his dick, tongue licking, cheeks hollowed, deep-throating Simon until his balls slammed against his body, his spine tingled and he emptied down that incredible throat. "Charles!"

As his lover worked him through his aftershocks, Simon sighed, sated and happy.

Charles released him, licked his chin to catch a stray drop, then gave him a kiss as he slid to his butt in the tub and leaned back, trying to catch his breath.

"Come here, let me finish you off," Simon offered.

"That's okay. I came when you did." Charles laughed. "Come on. Let's get clean and dressed." He got to his feet and offered Simon a hand up.

They showered, Charles took a leak, and they headed back to the bedroom.

"Damn!" Simon picked up his dress. "I don't have anything to wear but the dress from last night."

Charles burst into laughter. "You're going to be a sight walking to your car."

"Me?" Simon pointed as Charles slipped into his vest and picked up his jeans. "What about you? Together we look like we've just tried out for the Village People." He giggled.

"YMCA!" Charles sang out, doing the dance moves.

Simon lost it and flopped back on the bed in gales of laughter. "Stop! Seriously. We have to get dressed and out of here."

"Okay. Sheesh, you're the manager. Can't you do something?"

"No. Francis called. They need the room." He shrugged. "But he did invite us to lunch."

"Great! I'm starved!" Charles pulled on his jeans and buttoned them up.

"Worked up an appetite, did you?"

"Sure. I'm always hungry after I've had a little Chinese." Charles grinned and winked.

Simon groaned. "I'm Korean."

"Really?" Charles stared at him, eyes narrowed. "Yeah, right. Korean."

"Is that a problem?" Simon tensed.

"No. Is it for you?" Charles pushed his foot into one boot and looked up.

"What do you mean?"

"Well. You're Korean. I'm not. I just thought…" He trailed off.

"What?" Simon slipped on the dress and pulled it down over his hips.

"Your family? Are they okay with you seeing a white guy?"

Simon shrugged. "They're dealing pretty well with my being gay. Having a boyfriend who isn't Korean won't kill them."

Charles strapped the holster around his lean hips and put on his hat. "A boyfriend, huh?"

Simon picked up the wig and turned to face Charles. He searched deep into those beautiful blue eyes for a hint of the right answer.

"Well…" He shrugged. "Who else are you going to play cowboys and Indians with?"

Charles laughed. "Only my Indian princess."

"That's prince. I was in disguise, remember?"

"Right. My prince." Charles sauntered to the door. "Ready?"

Simon took a last look around the room. Other than the disaster of the bed, it looked clean and neat. "Ready."

Charles opened the door. "After you, baby."

Simon moved forward, but Charles stopped him with an arm across the doorway. "Wait."

Simon looked up just as Charles claimed his mouth in a hard kiss. Simon moaned and melted into it, threading his hand up the back of Charles's neck and into his hair.

A cough from the hallway broke them apart.

The maid stood in the corridor next to her cart piled high with clean white towels, small wrapped bars of soap and tiny bottles of shampoo.

Simon blushed and headed for the elevator, with Charles right behind him.

He pushed the button, the elevator clanged, and the lift started.

"I still think the eyeliner is sexy as hell, my prince," Charles whispered in Simon's ear.

The elevator arrived, the door opened, and Simon, shoved from behind, flew inside, landing against the bars at the back. Charles covered his body, pinning him to it and bit Simon's ear. What had to be Charles's erection pushed into his ass, making the muscles protecting his channel pucker and pulse with need.

Simon groaned. "Damn you, masked man."

EPILOGUE

One month later…

"Are you sure about this?"

"Positive."

Simon leaned forward, the eyeliner steady in his hand, and painted a perfect line across his eyelid. "See? I've been practicing."

"I wasn't asking about your abilities, just your decision to wear it to dinner with Francis." Charles kissed his lover on the temple.

Simon's thick black hair stood up in one-inch spikes all over his head. The black liner circling his eyes added to the sexy look. God, the man made him so fucking hard.

"We're going out after. I don't want to put it on in the car." Simon frowned.

"Okay, forget I asked." Charles held up his hands.

Simon closed the liner and laid it on the bathroom counter. "I'm ready."

Charles slipped behind his lover and wrapped his arms around Simon. "So am I." He bumped Simon's ass with the erection he sported under the black jeans.

"No, you're not." Simon shook his head and caught Charles's gaze in the mirror. "Did you forget?"

Charles groaned. "Really? Do I have to?"

"You lost last night, didn't you?" Simon glared at him.

Yeah, he'd lost the damn bet. Again. He should know better than to let Simon ambush him, tie him up like a wayward calf and go all outlaw on him.

"I lost." Charles sighed.

"Say it." Simon's eyebrow cocked upward.

"I surrender," Charles growled out.

"Now, just hold still. It won't hurt at all." Simon picked up the liner, unscrewed the cap and then turned to face Charles. "You're going to look so hot in this I'll have to beat the boys off you."

Charles held still as Simon applied the eyeliner. Simon finished, leaned back, and then gave a low, "Hot damn!"

He glanced in the mirror, bracing himself.

Shit. He looked *good.*

Simon closed the liner and tossed it down. "Let's go, baby." He swatted him on the ass.

Charles opened his mouth to say something, but words failed him. He wanted to protest, wanted to claim he was too butch to wear this stuff, wanted to… He took another look in the mirror.

Hot. Sexy. Dangerous.

He grabbed Simon's hand and pulled him against the door. Burying his hands in Simon's hair, he tilted Simon's head and claimed his mouth. Charles put all his desire, his lust and, most important, his love into that hard kiss and when he broke away, they were both gasping for air.

Simon sighed and pulled Charles to him again, their foreheads pressed together, noses touching, lips brushing.

Simon whispered, "Damn you, masked man. I surrender, too."

LYNN LORENZ

Ms. Lorenz lives in Katy, Texas, just west of Houston, with her husband, two teens and a neurotic dog. Originally from New Orleans, she's had gay men in her life since high school, so writing gay romance came naturally for her.

She started writing as a young teen, angsty poetry and short stories, attended the University of New Orleans as an English major, but switched to Fine Art, graduating with a B.A. She put down her paintbrush and picked up a pen just three years ago, and hasn't stopped writing yet.

Find out more about Lynn at www.lynnlorenz.com.

AMBER QUILL PRESS, LLC
THE GOLD STANDARD IN PUBLISHING

QUALITY BOOKS
IN BOTH PRINT AND ELECTRONIC FORMATS

ACTION/ADVENTURE	SUSPENSE/THRILLER
SCIENCE FICTION	DARK FANTASY
MAINSTREAM	ROMANCE
HORROR	EROTICA
FANTASY	GLBT
WESTERN	MYSTERY
PARANORMAL	HISTORICAL
YOUNG ADULT	NON-FICTION

AMBER QUILL PRESS, LLC
http://www.amberquill.com

Made in the USA
Lexington, KY
18 October 2010